DARE TO ENTER . . .

Will and his father took one corridor; Penny and her sister, Judy, another. Dr. Smith went with fighter jock Don West. All the rooms were the same—barren cubicles that opened from the outside only.

"This is a waste of time," Smith whined as Don opened door after door. "And of energy. We should be using more sophisticated techniques than just opening and closing doors."

"You're right!" Without warning, the brash young fighter pilot spun around and clamped a viselike grip on Smith's arm. He wrenched open a door, hurled the smaller man inside, and slammed it shut.

"I'll be back in an hour or so for a report on all the valuable info you've uncovered with your sophisticated techniques," he said, stomping off down the corridor.

Behind him he could hear Smith's muffled shouts. Then silence. What Don couldn't hear was Smith's gasp of terror as the alien nightmare began unfolding before his eyes. . . .

OTHER *LOST IN SPACE* TITLES
AVAILABLE FROM HARPERCOLLINS

Lost in Space
novelization by Joan Vinge

Lost in Space: Promised Land
by Pat Cadigan

THE VAULT

LOST IN SPACE

GENE DeWEESE

HarperEntertainment
A Division of HarperCollinsPublishers

HarperEntertainment
A Division of HarperCollinsPublishers
10 East 53rd Street, New York, N.Y. 10022–5299

This is a work of fiction. The characters, incidents, and dialogues are products of the author's imagination and are not to be construed as real. Any resemblance to actual events or persons, living or dead, is entirely coincidental.

ISBN 0-06-105910-2

HarperCollins®, ®, and HarperEntertainment ™ are trademarks of HarperCollins Inc.

Cover illustration © 1999 by Keith Birdsong
First printing: August 1999

Printed in the United States of America

Visit HarperEntertainment on the World Wide Web at
http://www.harpercollins.com

❖ 10 9 8 7 6 5 4 3 2 1

To Buck Coulson, 1928–1999:
For a fascinating half century of friendship,
from the symbiosis that was Thomas Stratton in the
early days of EISFA and YANDRO to the
aftermath of last year's Windycon and everything
in between. You'll have to excuse the surroundings,
but they are sort of appropriate, considering
how we used to figure a convention wasn't really
a convention unless we got lost on
the way at least once.

PROLOGUE

Dr. Zachary Smith was petrified with fear as he realized he was not dreaming.

He really *was* trapped in a grotesquely alien body, marooned on a world that was even more bizarre than the body. His eyes—and there were more than two—relayed the scene to his brain, but his mind, still human despite the shell that now housed it, could not make sense of the images. There were towering, kaleidoscopic things that resembled multicolored, metallic trees until one of his many eyes focused on them, causing them to flow into other, even more alien shapes that had no references in even his extensive memories. Colorless, crystalline masses hugged the ground like slabs of transparent granite—until his attention centered on them and they were transformed into things that may or may not have been alive but which writhed and slithered and exuded an overpowering stench that he absorbed not through nostrils but through every square inch of his body's surface.

And in the midst of it all, a creature from his worst nightmares suddenly loomed up before him.

For an instant Smith's panicked mind conjured up

images of the giant armored spiders from the Proteus, but then, as a dozen of his eyes involuntarily centered on the creature, it melted and reformed into something even more repulsive and terrifying, something with slavering mandibles and writhing, hairy tentacles and slit-irised eyes that glowed red with hatred and malevolence as it moved toward him, flowing like semicongealed slime over the other impossible shapes that surrounded him.

Suddenly released from his paralysis, he tried to back away. Impulses intended for legs moved other, boneless appendages, forcing them to spasmodically grip the jagged, razor-sharp surfaces beneath him, and he moved.

But it did no good. It was as if the creature were attached to him by an invisible, unbreakable cord.

He tried to scream, and found he had no tongue and no throat, no way of making even the slightest sound.

The creature moved closer and flowed around him like a smothering blanket, cutting off the light, cutting off the sulfurous air that he tried desperately to drag into his body through a thousand gill-like openings. He tried to strike out with his arms, and something—not an arm— lashed out uselessly, gripped and restrained by the thing that now completely enveloped him.

Slowly, horribly, not knowing what he was or where, Dr. Zachary Smith died.

And was resurrected, only to die the same death again.

And again . . .

And again . . .

2

1

"Diplomacy is almost always a dreadful waste of time," Dr. Zachary Smith complained loudly, his fear-wide eyes riveted on the bridge viewscreens and the black and gray ovoid that was rapidly overtaking the *Jupiter*, "but to attempt it in this particular situation is counterproductive folly as well."

"I hate to agree with that boneheaded traitor," Don West said, scowling as he tried to nurse a few more kps out of the ship's overworked engines, "but he's right."

"I suppose *you* think we should fight!" Judy Robinson, standing next to her father at the communications console, rolled her eyes. "That's your answer to everything!"

"Not *everything*!" West snapped, unable even under these circumstances to keep a trace of suggestiveness out of his voice. "And only if I have a chance in hell of winning!" he added, returning his full attention to the controls. "Which we don't! That thing may be less than half the size of the *Jupiter*, but unless our instruments are totally out of whack, it's ten times as deadly."

"What our musclebound friend is trying to say in his primitive way," Smith broke in, "is that turning tail and running has its advantages. Survival, for example, provided we don't waste even more precious time debating the issue!"

"We're already running," Judy pointed out, "thanks to Lieutenant West's 'lightning reflexes'! Fat lot of good it's doing us!"

"Run away and live to fight another day!" the robot volunteered in its thundering bass, giving voice to yet another of the annoying platitudes that seemed to be the most recent result of Will's tinkering with its AI software.

"Just because it has weapons doesn't mean it can't be reasoned with," John Robinson said irritably as he continued to work at the communications console, a look of grim concentration on his shaggy-bearded face. "We have weapons but we don't blast away indiscriminately at anything we encounter."

"We don't initiate high speed pursuit the instant we detect another ship, either!" West snapped. "That thing, whatever it is, *did*!"

"There could be a thousand legitimate reasons for that!" Robinson said. "If I can just get whoever's in charge to respond to a hail, I'm certain I'll be able to clear up whatever misunderstandings are behind its actions."

The bridge lurched as a pale greenish beam emerged from a faintly glowing circle on the hull of the pursuing ship and lightly grazed the *Jupiter*. An instant later, a rumbling voice even louder than the robot's filled the bridge.

"In case there was any doubt in your minds," it thundered, "that was a warning. Surrender immediately or be destroyed."

John Robinson looked up from the comm unit and darted puzzled looks about the bridge. Apparently the other ship had an even more advanced language translation technology than what Will and Dr. Smith had been improving and refining ever since it had fallen into their hands a couple planets back.

"Attacking ship," Robinson said loudly, "can you hear me?"

"Of course! And everyone in your vessel can hear *me*! I repeat, surrender or be destroyed. I do not *wish* to damage something that may have some value to me, but—"

"We are *not* your enemy," John shouted. "We are merely—"

"Who or what you are doesn't matter," the voice thundered back. "You have entered my domain and your ship is forfeit! Surrender or die!"

A spot on the hull of the pursuing ship glowed briefly, and a second beam shot out, barely grazing the opposite side of the *Jupiter* but shaking the bridge like a blow from a cosmic sledgehammer.

"I think," Don said, thumbing open a small panel on the navigation console even as he cut the drive, "it's time we headed through the sun again. Dr. Robinson?"

Robinson looked for a moment as if he were going to

argue, but then the alien voice battered at their eardrums again. "A wise decision to stop your foolish attempt to flee. We will take that into consideration when it comes time to determine your usefulness."

Robinson grimaced in resignation as he turned from the communications console to face Don, who was impatiently holding out his hand. Digging into a pocket for the two keys he always carried with him, Robinson handed one to Don, who instantly sent his pilot's chair shooting upward to the hyperdrive initiator console.

His finger to his lips in a "be quiet" gesture, Don inserted his key into the high console while John did the same below. His right hand on the key, Robinson held his left in the air, three fingers extended. A glance at Don, a nod of understanding, and he began the silent countdown. As the last finger folded into his palm, the keys were turned simultaneously.

Outside the ship, the hyperdrive segments extruded themselves into space and locked in position. An instant later they flared into life and a shimmering force field enveloped the entire ship, faint at first but building. Another few seconds for the field to peak, and—

"What are you doing?" the voice thundered.

"We would rather destroy ourselves than allow another to do it!" Don shouted back, improvising as the field continued to build. "I suggest you move away unless you're feeling suicidal!" he added with a grim smile.

"That field is not—" The voice broke off, and a telltale circular glow appeared on the hull of the ship, this one at least twice the diameter of the previous ones.

"You were warned!" the voice thundered.

"Looks like they're on to us. Everybody hang on!" Don shouted, engaging the hyperdrive moments before the field hit its peak. "It's sink or swim time!"

And the world went crazy around them. The violently shifting gravity fields of the hyperdrive shook the *Jupiter* like a cat shakes a mouse. On the viewscreens, wavering like fun-house mirrors, a distorted image of a beam of destruction, this one bright green rather than pale, emerged from the equally distorted image of the ship and—

—vanished.

Along with the alien ship and everything else outside the *Jupiter* itself.

But the crew of the *Jupiter* saw none of this. For them, time had ceased to exist moments after Don had engaged the hyperdrive. In fact, the *Jupiter* itself had ceased to exist in normal space and now spun blindly in the unknown dimensions of hyperspace, its unseen viewscreens and the bridge itself twisting into shapes that could be described by the multidimensional mathematics designed into the drive but could never actually be *seen* by eyes limited to three dimensions, not without twisting the minds behind those eyes into a nightmarish jumble that could never be untangled.

To the crew of the *Jupiter*, there was a brief but violent shaking as massive forces pushed and pulled them in a thousand different directions at once—and then a "flicker," as if they had all simultaneously blinked their eyes.

And with the flicker, the forces vanished, leaving only silence and seeming motionlessness.

But they all knew better. They knew that whatever velocity they had at the start of transition, they retained at the end—but in a new frame of reference, a new and distant part of space. It was as if, back on Earth, someone had "jumped" from an eastbound train to a westbound train. The jumper was motionless with respect to the train he jumped *from* but moving a hundred miles an hour with respect to the train he jumped *to*.

The same rules applied in jumping from one point to another through hyperspace. It was a form of conservation of momentum, one of the most basic laws of nature and, for the *Jupiter*, potentially one of the most deadly.

Which was driven home to Don West the instant his senses cleared and his eyes fastened on the planetary disk that filled the forward viewscreens and was growing larger at an alarming rate.

Luckily, he had managed to cling to the pilot's chair throughout the chaotic transition. He had the drive engines restarted in seconds, while the others were still blinking and picking themselves off the floor and fighting down the transition-induced nausea.

A quick glance at the velocity readings told him that full reverse thrust wouldn't stop them before the *Jupiter* burned a hole through the planet's atmosphere and produced a mile-wide crater in its surface. Fingers dancing across the controls, he applied full power, not in reverse for braking but at right angles to the ship's headlong path.

Abruptly, the disk began to shift to the left on the

viewscreens, but with maddening slowness as the drive fought not only the *Jupiter*'s massive momentum but the ever-increasing tug of the planet's gravity. No one made a sound, not even Smith, as the subsonic vibration of the overstressed engines threatened to tear the ship apart.

Alarms went off as a tiny dot appeared just to the right of the planetary disk. Almost without thinking, Don altered the thrust vector minutely and breathed a ragged sigh of relief as the alarms fell silent and the dot grew rapidly into a huge spoked wheel—a space station dozens of times the size of the *Jupiter*—and shot past with half a kilometer to spare.

"If there are a *lot* of those things up here, we could be in real trouble," he muttered, his gaze riveted on the viewscreens.

But there were no more—at least no more that lay directly in their gradually changing path. A half dozen much smaller artificial satellites skimmed by at safe distances, and they got a hurried glimpse of what looked as if it had once been a solar power array more than a kilometer in diameter, tumbling and useless.

Until, finally, the planet had expanded to fill almost half the sky.

For a moment a shower of sparks enveloped the *Jupiter* as it tore through the tenuous upper reaches of the planet's atmosphere—

—and emerged, the flaring curtain of sparks replaced by unfamiliar patterns of stars as the last traces of atmosphere were cleared and the planet fell behind them and began at last to recede.

Don cut the engines, letting a blanket of relieved silence envelop the *Jupiter* as it sped away from the planet on a skin-of-their-teeth hyperbolic trajectory.

"Good work, son," the robot thundered into the silence, one of its deadly metal claws coming up in what its AI software must've thought resembled a jaunty salute.

Don turned toward the robot with a scowl, but before he could speak, Judy Robinson laughed loudly, a sudden release from the tension of the last few minutes. "Yes, sonny," she said, still laughing, "a nice job indeed."

She was still laughing and Don was still scowling— at Judy now, rather than the robot—when Will came bursting onto the bridge, Penny close behind. He looked at the planet receding on the viewscreens, then at the unfamiliar star fields.

"You made another jump!" he said excitedly. "Where are we *now*?"

Penny glanced at the planet, her look of cautious hope turning instantly to glum resignation. "That's not Earth," she said, "so who cares?"

Her shoulders slumping, she turned and headed back toward the quarters she had just left.

2

Pocketing the hyperdrive keys, John Robinson stared at the planet, now centered on a single rearview screen.

"Take us back," he said, "and put us into high orbit. This world may have possibilities."

"You said very similar things about the last one," Smith pointed out, "and look what *that* got us!"

Tired of Smith's automatic objections and complaints, but most of all tired of Smith himself and his condescending tone and meticulously trimmed beard, John Robinson spun to face the doctor.

"I suppose *you* have a better suggestion?" he asked, raising his voice as he pushed his angry, shaggily bearded face within inches of Smith's. "Maybe you want us to go into cryostasis again and head for another star system that might or might not have any inhabited or inhabitable planets, maybe no planets at all? *If* we wake up after several years in cryostasis. For that matter, if you're so anxious to go into stasis, I'd be glad to oblige! It'd make things easier—not to mention *safer*—for the rest of us!"

Smith wilted uncharacteristically before the elder Robinson's vehemence. "I was only suggesting that we take a great deal of care, whatever we do."

"Thank you for your heartfelt concern!" Robinson snapped, turning away. "We always appreciate a helpful hint from the traitor who *put* us in this mess in the first place!"

Maureen, who had come to the bridge not long after Will and Penny, put a restraining hand on John's arm. He pulled in a breath and placed his own hand over hers, squeezing it for just a second. There were still problems between them, but one of the major ones— their almost constant separation because of their work on the *Jupiter* project back on Earth—had been removed by the very disaster that put them in this situation. Now they were together almost constantly, working on the dual problems of survival and finding a way to return to Earth. In some ways, it was more like the years before they had married, when both had been working single-mindedly—but together—on their educations, and some of those long-ago, happy memories now and again would surface. John was even beginning to think that, provided they survived long enough, they would someday recapture whatever it was that had drawn them together in the first place.

Somewhat calmed, he turned back to the view-screens and to Don, still at the navigation console, and realized that everyone, even an unusually silent Smith, was looking at him and his wife.

"As I was saying," John said, pointedly looking away from Smith, "unless someone has a better idea, we're going to take a closer look at that planet. And yes, a *cautious* look," he added, returning to the communications

console to begin a search for signals indicating that whatever civilization was responsible for the space station they
had so narrowly missed was still alive and kicking.

After two hours of listening from high orbit, John Robinson
was finally ready to throw in the towel. Except for static
from random lightning strokes generated by a half-dozen
storms that rolled and roiled across both land and water,
the planet was utterly silent throughout the entire elec-
tromagnetic spectrum. If the civilization that had built
the space station was still functioning, it was doing so
without radio communications of any known kind.

He turned from the comm unit and nodded to an
impatient Don West. "The space station first," he said.

"It's about time!" West groused, his fingers already
darting across the controls.

"As if we had anything *better* to do!" Penny said,
rolling her eyes. Tired of being alone in her room, she'd
returned to the bridge a few minutes earlier to stare
glumly at the not-Earth planet and now the approaching
space station.

"It looks big enough to support a population of thousands," Maureen said as the giant, spoked wheel grew to
fill an entire viewscreen.

"Not without supplies brought up from the planet,"
Don said, shaking his head. "I don't see any growing
areas, no transparent stretches to let sunlight in."

"So they didn't want to be farmers," Penny said, as if
surprised she had to point out something so obvious. "I
mean, who'd go into *space* to grow his own garden?"

"Not everyone thinks living in a Mega-Mall is paradise, sis," Will said.

Penny snorted. "Sure! I can just see you out there digging in the dirt, squashing bugs and stuff!"

Will shrugged. "I'd just build a robot to do it. An agricultural robot."

"If you two can stop sniping at each other long enough," Don broke in, "how about seeing if you can spot anything that looks like a docking port. I haven't had any luck yet."

"I don't think you ever will," John Robinson said, his voice hushed. "This never had a docking port."

"Not one that fits the *Jupiter*, maybe," Don said, still scanning the massive wheel. "But there has to be *something*."

John shook his head. "Not if this isn't the space habitat we first thought it was."

Don frowned as he glanced toward John. "So if it isn't a space station, what the hell is it?"

"Something I only dreamed about when we were designing the hypergate." Robinson leaned toward the viewscreen, pointing. "Look at the center, where a 'normal' station would have a hub—where the docking port you're looking for would be."

Instead of a hub and a docking port, the others realized, there was only open space. There was no hub. The half dozen ten-meter-wide spokes that arrowed in from the rim of the kilometer-wide wheel ended at a second, smaller ring that was still at least two hundred meters in diameter.

"And there," John went on, pointing at the inner surface of the inner ring, "see those stubs of metal sticking out?"

Don nodded. "So whatever happened to them, it kept them from completing the thing."

John shook his head again. "Look more closely. Those aren't the beginnings of a continuation of the spokes. Those are the start of—or more likely the *remnants* of—pylons that supported something that filled that entire area inside the inner ring."

"A hypergate!" Will exclaimed, his face suddenly bright with excitement as he strained toward the viewscreen in an effort to see more detail.

"But not a hypergate the like of anything we're capable of building," Robinson said, smiling at his son's instant understanding of the situation.

"Then how do you know—" Don began, but John cut him off.

"When we were working on the initial design for the hypergates, we did a little blue-sky speculation, just trying to see what we could do if we had all the energy and all the time we wanted."

He paused and looked again at the slowly tumbling wheel, a glimmer of envy in his eyes. "If we'd had enough energy to power not just a city—which is what the actual hypergate requires—but enough to power a country, or even an entire world, and if we'd had three or four decades to work instead of three or four years, then we might've designed and built something that looked a lot like this. . . ."

3

The next two hours proved John and Will right. Each of the six spots on the inner ring did indeed contain the remnants of support beams made of alloys beside which carbon steel had the tensile strength of warm butter. Even so, their ends were fused by the kind of heat that only existed in the heart of a sun.

And in the middle of each cluster of support beams was an opening through which protruded the equally fused remains of massive power conduits. The outer ring, as best they could tell from what little data the *Jupiter*'s instruments could extract through the more conventional steel and iridium walls, was a series of highly advanced fusion power generators, while the inner ring contained a half dozen super-conducting storage devices. Each had once been capable, John suspected but did not say, of delivering in a fraction of a second a concentrated pulse of power that would have sucked all of Earth's generator's dry.

It could certainly deliver enough energy, he thought uneasily, to vaporize the entire hypergate structure that he was certain had once occupied this now-empty space. If something had gone wrong . . .

Not that there was any danger of that now. The power generators had long since ceased functioning, and there was no indication that even a milliwatt of power remained in the storage devices.

But information . . .

If these people had developed gates as advanced as this, then who knew what else they may have had? Maps of hyperspace itself? Methods of controlling and directing the forces of a hyperdrive so that, even without a hypergate, destinations could be chosen?

John turned toward the image of the planet. Even if the civilization that constructed this marvel had collapsed—or, more likely, had been destroyed—surely there would be records of *some* kind.

Or survivors.

"It's time to look at the planet," he said.

Minutes later Don had maneuvered the *Jupiter* into a low polar orbit that would take them, strip by strip, over every part of the planet twice in its twenty-nine-hour day.

They quickly realized, however, that prospects for finding either information or survivors were not good. During the first eighty-minute orbit, on a plain about a quarter of the way from the planet's equator to its south pole, the remnants of a city slid by beneath them. Their first fleeting impression was of a metropolis in ruins, hardly a building standing, vegetation eating its way in from the periphery and growing outward from dozens of spots within the city.

But with computer enhancement of the recorded image, a puzzlingly different picture began to emerge.

The buildings weren't disintegrating and collapsing. There wasn't a jagged edge or a broken wall or a collapsed roof anywhere. The buildings and the streets looked as if they were *melting*. It appeared they were being absorbed by—or converted into—the soil, from which sprouted the grasses, trees, and bushes that were supplanting the city.

It was as if the city was biodegradable, John thought wildly. And more. As if it had been organically grown and was now well along in the process, not of dying but of being reabsorbed—of being "ungrown."

Despite such a seemingly alien technology, the city had been laid out in a very Earthly checkerboard pattern. Assuming urban population densities similar to Earth's, at least a million beings—people—had once lived there.

And, apparently, died there.

A half orbit later, two thousand miles north of the equator, the pattern of a second, even larger city was evident in the irregularities of a forest the size of Texas.

Another orbit later, almost on the equator, they drifted over what had once obviously been a major seaport but was now half submerged by a rising ocean level and half devoured by a jungle, a rain forest that would've more than matched Earth's nineteenth century Amazon basin.

"Greenhouse effect?" Will wondered glumly when they found the fading imprint of a fourth dead city in the midst of another jungle. "Maybe they did the same thing the people back on Earth were doing."

"I doubt it, son," his father said as he studied the images on the viewscreens. "For one thing, the atmosphere looks as clean as Earth's back before the industrial revolution took hold and started muddying it up. And from the looks of the vegetation, the ecosystem is in ter-rific shape, which isn't surprising if their structures were all as ecofriendly as these *appear* to be."

John Robinson shook his head. "No, something else killed this civilization. And it wasn't war, either, at least not the kind we're familiar with. There's obviously not been a large scale nuclear conflict. Those cities would be fused scars. And there's no radiation, at least not enough to detect from up here."

"So what killed them?" Judy asked. "Alien invaders with 'clean' weapons? Maybe a world full of belligerent idiots like the one we just got away from?"

"Anything's possible," John replied.

"I make it a practice," the robot rumbled conversa-tionally, "to believe in at least one impossible thing before my morning self-diagnostic routine."

Will grinned while most of the others grimaced. He still hadn't figured out exactly what it was in his last over-haul of the robot's AI software that accounted for gener-ating mangled quotations and platitudes, but as far as he was concerned, it was definitely more "spontaneous" and therefore more "human" than it had ever been before. Maybe, by the time they finally found their way home—

If they found their way home, his darker half reminded him, as if taking perverse pleasure in raining on his Pollyanna half's parade.

"Shut up, Robot," Will muttered under his breath as he turned back to the others, who were still arguing about what might or might not have taken a planetwide civilization from space travel to dead cities and radio silence in only a century or two, maybe wiped it out altogether. Listening to the argument—and remembering Earth—he decided the planet probably hadn't needed to be invaded. If the people of this world had been anything like grown-up humans, they could've done it all by themselves. Maybe they'd just found a neater way to do it than nuclear war or rampant pollution.

After another orbit and two more similarly absorbed cities, John Robinson announced that, when their initial orbital survey was completed, they would switch from polar orbit into the equatorial orbit currently inhabited by a number of smaller satellites, some of which, at a distance, resembled conventional space stations. While they were discussing—arguing over—who would transfer to one of the stations for a close-up look, their attention was caught by a sixth fading city as it appeared on the curved horizon of the world below them.

But as it grew closer, they saw this one was not only larger than any of the previous cities, but different. Despite its near-complete reabsorption by the surrounding wilderness—thicker than a forest but not quite a jungle—it was obvious that the city had been almost perfectly circular. The remnants of the streets—imprints, really—showed hundreds of concentric circles connected by hundreds of arrow-straight spokes.

And at the center was not a ruin, but a seemingly intact building, similarly circular and squat but nearly half a kilometer in diameter, surrounded by a comparatively narrow ring, perhaps two hundred meters wide, of what looked to be carefully maintained grass, trees, and shrubs. The encroaching forest—unkempt and shaggy, as forests tend to be—stopped abruptly at the outer edge of the ring.

Whatever it was, John Robinson decided, they could not afford to pass it by without a thorough investigation.

"Set us down, Major, as close to that building as possible."

Word spread quickly among the Watchers: The day they had hoped and believed would never come had apparently finally arrived.

Ever since the last trace of the Invaders had vanished from Rellka more than five generations ago, groups of families had taken year-long turns watching the Vault and the surrounding area, though what it was they were watching for had never been precisely defined. What they feared, of course, was that the Invaders, who had long ago slaughtered at least ninety percent of the population, would someday return.

What they knew—virtually *all* they knew—was that the Invaders had been associated in some way with the Vault, which had once been the key to keeping their world free from other, earlier enemies.

And so, for nearly two centuries, they had watched for they knew not what. Occasionally they turned away a traveler foolhardy enough to want to enter the Vault itself. The only "Invader" they had seen, however, was the welcome one of nature itself, which, as expected, had quickly reclaimed virtually the entire city. Except for the Vault and the few hundred square meters surrounding it, the only buildings still functioning were a few low-profile residences that those same generations of Watchers had occupied during their year-long stints, thereby keeping the buildings in a constant state of renewal.

But now . . .

Now a ship had settled to the ground within a few thousand meters of the Vault itself, a ship larger than anything their own world had produced in the millennia before the Invaders.

Was it a new Invasion?

Or just a visitor, an explorer like their own ancestors had been — before the Invasion?

They would watch and wait and take what action they dared.

And hope that the truth would, somehow, reveal itself . . .

"Go ahead and make fools of yourselves if that's your desire," Dr. Smith said firmly. "I will stay here in the *Jupiter*, where it is at least marginally safer than out there in that dreadful wilderness. I will 'hold down the fort,' so to speak."

"'Fly away with the fort,' you mean!" Don West said, glowering at the doctor and, almost instinctively, tightening his grip on the strap of the plasma rifle slung over his shoulder. "The only way we leave you alone in here is if you decide you really do want us to stash you in a cryotube."

Smith managed to look offended. "*What* does one have to do in order to gain a modicum of trust in this nepotistic organization?" he asked plaintively.

"Trust? You?" Don snorted derisively. "How does 'when hell freezes over' grab you?"

"Now, now, children," Judy Robinson interrupted, "play nice or we might have to consider freezing both of you."

John Robinson sighed loudly as he looked up from the readouts he'd been studying since Don had expertly set the *Jupiter* down in a stadium-sized clearing a few hundred meters from the perimeter of the city. Once, long ago, it might have been an area cleared for a small farm, so regular were the edges, but it obviously hadn't been used for that purpose for years, if not decades.

"In case any of you are interested in such mundane matters," John said sternly, giving his daughter Judy and the pilot a patient scowl, "the atmosphere is eminently breathable and the temperature almost comfortable, though the humidity is a little high.

"And," he added, pausing for effect, "there *is* a functioning power source somewhere, providing electricity and possibly other forms of energy to at least the central area of this . . . city."

Judy's thoughts immediately refocused on their reasons for being here. "But still no sign of life," she said with one last check of the comm station readouts. "And no response to any of our signals."

Her father nodded. "Which could mean anything. The power source may be self-repairing and simply continuing to supply energy without supervision. Or the inhabitants may not want anything to do with us and are hoping we'll go away."

"Or they're hostile and will kill us all the moment we move away from the ship," Smith added.

"In that case," Don said flatly, "I suggest we send *you* out to look around." He grinned. "I *knew* you'd eventually turn out to be good for *something*."

John shook his head. "And if they're waiting to give him the key to the city instead? No, we go out together."

"We could send the robot out," Will volunteered eagerly. "I've got him configured so he's all-terrain now. He can go anywhere."

"*It* can also scare the stomach contents out of anyone it runs into." John shook his head again. "No, that rifle Major West refuses to leave behind is ominous enough! If there are people out there, and if we want to be able to communicate with them, we'll have a better chance if we don't instantly confront them with a walking, talking weapon of mass destruction."

"He's not—"

"I know *it* has several other functions, Will, but it is still not your ideal goodwill ambassador. And if it turns out we need its help, we can always signal it." John looked down at his son. "We *can* still signal it to come give us a hand, can't we?"

"Sure!" Will grinned. "I've been working on a new remote control, but the old ones all still work. And with what I've been doing with his AI software, we can even tell him before we leave that he should come and check on us if we don't come back. Or you can just send regular radio messages back to the ship, and he'll hear them.

Or you could have him follow along behind us, you know, just in case, and—"

"Do not worry, Robinsons," the robot thundered helpfully. "I will not by inaction allow any of you to come to harm."

"And what about *me*?" Smith asked.

"You are not a Robinson, but you are included in my programming," it rumbled noncommittally, "as is Pilot West."

"Now that we have all that settled," Don said with a suspicious glance at the robot, "maybe we should get started."

"Agreed," John Robinson said, casting one last disapproving glance at the rifle still slung over West's shoulder as he led them to the *Jupiter*'s main airlock. Whenever Smith slowed or held back, Don put a viselike grip on the doctor's arm and kept him moving.

Outside, as promised, it was shirtsleeve weather, late morning on this particular part of the planet. Even Penny, who had lobbied briefly to stay behind in the *Jupiter*, smiled faintly as she felt the real, not recirculated, air cool her face and brush at her hair. Overhead, puffy clouds and a startlingly blue sky reminded her of the EnviroVids they had seen that simulated Earth as it had been a century or two earlier.

John, meanwhile, couldn't help but think that whatever these people did to kill themselves off, they didn't take their entire world with them, the way Earth had been threatening to do for the last century or two.

Suddenly, the idea of living out his life on a world

like this—on *this* world—was overwhelmingly attractive. Their search—their fool's errand—to find a way back to the dying world that was Earth no longer seemed as urgent or even all that sensible. What's more, the evacuees of that dying world would almost certainly overrun any new world they were given and quickly infect it with their own cancerous blight.

Except, John reminded himself reluctantly, he had worked most of his adult life to give them that second chance. His hope, doubtless naive, had been that humanity, having learned from its mistakes, would do better. He couldn't abandon that hope, not even for his entire family.

And not for Earth.

Not yet.

Pulling in a thought-focusing breath, he turned toward the distant center of the phantom city.

And saw that Will was already fifty meters ahead, waving to the rest of them impatiently.

With Smith continually grousing, it took nearly two hours for them to pick their way through the wilderness that a century or two ago had doubtless been broad, well-kept streets. The seemingly biodegradable nature of the streets and buildings was even more evident close up than it had been in the computer-enhanced images generated from orbit. What had formerly been streets now looked essentially like shallow ten- or twenty-meter-wide riverbeds; their gentle, at times barely noticeable banks made up of the collapsed or melted buildings that once lined the street. Even the artificial pattern, so obvious from space, was virtually invisible at ground level. If not for occasional patches of stubbornly unrecycled building material peeping out here and there, it could have been a completely natural wilderness of trees, brush, grasses, flowers, and occasional vines.

Then they were at the central clearing. The transition from the wilderness was startlingly abrupt, even more so than it had appeared from orbit. It was as if the two areas were separated by an unseen wall, the almost-jungle on one side, and what looked like meticulously maintained park land on the other. Carefully but irregularly placed trees and shrubs alternated with stretches of geometrically smooth lawns of faintly bluish grass and beds of pastel flowers. Paths, not of stone or concrete, but of some milky-white, perfectly smooth substance, crisscrossed the area. In the shade of many of the trees stood what John could think of only as graceful combinations of park benches and chaise lounges, made of slightly different colored versions of the material in the pathways, which itself, he suspected, was the undegraded form of what the rest of the city had once been made of.

Tentatively, he extended a hand into the oasis of order, half expecting to be repelled by the invisible force field that obviously held the outer chaos at bay.

But nothing held him back, nothing resisted the slow forward motion of his fingers.

Until—

Abruptly, he jerked his hand back.

4

"What's wrong?" Maureen asked worriedly as her husband inspected his hand, wiggling his fingers experimentally.

"Nothing," he said, shaking his head. "At least I don't think so. There was a tingle, that's all, like an electrostatic field."

More slowly than before, he extended his hand again. This time he felt nothing.

"Nothing at all," he said. "Or it could've been nerves the first time."

Or, he thought bemusedly, it just sniffed at me and learned all it needed to the first time.

The others, when they followed him across the boundary moments later, felt nothing, although Smith managed to twitch nervously anyway. Overhead, a pair of colorful birds the size of pigeons swooped through the boundary and looped back out a dozen meters away, all with no obvious effect. John wondered what would happen when something—or someone—that *wasn't* wanted tried to cross the line.

The temperature and humidity, he realized after a moment, were subtly different, slightly cooler and drier.

Yes, *something* was still operating here, supplying power and maintaining this park area, whatever it was. As he stood there, looking around, he realized it reminded him somewhat of the campus of the university he and Maureen had attended—or rather, the university's holodisplays of what the university had been like in the twentieth century.

Was *that* what this had been?

An alien version of a university?

He looked more closely at the huge building that lay before them. Like the paths and the "benches," its walls were perfectly smooth and featureless, looking like a cross between tile and plastic. But even as he watched, blur-edged sections of the walls began to change color, not suddenly or radically, but slowly and soothingly, like a hundred overlapping pastel rainbows coming gradually into existence, each at its own pace, dancing in the breeze, and just as gradually fading, only to be replaced by others, a visual equivalent of elevator music.

It's waking up! he realized, a mixture of uneasiness and anticipation sweeping over him.

As if to add to the illusion of a creature awakening, a pair of double doors appeared like eyes, the same way the shifting rainbows had, but permanently placed, square-edged, and striated glossy brown like oak or mahogany.

John Robinson pulled in another deep breath and looked around at the others. All of them, even Smith, were staring blankly at the building.

"Judy," he said, "any signals now that it's active?"

Pulling her eyes from the hypnotically shifting patterns on the walls, she checked the link to the comm station back on the *Jupiter*.

"Nothing," she said after a moment, then nodded at the newly appeared doors. "Maybe they just *outgrew* radio."

John nodded uneasily. "In which case, what killed them off? And is it still around?"

"My thoughts precisely, Dr. Robinson," Smith said quickly. "If you will only—"

"Put a sock in it!" Don West snapped, then turned to John Robinson. "Whatever happened here happened a long time ago, a century at least. And if whatever did these people in was still around—and *wanted* to do us in—it's had all the time in the world, and we're still alive."

"Don's right," Judy agreed reluctantly. "Whatever or whoever wiped these people out is long gone."

"And if we set off an alarm they left behind to alert them to trespassers?" Smith asked. "They could be on their way back right now!"

"In which case," Don said loudly, "why are we wasting time with our little debating society? If there's information inside there, let's get it and get the hell out."

"Then let's go," John agreed, heading for the double door.

Smith snorted derisively, wincing as Don gripped his arm and hustled him along on John's heels. As they approached the "door," it slid almost soundlessly upward and to the right, vanishing into the surrounding wall.

Another faint tingle swept over John as he entered the building, but he couldn't be sure if it was real or imagined. The others followed, Don herding a reluctant Smith ahead of him.

The building, they saw immediately, continued the spokes-and-concentric-circles pattern of the surrounding city. An arrow-straight corridor shot ahead toward the center of the building, with intersecting corridors every eight or ten meters. Except for a softly glowing strip that ran down the middle of each corridor's ceiling, casting shadows so diffuse they were almost nonexistent, the corridors were utterly empty and featureless.

"Haven't these people ever heard of signs?" Don grumbled, scowling at the walls. "Or control panels?"

"There's something down here!" Will shouted, starting at a run down the first corridor to the left. Despite the emptiness and the blank walls, there was no echo, no reverberation, either from his rapid-fire footsteps or from his father's shouts to be careful. A few meters in, Will stopped and tugged at something protruding from the wall a meter above the floor. The same color as everything else, it was invisible unless you knew where to look. When nothing happened, the boy twisted at the protrusion, first one way and then the other.

A door handle? John wondered, hurrying along the corridor toward his son.

Apparently so, because even as he came up behind Will and put a cautioning hand on the boy's shoulder, a door-shaped section of the wall hinged open.

"Have to twist it counterclockwise," Will said triumphantly, as if he'd just hacked into a particularly resistant computer, "and push down and to the left."

But as the door swung open and he saw what lay beyond, Will's face fell. It was nothing but a cubicle, no more than three meters on a side and just as featureless as the corridors. Directly across the gently curving corridor, Don West followed Will's formula and snatched open an identical door.

And found an identical cubicle behind it.

Frowning, he stepped inside, peering closely at the walls, tapping at them as if searching for secret panels. But the cubicle walls, even more than the corridor walls, muffled and almost completely absorbed the sound.

Shaking his head irritably, Don stomped out of the room, his purposely heavy footsteps as muffled as his tapping had been. He lumbered down the corridor to another pair of handles. Yanking them both open revealed only two more seemingly identical cubicles. Two more cubicles were found several meters farther on.

And two more beyond that.

Instead of tapping at the walls as he had in the previous cubicles, Don slammed his fist hard against one wall. And found the force of the blow absorbed as if by a pillow. Judy Robinson, who had been bemusedly watching his "inspection" routine, stifled a laugh, earning a glower from the frustrated pilot.

"What the hell *is* this place?" Don asked, looking up and down the seemingly endless corridor. "And why would anyone waste the planet's only functional power source on it?"

"Padded cells, of course," Smith said, emerging from

one of the cubicles himself, smiling derisively. "In the event you haven't noticed, the inside of these doors are completely bare. It appears that they can only be opened from the outside."

"An asylum? Or maybe a prison?" John Robinson shook his head. "I can't believe that."

Smith shrugged. "As you wish. But whatever it is, I do not foresee any particularly bountiful harvest of information."

"Perhaps not," John said, looking down the corridor to where it curved out of sight. "But there has to be more to it than these . . . cells, if that's what they are. Don is right. These people must have had a reason to want to maintain power to this complex above all others. And I'm not about to give up after a cursory inspection of twenty or thirty meters of one corridor out of dozens."

John assigned Maureen to stay by the outer door, "just in case," and divided the rest of the group into pairs, Will with him, a protesting Penny with her sister Judy, and an even more vehemently protesting Don West with Smith. Each pair would take one corridor and continue around it until they came back to the radial corridor they'd started from—or until the corridor they were following ended.

"This really *is* a waste of time," Smith said as Don opened the twentieth or maybe the twenty-fifth pair of doors along their assigned corridor, "and of energy."

"If you have any better ideas, feel free!" Don said, moving on to the next pair of doors.

"Almost anything would likely be more productive than mindlessly opening and closing doors on empty rooms. For example, you might try to learn something about them, using more sophisticated techniques than occasionally slamming your fist against the wall."

Without warning, West spun around and clamped a viselike grip on Smith's arm. "You're right!" the pilot snapped. "We *have* been wasting time."

"And just what do you think—"

"I *think* I'll let you do all the 'sophisticated' investigating you want!"

As he spoke, Don wrenched open a door, saw that it contained yet another identical cubicle, and literally hurled the smaller man inside. "I'll be back in a hour or two for a report on all the valuable information you'll no doubt uncover," he said, attempting to slam the door but succeeding only in closing it with a soft whoosh.

He could hear Smith's muffled shouts but couldn't make out the words as he stalked off down the corridor to the next pair of doors. For a moment he thought about going back and letting Smith out, but shook his head. It would be safer this way for both of them. If he had to spend the next hour listening to Smith's snide remarks, there was no way he could resist the constantly recurring impulse to smash a fist into the man's supercilious face.

"Come back here and release me, you pea-brained mental midget!" Dr. Zachary Smith shouted, pounding on the frustratingly absorbent wall of the cell.

There was no response. Not that he had expected any, not after the way that cretinous mesomorph had pitched him through the door, accompanied by what passed for a *bon mot* among such creatures.

Lowering his fists, Smith stepped back from the wall and stood silently. In truth, he was much calmer than his shouting would indicate. Not being claustrophobic, he knew he didn't have anything to worry about except a few minutes or hours of boredom. West or one of the others would eventually be back to let him out. They couldn't help themselves. It was in their misguided nature not to allow even an enemy to die if they could prevent it.

Except, perhaps, for West. He was a soldier, after all, and that overly soft, counterproductive aspect of his personality had been at least partially submerged by his training.

Therefore, Smith decided, it had been a mistake to continue to goad West when the others weren't around to ride herd on the pilot. In the future, he would have to exercise more restraint when he was alone with the big oaf. There was too much risk involved for the minor, fish-in-a-barrel pleasure it afforded him.

Sighing mentally, Smith looked around, wondering if his semiserious suggestion as to the purpose of the cubicles was actually correct. This one at least fulfilled the basic function of a padded cell: restraining a person while preventing him from harming himself. Whatever these walls were made of, they were the ultimate shock absorber. Even the dully glowing patch in the ceiling—

A faint rustling sound somewhere behind him cut off his train of thought like a guillotine. He spun around, eyes searching the blank wall and finding nothing.

Rats in the walls? he wondered. High-tech rats of some kind, of course, but—

Another sound spun him around to face the door—if it was indeed the door. With four identical walls, he realized he couldn't be positive of anything, even that the walls were still there. It was more like being in an incredibly dense fog than in a room, a fog that was growing thicker and more disorienting every minute, closing in like a—

Shaking his head violently, Smith closed his eyes, trying to get rid of the feeling of vertigo that had begun to grip him.

Something touched his back.

Jerking around again, his eyes snapping open, he saw that whichever wall he was now facing was no longer featureless. A portion of it had darkened to a dull gray and was bulging out toward him like a grotesque plastic tumor.

It's *alive*!

For the first time since they had landed, Dr. Zachary Smith was truly afraid. West might not have *intended* to kill him, but if someone didn't let him out before—

Heart pounding, Smith backed away, but realized that the same rustling sound was coming from behind him as well, from the opposite wall.

And from the floor beneath his feet, which, he realized with a new wave of terror, was shifting and undulating just like the wall.

And the ceiling—

Abruptly, the light went out and he was left in darkness.

Then Smith felt something warm and gelatinous oozing up his legs.

He screamed and struggled as long as he was able.

5

"You did *what*?"

Maureen Robinson frowned angrily at Don West, who shrugged uneasily under her gaze.

"He was getting on my nerves," he said defensively. "It seemed like a good idea at the time."

She looked at him with exasperation, as if he were a misbehaving child.

"What's going on?" John Robinson emerged from another corridor, followed closely by Will. A dozen meters in toward the hub, Judy and her sister appeared at the mouth of another corridor.

"It's nothing," the pilot said, waving a hand dismissively. "I just stuffed Smith in one of the cubicles to get him out of my hair for a while. Don't tell me the thought hadn't occurred to any of you."

"Not as much trouble as a cryotube, I suppose," John admitted, unable to completely suppress a flicker of a grin. "Where is he? You *do* remember which cubicle you left him in, don't you?"

"Approximately," Don said with a sigh. "I'll go let him out."

"We'll all go," Maureen said sternly, although all of

the others, particularly Judy, seemed to be holding back grins.

"One of these," Don said a minute later, gesturing at a string of half a dozen doors along the interior curve of the corridor he and Smith had originally been assigned to. "I'm not sure exactly which one, but—"

Maureen snatched open the first door, revealing an empty cubicle. John was already at the next, opening it with the same negative result. Giving Don and her husband a disapproving glance, Maureen moved to the next door and twisted at the handle.

It wouldn't move.

Frowning, she tried again.

"It won't open," she said, a mixture of nervousness and accusation in her voice.

"Let me try, Mom," Will said, hurrying over.

She hesitated before stepping back and turning toward Don and her husband. "Don't just stand there," she said sharply, "try the others!"

The two men hurried past her to comply, but the next two doors, then the next four, the next ten, all opened on empty cubicles. Don shook his head as the last one opened. "I *know* it wasn't this far. It *has* to be that one back there."

"Something's moving around inside," Will said, his ear pressed to the door next to the still-unbudgeable handle.

John pulled the boy away from the door. "I'll do it," he said, wishing he could give in to the impulse to simply stand back and let whatever was happening to Smith—if anything—continue to happen.

As he twisted at the handle, he felt it shift in his grip, as if it were alive, and he snatched his hand back.

A moment later the door swung open.

On an empty cubicle.

"I thought you said—"

John froze as he realized, first, that the walls were gray, not white, and second, that the far wall was bulging out, wriggling like a giant plastic cocoon.

As they all watched in gape-mouthed silence, a slit appeared in the bulge, extending from floor almost to ceiling, revealing a catatonic-looking Dr. Smith.

A moment later the slit expanded and the lips retracted, becoming once again part of the wall. Smith slumped bonelessly to the floor.

"I think he would've preferred a cryotube," Don muttered. Feeling an unexpected pang of guilt, he pushed past everyone, scooped Smith up, and headed back toward the radial corridor at a heavy-footed trot, the others following.

He was about ten meters from the door to the outside when his burden woke up abruptly, gave an earsplitting shriek, and began thrashing so violently he wrenched himself free and thudded to the floor, almost tripping Don.

"Smith!" the pilot shouted as the doctor continued to scream and thrash on the floor, his eyes tightly closed. "It's all right! You're out! We got you out!"

As quickly as the outburst began, it stopped. For a moment Smith lay perfectly still. Then, swallowing audibly, he opened his eyes, which darted from side to side.

Judy, carrying her small "just-in-case" medical kit, was already kneeling next to Smith. When she tried to slip the tiny, self-adhesive transmitter unit of the stethoscope beneath the fabric at the neck of his tunic, he batted her hand away and scrambled backward, coming up against the nearest wall, cowering.

"Whatever happened," Judy said calmly, "it's over. You're safe now."

Smith blinked. "It's really you?" He darted suspicious looks at them all. "You're *real*?"

"As far as I know," Don said. "Now what the hell happened in there? I didn't think—"

"That is precisely the problem!" Smith snapped at the pilot, his terror of a moment before seemingly erased by the healing power of angry contempt. "You had no idea what those cubicles are or what they can do, and yet you locked me inside one without a second thought!" He glared at the rest of them. "And where were *you*? How many days did you leave me *in* there?"

"You weren't in there much more than an hour!" West said. "Look, I'm sorry, all right? But—"

"That is utterly impossible!" Smith protested as he climbed shakily to his feet. "I was trapped in there for several days, at the very least."

John Robinson shook his head as he glanced at his watch. "We entered the building only an hour and a half ago."

Smith glared at them, then belatedly looked at his own watch. His eyes widened in surprise.

"Now what exactly happened in there, Doctor?"

Robinson asked. "It *looked* as if the wall had . . . eaten you."

"An apt description," Smith agreed with a shudder, "but that was only the beginning." He scowled at the nearest door, but after a moment his expression morphed into a thoughtful frown. "However," he went on, "I do believe I now understand the function of these cubicles."

"And are you going to share your insight with us?" Robinson asked when Smith paused, probably for dramatic effect. "Or do we have to go in and find out for ourselves?"

Smith smiled, seemingly fully recovered from his experience. "Now *that* is something I would indeed enjoy seeing," he said, darting a glance toward West.

"And maybe I'll throw *you* back in," Don threatened, reaching toward Smith, "if you keep beating around the bush."

Smith twitched backward. "They're torture chambers," he said stiffly, then relaxed as West lowered his hand. "Of exquisite efficiency, I might add, if the time I spent in there is indeed no more than you claim."

"Torture chambers?" West shook his head disbelievingly. "You look pretty much the same as when I left you."

"I *said* it was highly efficient," Smith retorted, a trace of admiration entering his voice. "These devices could punish some recalcitrant individual—punish him *severely*—for several hours of subjective time while actually taking only a few minutes of real time." A faint smile pulled at the corners of his mouth. "A full day of punishment would still leave time to get a good day's work out of the troublemaker. There wouldn't even be any debilitating physical damage, nor any unsightly mess to clean up afterward."

"And you underwent this torture for what seemed like *days*?"

"Not by choice, I assure you!" Smith shrugged. "If you don't believe me, try it for yourself."

John frowned at the doctor skeptically. Smith was up to something. He was probably constitutionally incapable of *not* being up to something. And he *had* been alone in one of the cubicles for over an hour, apparently in complete and intimate contact with—

With what?

With whatever this building really was. And the story Smith was telling now could hardly be better designed to keep everyone *else* from entering a cubicle. Not that anyone in his or her right mind would volunteer in the first place, after seeing Smith disgorged from the wall like a bad meal.

All of which meant . . . ?

For one thing, it was clear that Smith didn't *want* anyone else to enter a cubicle and experience whatever it was he'd experienced in there.

Which meant, of course, Robinson realized, someone had to do exactly that.

Handing the second earpiece to her mother, Judy Robinson carefully held the stethoscope transmitter against the door they had just closed behind her father. Will and Penny both watched anxiously while Smith leaned against the opposite corridor wall, smiling with smug expectancy.

Maureen, for one, was beginning to doubt the wisdom of her husband's action, but no one had been able to talk him out of it. Even pointing out how much Smith seemed to be enjoying himself hadn't swayed him.

And now he was inside.

"I'm fine." The stethoscope picked up the words easily, though they were muffled. "Nothing at all is happening so far. Except that it's a little disorienting, these walls are so completely blank. But I don't see or hear anything at all, except my own voice. And even it—"

"I hear something!" Judy said abruptly. "A rustling of some sort."

"I do, too," Maureen said, leaning close to the door. "Can you hear that, John?"

"He's about to realize I was telling the truth," Smith said cheerfully. "The walls will start reaching out for him any second now."

"John?" Maureen almost shouted.

"He was right," John's voice came back, but each word was more muffled than the one before. "The walls *are* changing shape, as if . . . "

And then his voice was gone even from the supersensitive pickup in the stethoscope that Judy pressed more tightly against the wall. Now she heard only the rustling sound increasing rapidly, like a growing windstorm, until it was audible even to those without earpieces.

Abruptly, it stopped. Total silence.

"The handle!" Will exclaimed, and everyone looked toward where he was pointing.

The handle changed color just slightly, as if to mark this door from the others. Had the other one, behind which they'd found Smith, done the same? No one could remember. They'd been concentrating on opening it rather than on minute color shifts of the handle.

"I think he's been in there long enough," Maureen said in an unsteady voice.

Smith shook his head. "There's really no hurry, dear lady. He's probably only been killed once or twice so far."

"*Killed*?" Don spun around to tower menacingly over Smith. "You didn't say anything about being *killed*!"

"I told you they were torture chambers," Smith said with a shrug. "What better way of torturing someone than by killing him slowly and painfully—over and over?"

"And you let him—"

"*You* let *me* stay in there for over an hour!"

"I didn't know!"

Listening to the exchange, Maureen's face had turned ashen. Now she grasped at the door handle and twisted.

It wouldn't turn.

6

"I'll call the robot," Will said quickly, pulling the latest remote from his pocket. "He'll get Dad out!"

Maureen shook her head decisively. "If that room 'absorbed' your father the way it did Dr. Smith, John could be *in* the wall that the robot tears through or burns down."

"She's right," Judy said, preempting Will's protest. "We don't know *what* is happening in there. Besides, if we damage it, it might not be *able* to open—or to release Dad, ever."

"Like a cryotube," Don said, grimacing, remembering how Judy had almost died when the robot, sabotaged by Smith before their launch from Earth, had destroyed her cryotube's thawing engine before she could be revived.

"Exactly," Maureen said, her face grim, her hand still on the door handle.

"Let me try, Mom," Will said. "Maybe it works a little differently when there's someone inside."

The boy stepped past her as she released the handle. He looked at it more closely before putting his own hand on it. "I *think* it's changing color again," he said, "going back to the way it was before."

His mother leaned down to Will's eye level, squinting as he gripped the handle. It still wouldn't turn. But the color change continued, or so it seemed. The change was so subtle —

Without warning the handle turned under the pressure of Will's fingers. And the color now matched the rest of the door perfectly.

The door swung open.

"I bet it's like a status light!" Will said excitedly. "It tells you when it's safe to open it! Just like the cryotubes!"

Inside the cubicle it was just as it had been with Smith. The cocoon the wall had formed was slowly retracting, allowing John to slump to the floor.

Maureen jumped inside, followed closely by Don West, who knelt down, intending to scoop Robinson up the way he had Smith. But even as the pilot was leaning down, John's eyes snapped open, darting from side to side, his mouth opening as if to scream.

He froze, as did Don, his arms not quite touching Robinson. "You're out of that thing, John," Maureen said, kneeling next to Don. "You're all right."

For a moment John remained teeth-clenchingly stiff, then let out a relieved whoosh of air.

"How long?" he asked weakly.

"A couple of minutes," Maureen said anxiously, "that's all."

He shuddered, glancing toward Smith, who smiled and inclined his head in brief acknowledgment. "Marvelously efficient, wouldn't you agree?" Smith remarked.

• • •

"I simply do not believe it," John Robinson said as the group made their way back toward the *Jupiter*. "This civilization was not only more scientifically advanced but—well, 'enlightened,' for want of a better term."

Smith laughed. "Ecofreaks need not also be altruists when it comes to dealing with others of their own race. Just because they built houses that turn to mulch once they're abandoned doesn't mean they didn't recycle their enemies with great gusto."

John shook his head vehemently. "Only a world of sadists would build thousands upon thousands of devices solely to torture their enemies."

"Perhaps they used them on their friends, as well," Smith said, still perversely enjoying himself. "Perhaps that's how they made sure their friends remained friends."

"Maybe torture is the only way *you* can hang on to your friends," Don snorted, "but most people have better ways."

"I simply don't buy the idea that the purpose of those thousands of cubicles *is* torture!" John said. "Look at where the building was located—in the middle of what amounts to a ring of park land, itself in the center of a major city! It would be like surrounding Auschwitz with a rose garden and sticking it in downtown Berlin!"

"Everyone likes their workplace environment to be pleasant," Smith said with a shrug. "But perhaps you're right, Professor Robinson, in which case the Roman Coliseum would be a better analogy than Auschwitz. Perhaps, instead of a torture palace, it's the ultimate entertainment complex—ten thousand screens, no waiting!"

"*Entertainment?*" most of the Robinsons virtually chorused incredulously.

"Of course," Smith said, enjoying their reaction. "A virtual reality 'theater.' It was just our luck that today's matinee was a horror story."

John shuddered at the thought of a race who considered what he and Smith had gone through "entertainment." Even so, a dark but logical corner of his mind told him, it wasn't entirely beyond the realm of possibility. He remembered some of the gross-out Surroundvids he and his pals had subjected themselves to back in grade school and realized that maybe, just maybe, the difference was not in kind but in degree. Except . . .

"No," he said. "This was just the same thing repeated over and over."

"I didn't say it had an award-winning script." Smith shrugged again. "Or perhaps, after a hundred years, a malfunction developed and the program became stuck in a continuous loop. Although I have to admit, this does not explain why the complex itself, whatever it is, is still functioning while every other structure seems to have been designed to return posthaste to the environmental womb, so to speak."

Abruptly, John stopped and raised his hands in a shushing gesture. "Did you hear something?"

Everyone halted while Major West quickly unslung the plasma rifle and scanned the clearing they were just entering, a thirty-meter irregular oblong area surrounded by a dense stand of trees the size of earthly oaks. In the center of the clearing was an amorphous, undissolved glob of the material the city had been made of. Apparently it wasn't degrading as fast as the rest, resulting in the clearing surrounding it.

As they watched, warily, something moved in the shadows of the trees directly ahead. Don's plasma rifle twitched toward the movement like a compass needle.

An animal? They had seen countless birds and caught glimpses of small, furry animals on the way in, but nothing larger than a small dog.

Cautiously, they emerged into the clearing, itself in the lengthening shadows of the surrounding trees. A moment later a young man stepped out of the trees ahead into full view. Clad in what looked like nondescript homespun shirt and pants, he was holding his arms stretched out to either side, palms up, as if to demonstrate he was holding no weapons.

Will started to dart forward but his father caught his shoulder and held him fast.

"Major West!" John hissed. "Do *something* with that weapon besides pointing it at him!"

Reluctantly, West lowered the weapon, and then, even more reluctantly, reslung it across his back in response to John Robinson's scowling gesture.

"Everyone take it slowly," John went on. "No sudden moves, and stay behind me."

Holding his own arms outstretched in imitation of the stranger, John moved forward slowly, out of the shadows of the trees into the clearing, onto an uneven rivulet of the undegraded building material. When West and the others followed a moment later, another half-dozen natives, both men and women, joined the first, their arms similarly outstretched.

"Beware," Smith said softly, hanging back as the others moved forward. "People whose ancestors considered what happened in those cubicles either torture *or* entertainment do not strike me as people on whom it would be wise to turn one's back."

"Your concern is duly noted," John said, not taking his eyes off the natives. West's hands twitched toward the rifle but didn't touch it.

"And you, young man," Smith went on, directing a purposeful look at the back of Will's head, "I trust you are able to summon your metallic friend on short notice."

When no one replied, Smith sighed uneasily and reluctantly followed. The natives, he could see, were moving forward as well, as if to meet them halfway.

For five meters, then ten, both groups walked in slow silence, but then, when they were separated only by the ten meters of the glob of building material, the natives stopped. Until then their eyes had been focused straight ahead, watching the advancing Earthers, perhaps warily, at least alertly; but now, for just an instant, the eyes of the young man who had first stepped out of the shadows darted to one side, toward the densest, darkest part of the surrounding wilderness.

Too late, John sensed motion out of the corner of his eye. Turning abruptly, he saw a dozen riflelike objects poking out of the shadows.

Even as Don West snatched at his plasma rifle,

Robinson shouted their peaceful intentions, though he knew that until the translators kicked in, anything he said would be gibberish to the natives. His arms were still outstretched, but as the words emerged and the rest of the group spun to look in the same direction, Don was bringing his weapon around to point in the general direction of the would-be ambushers. At the same time there was a rapid-fire series of popping sounds, and a half-dozen tiny darts appeared as if by magic on West's arm and chest. The rifle flared, but the energy beam tore at the ground and then splattered off the glob of building material.

A moment later John felt a beelike sting in his own shoulder.

The last thing he saw before his vision blurred and darkened and the world spun out of control around him was Don West thudding to the ground, the plasma rifle falling from his limp fingers.

7

Judy Robinson grimaced as a surgical assistant wiped the frost from her microgoggles, giving her once again a clear view of the frost-rimed chest cavity visible through the opening in the surgical draperies. Operating in a giant cryotube was *not* a good idea. No matter how much it slowed down the patient's metabolism, it was no substitute for a reliable anesthetic. Besides, her surgical gloves did virtually nothing to keep her own fingers insulated from the nerve-numbing, near-absolute-zero environment, and open-heart surgery was both delicate and demanding. Performing it when one's fingers were stiff from the cold—

Something touched her arm, startling her into letting the laser scalpel fall from her icy fingers into the chest cavity. Looking away from the slowly pulsing heart, she saw a bare hand and arm reaching out from under the surgical draperies and gripping her arm tightly.

And a voice: "You didn't think a little thing like open-heart surgery could distract me from your charms, did you, Judy baby?"

The draperies slithered away as her patient, a smirking Don West, sat up on the icy operating table.

With an annoyed gasp, she woke up.

She tried to identify the sources of the dream, but before she had gotten beyond the obvious—her own near-death in the cryotube and West's crude come-ons and macho posturing—she realized she wasn't on the *Jupiter* but slumped on the floor of a five- or six-meter-wide room as plain and featureless as the tiny torture cubicles.

Suddenly her heart was racing, her every nerve tingling as she remembered the ambush and the darts. At the same time, her right hand went instinctively to the spot on her left arm where the dart had struck, the same spot that, in her dream, West had grabbed. It was, she saw, puffy and tender, like a spider bite. Her pulse accelerating even more at the thought of an alien drug coursing through her body, she reached for the medical kit at her waist.

But it wasn't there.

Nor was her watch, she realized a moment later as she tried to find out how long she'd been unconscious.

Nor her communicator.

At least, she thought with minor relief, they had left her her clothes.

And they hadn't dumped her in one of the cubicles.

Or had they? This didn't seem, so far, anything like what Smith and her father had described, but who was to say all ten thousand cubicles were running the same show?

But no, there was no point even considering that possibility. Assume her current surroundings were real and work from there, she decided. It was the only reasonable course to follow.

So where was she? Struggling to her feet, she realized the ache was not, after all, confined to the area where the dart had struck. Her entire body felt as if she had a low grade fever, and she wondered how the others were doing. Particularly her brother. With Will's much smaller body weight, the effects of the dart would be proportionally stronger.

Still unsteady on her feet, she looked around for some indication of a door.

Nothing. Not even a semidisguised "handle" of the sort that had been on the outside of the cubicles.

But whatever this was, she was *inside*.

A prisoner.

"Hello?" she called loudly. "Is anyone there?"

There was no response, but at least the translator had kicked in. Her captors must have talked enough while they were transporting her for it to have generated at least a rudimentary vocabulary.

"Hello?" she repeated, this time banging on the nearest wall at the same time.

To her surprise, a door flowed open almost directly in front of her. At the same time, a half-dozen smaller holes—ports?—appeared at various points around the room. An instant later the barrels of some kind of weapon poked through. They could be anything, but as far as she could tell, they looked like the barrels of the dart rifles she had glimpsed in the seconds before unconsciousness had overcome her.

An elderly woman in a shapeless, homespun robe appeared in the doorway and stood there looking at her, as if inspecting her.

"Why have you done this to us?" Judy demanded. "For all you know, those darts could've killed us, not just knocked us out! And you took my medical kit—"

"*Your* friend's weapon *would* have killed *us*! We saw what it did!"

"It was only for protection," Judy protested. "He fired only when you fired on us!" she added, trying to remember if it were so.

"In any event," the woman went on, "your possessions will be returned to you, except for the weapon, as soon as we are satisfied it is safe to do so."

Judy glared at the woman. "And how do I 'satisfy' you? What is it you want?"

"We wish—we *need* to know why you have come to our world."

Judy blinked. Well, at least these people knew there *were* other worlds. They hadn't forgotten *everything* when their civilization collapsed. "You know about other worlds, then?"

"We do," the woman said. "But we also know that many of them pose a danger to us."

"Is that what happened to your people? They were killed by people from other worlds?"

"The Invaders, yes, that is what we are taught. Our entire world fell victim to such people."

Which wouldn't be all that surprising, Judy thought, considering the so-called "civilizations" the *Jupiter* had

55

run into, particularly whichever one had spawned the space-going privateer that had driven them into hyper-space little more than a day ago.

"Where are they now, these Invaders?" Judy asked.

"No one knows. You could be their emissaries for all we know."

Judy scowled. "So that's why you took us prisoner? Just on the off chance we might be—"

"And what would *your* people do, if someone came to *your* world as you came to ours? Openly carrying what is obviously a deadly weapon?"

Judy's frown faltered as she recalled the kinds of things her people *had* done, not to aliens but to each other, for far less serious perceived threats. Thousands of years of wars because humans hadn't trusted—had *refused* to trust—their friends and neighbors, let alone complete strangers.

"You're right, of course," Judy said, lowering her gaze. "My people would probably do far worse in similar circumstances. What can I do to convince you we mean you no harm?"

Dr. Zachary Smith was lost in a saccharine nightmare of self-sacrifice and forgiveness. A positively beatific-looking John Robinson loomed over him, his arms spread wide as if waiting blissfully to be nailed to an invisible cross.

"We all know that Will's death wasn't your fault," Robinson said, a tear trickling down across his cheekbone and disappearing into his unkempt beard. "You simply had to save yourself, a perfectly natural reaction in a moment of stress and danger."

That was when Smith realized he was cradling the boy's body in his arms.

But he was alive, not dead.

"You *meant* to kill me, Dr. Smith," Will Robinson said.

"Of course I did, you foolish child! You're an annoying distraction and you *deserve* to die!"

"Even so, we forgive you," John Robinson said, the words echoed a moment later like a Greek chorus by his wife and daughters, who had appeared behind him sometime in the last few seconds.

"Then you're utter fools, all of you!" Smith shouted, heaving the boy's body at them. "None of you deserve to live!"

"Your thought is our command," they chorused in annoying, cloying tones and promptly fell dead, their expressions remaining beatific and forgiving.

Except, Smith suddenly realized, they weren't the Robinsons!

The bodies now wore the faces of his own family, not only parents but long-forgotten—until now—uncles and aunts. But what were they doing *here*? Hadn't they done enough, the self-righteous fools!

But at least they were dead and couldn't waste his time delivering more of their sanctimonious lectures. He didn't have time to listen to such foolishness, not now, of all times! He had to get out of here before—

Abruptly, without warning, he was awake, a cold floor hard beneath him.

Where . . . ?

The trek through the forest that had once been a city, and the ambush that had ended it, flashed through his mind. Had the attackers captured him and returned him to one of the cubicles? Was this another—

He looked down at himself in the dim light and saw, with stomach-wrenching relief, that he was still himself, not yet another bizarre alien creature. So this was *not* another torture session, at least not so far, although the grayish room he was in wasn't all that different from a large version of the cubicles. But the walls weren't bloating out to smother him, not yet, and whatever was happening to him was, in all likelihood, real.

On the other hand, whoever had captured him was almost certainly not as mindlessly forgiving as the Robinsons of his dream. If they were in fact the descendants of the people who had built—and used!—those cubicles . . .

Smith shuddered silently. The admiration he had felt for the efficiency of the cubicles was rapidly mutating into fear at the thought of once again being the object of that efficiency.

What he needed, he thought dismally as he looked around the gray-walled, featureless room, was a plan.

Or at least a door.

But even as the thought came to him, the light brightened and a doorlike opening "appeared" in the wall before him, along with a half dozen of what he realized instantly were gun ports.

Scrambling to his feet, he ignored the feverish ache that he only then realized pervaded his entire body, radiating out from where the darts had struck him. Momentarily surprised at his ability to block out the discomfort, he wondered if his experience—his countless agonizing deaths, more accurately—had anything to do with it. Had it raised his normally low tolerance for discomfort? Torture could, he imagined, have that effect—if you survived. With the torture taking place in your mind while your body was restrained and protected by a life-supporting cocoon, you were pretty much guaranteed to survive.

And he wondered: Was *that* the cubicles' intended function? Not to torture, per se, but to *condition*? To inure people to pain so as to make them better soldiers? A high-tech version of the "toughening up" that the military subjected its new recruits to?

The sound of footsteps from beyond the door drove all such pointless speculation from his mind. His captors were doubtless coming to check on him, but they might not expect him to be awake yet. Frantically, he looked around, but the newly brightened light revealed only how completely featureless and weaponless the room was.

A man appeared in the doorway, and suddenly, without warning, Smith was once again immersed in his torture cubicle nightmare. It wasn't a man coming toward him through the door but a *creature*, the same hideous thing that had killed him a hundred—a *thousand*—times while he had been trapped and cocooned in that room.

But this was different, he saw instantly. The creature

that advanced upon him now was not the suffocatingly solid monstrosity that had tortured and killed him so many times. It was a translucent *ghost* of that creature, and through its insubstantial body he could see the open door and the man still bearing down on him.

Then the man was plowing *through* the creature with no more resistance than if he were moving through a hologram.

Or through a drug-induced hallucination, Smith thought with a new rush of terror, wondering if this could indeed be a result of whatever had been on the darts that had felled them all.

But then, just as suddenly as he had been swallowed up in this seeming hallucination, Smith remembered— was somehow *urged* to remember—the torture itself, not just the sights and sounds, not just the pain and the odors, but the torrent of out-of-control thoughts and emotions that had torn at his shattered and traumatized mind as that death scene had played itself out again and again until, finally—

As if plucked from a raging maelstrom, one particular memory emerged and presented itself to him, but it was a memory not of what had been done *to* him, but what, during the thousandth or the ten-thousandth excruciating repetition, *he* had done to the thing that, until then, had been his unstoppable executioner.

Most of Judy Robinson's subsequent sessions with her captors—six or eight hours of them—seemed to have gone well, especially considering the chip-on-her-shoulder start she'd gotten off to. The first of the three women and one man who had talked to her and questioned her had soon become positively apologetic, although the workings of the translator implants always left room for doubts. They had the language down cold after a few minutes, but intonation was something that even computers this advanced had trouble with, and she was totally on her own in trying to interpret body language. The only questioner who had been openly hostile was the man. He had not only refused to answer any of her questions, but had clearly been displeased at the others' openness. He even seemed unhappy that the previous questioner had revealed his name, Zolkaz, as if even that tiny bit of knowledge could prove dangerous in Judy's hands. He also hadn't so much questioned her as cross-examined her, often asking the same questions a half-dozen different ways, his skepticism at her answers obvious.

On the other hand, the first woman—Kelwyn, her name proved to be—had, after her brief, early reluctance, freely answered Judy's questions about the history of their own world called Rellka. As much of it as they knew, at least. And they *did* appear to know a fair amount. They were even aware of the orbiting hypergate, which they called, aptly enough, a "window in the sky." Their ancestors had built it, Kelwyn said, and had used it for "exploration among the stars" for several generations.

They had met and dealt with a number of unpleasant species during that time, but finally encountered something so dangerous that they had purposely destroyed the hypergate themselves in order to keep whatever it was from coming through. But the action hadn't saved them. The Invaders had gotten through before the hypergate could be closed. But the Invaders hadn't been warships and armies. According to most versions of what had happened, the Invaders had never even been *seen*. Whether that was a result of their technology or their nature, no one knew.

But whatever the Invaders were, they had been real enough to destroy the Rellkan civilization. They had not used nuclear weapons but some form of "possession" that drove Rellkan to kill Rellkan. The plague had struck this very city first. From there it spread inexorably around the planet like a virus of madness. Within a decade, all but a few thousand "immunes" were dead at the hands of one-time friends and family.

Listening, Judy couldn't help but wonder if the so-called possession had not actually been a form of biological warfare. Perhaps a small cadre of Invaders had come through the hypergate and simply released an airborne biological agent of some kind, something that attacked the Rellkan central nervous system, driving everyone mad that it touched.

As for the still-functioning Vault and its torture cubicles, Kelwyn knew only that it had once been a major part of a defense system devised during the early years of the hypergate's use. It was assumed that was the reason this city had been the focus of the attack when it came. Disable the defense system, what*ever* it was, and the rest of the world would be helpless.

And so, apparently, it had proved to be. Whatever

the system had been intended to do, it had obviously failed. For her part, Judy simply couldn't imagine what the torture cubicles could possibly have to do with a defense system. But then, remembering again the ruthless, slaver mentality of the privateer who had driven them here, she found herself wondering if the Vault had been modified into its present form by the Invaders themselves, the actual beings she suspected had come through the gate in order to release the biological agent. It made a warped kind of sense that the Vault could serve as a "playground" for people who had no compunctions about slaughtering an entire planetary population. People like that would probably enjoy a technological version of a Roman Coliseum, in which the lions could kill a Christian not just once, but over and over for the delectation of the audience.

She shuddered, imagining a battalion of such alien de Sades hooked into the circuit, savoring and slavering over each prolonged and grisly human death.

And wondering if, light-years away, an entire planetful of such creatures actually existed. And if there was any basis in reality for Kelwyn's fear that the creatures might someday find their way back to Rellka.

8

Relief flooded over Judy Robinson as her captors ushered her into a large, plain room the next morning and she saw that everyone else from the *Jupiter* was already there. Aside from the stubble visible on Don's and Dr. Smith's faces even at this distance, no one looked any the worse for wear. Her parents gave her a forced but encouraging smile while Don West managed a protective swagger while standing perfectly still. Penny, looking only slightly more glum and petulant than she normally did on board the *Jupiter*, stood between her parents and a disconcertingly eager-looking Will. Judy assumed her brother's questioners had been as free with their answers to him as they'd been with her. It would certainly account for his expression. As long as he was learning something— "hacking into knowledge," their father sometimes said— he was happy, no matter what the circumstances.

Black-clad Dr. Zachary Smith stood apart from the group, arms folded as he pointedly ignored both the *Jupiter* crew and the score or more of natives— Rellkans—at least half of whom held dart rifles at the ready.

No one moved to stop Judy as she crossed the room

to her family, but before she could do more than give a squirming Will a brief hug, one of the unarmed natives pounded a crooked stick as tall as himself—a staff?—on the floor like a gavel.

It was Zolkaz, Judy realized with a sinking feeling, the man who had been so hostile in his questioning. If *he* was in charge, they were in real trouble.

"Did that one—" she began to whisper to her parents, but was cut off by a second gavel-like slam and an angry-sounding voice.

"There are those among us," Zolkaz was saying, "who believe you should be present while your fate is discussed and determined. I do not share that belief, but I bow to their will. I will not, however, tolerate disruptive behavior. You will be allowed to speak, but only at the appropriate time."

"And when will *that* be?" Kelwyn, until then standing quietly in the background with the others, spoke up in a harsh voice, totally unlike the tones she had used during her questioning. "Will you allow them all some final words before their executions?"

Zolkaz scowled as he turned to face the older woman. Several of the others turned toward her as well, startled.

"What nonsense is this?" he asked angrily, his grip on the staff tightening. "No one has spoken of execution!"

"You don't have to!" Kelwyn's gaze swept over the others, two of whom Judy recognized as her other interrogators from the day and evening before. "We all know how you feel! You have spoken often enough of the need to 'play it safe' if this situation ever arose. And now it has!"

"And that is precisely the reason we are here. We are here to *decide* what to do! There has as yet been no decision made!"

"Not by the rest of us, perhaps, Zolkaz, but—" Abruptly, Kelwyn stopped. Looking around, she blinked, appearing puzzled.

"Yes?" Zolkaz was still scowling at her.

"I—I only wanted to be certain the strangers are given a complete and impartial hearing," she said, her voice still firm but lacking the harshness and anger of a moment before.

"They will be, of course," Zolkaz said sternly. "And it is insulting that you apparently consider me incapable of conducting it. Now shall we begin?" He looked around with a questioning scowl, as if daring someone else to challenge him or his impartiality.

"Very well," he said when no one spoke up, "we will begin. Kelwyn, you have spoken to them all. Report."

Uneasily, Kelwyn looked around as all eyes focused on her. "It is my belief," she began, "that these people are in no way connected with those who destroyed our world. It is my recommendation that they be released and allowed to return to their ship and continue on their way."

"You believe them, then?" Zolkaz demanded, obviously spoiling for a fight. "You believe that it is sheer chance that brought them here? Not only to our world but to this place, of all places?"

Judy suppressed a grimace. The man was persistent, if nothing else. He had asked different versions of the same question again and again the evening before, and she assumed he'd done the same with the others. Where else *would* they land? she had asked sharply. They had surveyed virtually the entire planet and found this city to be the only one containing any functioning technology, she'd told him repeatedly, but no amount of explaining had cut any ice with him.

"I do believe them," Kelwyn said flatly, scowling at Zolkaz as if he were a stubborn child.

"And you," Zolkaz said, turning abruptly to another of the woman questioners, "I suppose you—"

"You're an idiot, Zolkaz!" the woman cut him off angrily. "It's people like you that have kept us from regaining—"

The woman was cut off in turn by an explosive curse, not from Zolkaz or Kelwyn but from one of the guards, who was moving toward his neighbor, glowering and wielding his weapon like a club. His startled would-be victim brought up his own weapon defensively, but as the two stood facing each other, the first man's expression shifted from anger to confusion. His eyes widened as they fastened on his weapon, still held threateningly aloft like a club. At almost the same moment, a third guard lurched forward as if shoved from behind, his weapon clattering to the floor as he tried to regain his balance before he crashed to the floor. Others, trying to get out of his way, bumped into yet others until, in a matter of seconds, it seemed that everyone was shoving everyone else and everyone was talking or shouting at once, a mixture of anger, confusion, and fear in their voices and in their actions.

"Stop it, all of you!" Kelwyn's angry voice cut through the chaos, but even as she spoke, someone lurched against her, sending her reeling toward Zolkaz, who tried to fend her off with his staff but succeeded only in tangling her feet and sending her crashing to the floor, her right leg twisting under her as she fell.

Where her shouted admonition had had little effect, her scream of pain brought sudden silence.

Instantly, it seemed, everyone but the Earthers were clustering around her. Then Judy was pushing through the crowd, eluding the grasping hand of Dr. Smith, of all people. Was *he* looking to help? she wondered disbelievingly. He might be a doctor, but not one who placed any value on the Hippocratic oath.

As Judy got close enough to see Kelwyn's twisted features, she wished her captors had seen fit to return her medical kit. Would they now, finally, get around to it?

"I'm a doctor," she said, elbowing her way into a kneeling position next to the woman. "I could be more helpful," she said loudly to anyone who was listening, "if someone would return my medical kit."

By the time the kit was handed to her apologetically by one of her other questioners, however, she knew that nothing it contained would be of much help. Kelwyn's leg was broken. She could reset it and monitor her vital signs, but—

"Kelwyn," she said, "I can't do much for you here,

but if you let us take you to our ship, I have all the supplies and equipment there that I need to—"

"All the equipment you need," Zolkaz broke in angrily, "to turn the tables on us and kill us all!"

"Keep the plasma rifle," said Maureen Robinson, who had argued against West's carrying it in the first place. "Keep the rest of us here. Make us hostages, if that's what it takes to show we're only trying to help."

"And assign us however many guards you want!" Judy said, looking up from her patient. "Never let me out of your sight, I don't care!" She glared around at the crowd. "Now does anyone have something we could use as a stretcher?"

Unexpectedly, Smith was hovering over Judy and the injured woman. He looked around at the crowd not with a glare but with a reassuring smile, his eyes finally coming to rest on Zolkaz.

"One of your men and I can take turns carrying her," he said, his voice startlingly smooth, even calming, though until that moment "calming" was not a word Judy Robinson had ever thought to associate with Smith in any capacity. "I too am a doctor," he added.

Judy turned her scowl on Smith, shaking her head, but before she could formulate a warning that wouldn't tar all the Earthers with the same brush, Kelwyn spoke up, raising herself painfully on one elbow. "That is what we will do," she said, wincing, as even that simple movement stressed the break. "Zolkaz, you will help them transport me. Bring as many guards as you need to feel secure."

For a moment Zolkaz's scowl turned into a puzzled grimace, but finally he nodded. "If that is your wish, so be it," he said with a slight, head-bobbing bow.

"Hold on a second!" Don West exploded. "Judy— Dr. Robinson doesn't need that quack's help! And I can carry—"

"A representative of the military is not required," Zolkaz interrupted stiffly, eyeing Don's leather battle garb, then turning back to Kelwyn and the others. Motioning to half a dozen guards to accompany him, he turned again to Kelwyn. Judy had by then applied an antiswelling compound and immobilized the leg as much as possible with her limited resources. She stood back as Zolkaz knelt and gently lifted the injured woman, cradling the fragile, almost wispy body in his arms while Kelwyn draped a steadying arm over his shoulders.

"Keep the remainder here until we return," Zolkaz said as the door opened for him and Smith.

"Watch out for that weasel!" West called after Judy as she followed the others through the door. She didn't bother acknowledging such an obvious warning but did glance briefly at her parents and siblings, who watched her leave with various degrees of concern on their faces.

Outside, Judy saw that their "prison" was a smaller, rectangular version of the Vault, and she wondered if *all* buildings on this planet were equally featureless. Or if, perhaps, the buildings—private residences, anyway, if such things existed—were so completely malleable that they could be reshaped at the will of their occupants.

Maybe this total featurelessness was merely a default configuration.

"Which way to our ship?" she asked. For all she could tell, they could be anywhere. One of the overgrown "riverbeds" coursed past the building, but that told her nothing except that they were probably somewhere within the remnants of the city.

"This way," Zolkaz replied, sighing as he set out to lead the way. His tone was teeth-pullingly reluctant, as if he were still hoping for a reprieve, despite Kelwyn's order.

The six guards, each armed with a dart rifle, formed a watchful envelope as the group made its way through the not-quite-jungle. Judy, staying close behind Zolkaz and his fragile burden, glanced now and then at Smith, who strode easily along beside Zolkaz.

When they got to the ship, she knew she would have to be very careful—and hope that Smith hadn't completely conned Zolkaz. Presumably, Smith had been questioned as long and as repetitively as the rest of them, but who knew what kind of lies he'd told them? He had likely told the truth about the basics—how they had come to be there, for instance—but when it came to answering questions about the others, about she herself and the rest of the Robinsons, and particularly about Don, there was no telling what wild fantasies Smith had spun. Anything to make himself look good, she assumed, and the rest of them to look bad.

Why else, she wondered, would they have so easily acquiesced when Smith suggested he accompany her and Kelwyn to the *Jupiter*? Almost certainly all he wanted was an opportunity to gain control of the ship.

Or of the robot, Judy thought with a shudder, remembering Smith's original sabotage, which had sent the robot on a murderous rampage on the bridge of the *Jupiter*. And that wasn't the only time he'd taken it over, despite the safeguards Will had designed and installed after each incident. Even now, given enough time, Smith could probably bypass them all and send the robot off to do his treacherous bidding.

He might even be able to gain control of the *Jupiter* itself, circumventing the lockouts that Don and her father had put on the ship's controls, in which case she, her family, and their pilot would almost certainly no longer be lost in space, but stranded on a planet.

This planet.

Forever.

9

After a few hundred meters, Smith, to Judy's surprise, took Kelwyn gently from Zolkaz's arms and continued that way for almost as long before Zolkaz took her back.

Could Smith have *reformed* in some odd moment when she hadn't been watching? Judy wondered. But no, the idea was pure fantasy. She recalled, not so long ago, her mother confronting him about the ruthless deception and treachery that culminated in the sabotage of the *Jupiter* and the loss of what had probably been Earth's last chance for long-term survival. Smith had said then: "Do not mistake my deception for a character flaw. It is a philosophical choice, a way of life."

No, despite a few seeming lapses in recent months, there was no way someone like Smith would *ever* consider someone else's welfare before his own. Or even on a par with his own. Whatever he *appeared* to be doing now, Judy told herself, he was in fact looking out for number one: Dr. Zachary Smith.

But the thought that he might have changed wouldn't stay away, no matter how hard she pushed, no matter how absurd it seemed. The lapses *had* happened. True, they had all been relatively minor and had mostly occurred in the period after she'd helped him through detox, when it was impossible for even a viper like Smith to not be at least briefly grateful that the agony of withdrawal had finally ended. But . . .

She glanced at him surreptitiously as they walked, and a moment later he lagged back from his position at Zolkaz's side and fell in beside her. He *was* handsome, she found herself thinking, then shook her head in an effort to dislodge the traitorous thought. Even a *handsome* Zachary Smith was little better, morally speaking, than pond scum.

And even handsome, pheromone-emitting pond scum is still pond scum.

"If you want to save your family," Smith whispered in her ear as they walked, "follow my lead."

Her heart leaped at the words before she had time to consider their source. Or to wonder why neither Zolkaz nor any of the guards had reacted when he'd spoken to her. They couldn't have understood him, even had they heard his words, since he'd apparently disengaged his translator implant, but how could they have missed the conspiratorial way he'd leaned toward her?

As Smith sidled away from her, slowing and letting the rear guards almost catch up with him, she noticed that the smile that had been pasted on his face since their departure from the makeshift jail faded, giving way to a fierce frown of concentration.

What the *hell* was going on?

She almost blurted out the question, but the very air around her seemed to thicken, making every movement a chore, dragging at her limbs as if she were trying to walk underwater. Even her lips and tongue felt heavy, almost paralyzed, and she knew that anything she tried to say would be muffled and probably unintelligible.

The others slowed as well, as if the whole world had shifted into some grotesque slow motion parody of itself.

Suddenly there was chaos as three of the six guards tripped, simultaneously, falling headlong into the dense undergrowth and vines, sending their dart rifles flying. Judy and the other three guards only stumbled, catching themselves before they fell, as did Zolkaz, despite the injured woman in his arms.

But Smith . . .

Seemingly unaffected, he lunged toward the nearest of the fallen guards, grabbing up the dropped dart rifle and firing at the unfallen guards. Two more of them had joined their comrades on the ground before Judy, released from whatever had been clouding her mind and weighing down her body, decided that whatever Smith was doing, it couldn't be good. Instinctively, she leaped on his back, straining for the dart rifle he was trying to turn on another guard.

Startled, Smith struggled to throw her off and break her grip on the weapon, but somehow she hung on.

"You fool!" he grated through clenched teeth.

Suddenly, the sluggish feeling came over Judy again, as if weights had attached themselves to her limbs, to every part of her body. She felt herself being thrown backward, her nearly numb fingers dislodged from their no-longer-viselike grip on Smith's gun.

As she tumbled to the ground, she saw the gun falling too, as if whatever was numbing her own limbs was doing the same to Smith. And all four of the still conscious guards now had dart rifles in their hands, and Judy wondered if her attack on Smith had been such a good idea. But though the guards had seemingly firm grips on their weapons, they were moving no more rapidly than Judy. Smith, motionless now, looked apoplectic, teeth and fists clenched, cordlike tendons standing out on his neck, as if he were straining mightily against an even stronger force than the one that gripped Judy and the natives.

Abruptly, as if released from an invisible force field, he lurched forward, almost falling, then quickly regained his balance and sprinted away, racing through the underbrush and vanishing within a dozen meters. The guards almost dropped their weapons as they tried to spin about to fire after him, but for those few seconds they could only lurch uncontrollably.

And then, whatever had happened, it was over. Whatever had been gripping them all, it was gone.

"Don't let *this* one escape too!" Zolkaz said, his voice cutting through the silence.

All of the weapons swiveled toward Judy, some of them hesitantly while the guards glanced nervously over their shoulders in the direction Smith had escaped.

"In case you didn't notice," Judy said, scowling at Zolkaz, "I probably saved all your butts just now when I jumped on him! And—"

"A trick, nothing more! And now that we have seen

you cannot be trusted, we will return you to the others."

Dumbfounded at the man's obstinately one-track mind, Judy could only shake her head. She turned to the injured Kelwyn, whom Zolkaz had set down on the ground sometime during the fracas, her back against a tree. "Kelwyn, *you* saw what happened!"

The woman nodded. "Of course I did," she said sternly, turning toward Zolkaz. "We will continue to their ship—if she thinks it wise after what has happened." Ignoring Zolkaz's sputtering reaction, Kelwyn looked questioningly at Judy.

Relief washed through her, though she knew she was still far from being out of the woods, as were they all. With Smith on the loose, pursuing his own unique goals, no one was safe.

"Yes," she said to Kelwyn, "we have to continue, and not just for the sake of your leg. But first you have to send someone back to my family and warn them—your people *and* mine—that Smith has escaped. No matter what he may have told all of you when you questioned him, the only time you can trust him is when he's asleep, and I wouldn't put a lot of money even on that."

"He poses a danger to you as well as to us?" Kelwyn asked, still ignoring Zolkaz, whose look had changed from a glare to resigned skepticism.

"Definitely," Judy replied. "No matter what he told you, he's tried to kill us more than once. And don't ask why he's still with us. If it were up to me—" She broke off, shaking her head. "Look, as soon as you send someone back with a warning, we have to get to the *Jupiter*.

Quickly, before *he* does. It's locked, and he doesn't have a key—not that I know of, anyway—but all he needs is enough time. And if he *does* get inside while we're not there to stop him, we're *all* in big trouble."

It was obvious that Zolkaz still didn't entirely believe her, but he dutifully dispatched a pair of the guards before gently scooping Kelwyn up in his arms again and setting out once more in what Judy hoped was indeed the direction of the *Jupiter*.

As they traveled, Zolkaz setting a rapid pace despite his age, Judy tried to get a grip on what had happened.

The only totally obvious fact was that Smith had escaped and had intended for Judy to accompany him. He had even, in his self-delusional way, *expected* her to. But *how* had he escaped?

Was he responsible for the bizarre, incapacitating sluggishness she'd felt, which had, presumably, over-taken the others as well? For the feeling that every muscle was held in check by an invisible counterweight? For the seeming clumsiness that had sent three of the guards tumbling to the ground and kept four of them from firing at his retreating back until it was too late?

Or had Smith simply taken advantage of them? Did he for some reason have a partial immunity to whatever had swept over them all? The same kind of immunity that had allowed a few thousand Rellkans to survive the Invaders? Had Smith simply been able to resist more effectively than everyone else, leaving him with enough motor ability to shoot the dart gun and then escape while everyone else was still immobilized?

Either way, she thought—whether Smith was the source or merely the beneficiary—what had actually *happened* to them?

It had to have something to do with that building the natives called the Vault, she decided, and with its torture cubicles. According to Kelwyn, it had once been part of a "defense system," the nature of which was long since forgotten. Had this been a manifestation of some aspect of that system? Smith had been trapped inside one of the cubicles for more than an hour. Had his presence reactivated the system in some way? Had he even, during that time inside, somehow established a link to it? Or, more likely, it to him? Had he then been able to call upon this defense system, whatever it was, to produce the effects she'd seen and felt?

She recalled what Kelwyn had said: that the system, when the invasion had finally come, had obviously failed. No wonder it failed, Judy thought, if it operated by interfering with the physical workings of an enemy's body. The Invaders, if Kelwyn was right, had operated by "possessing" the bodies of the natives. Judy had assumed, when she first heard Kelwyn's story, that the truth was elsewhere, that the so-called possession had been nothing more than some form of biological warfare, a virus or a chemical agent that drove people mad or incapacitated them.

But now . . .

Now she wondered if perhaps those long-ago Invaders, whether corporeal or some life-form of pure energy, really *had* possessed their victims' bodies. And if the Vault's defense system, unable to distinguish between Invader and invaded, had in the end destroyed them both.

If that system had been reawakened now or, worse, not only reawakened but come under Smith's control . . .

Her heart pounding, Judy peered through the trees and underbrush ahead, hoping ever more urgently for a first glimpse of the *Jupiter*.

10

When finally a patch of the ship appeared through a break in the canopy of trees, Judy forced her mind to ignore her body's exhaustion and raced ahead, leaving an irritated and possibly worried Zolkaz behind. Erupting into the clearing where the *Jupiter* stood waiting, she sprinted across the few intervening meters. At the entrance, she hastily inspected the readouts of the security systems Don and her father had installed and programmed. She sighed with relief when she could find no evidence of tampering. Nothing had touched them during her absence, either physically or electronically, so far as she could tell.

But then, she knew that Smith would have known he didn't have time to do much experimenting before she and the others arrived, so he probably hadn't tried. And, no matter what sort of "connection," if any, he had with the defense system in the Vault, he obviously wasn't yet proficient with it and was still highly vulnerable. His almost-thwarted escape had proven that.

But she didn't doubt that if the connection did exist, he would get better with practice. Smith was nothing if not determined. And, to give the devil his due, brilliant.

Careful not to trip any of her own booby traps in her

haste, Judy deliberately entered all the proper codes and pressed all the buttons and keys in the proper order with the proper fingertips and timing.

Finally the airlock hissed open, revealing the robot, standing only a meter or so beyond, towering over everything on its "all-terrain mobility enhancement module," which is to say, the three multijointed, gyrostabilized legs that Will had improvised for it.

"Where have you been?" Will's AI program rumbled accusingly from the robot's speakers. "You haven't called once since you left. And who are your new friends?" It swiveled its all-spectrum vision receptors toward Zolkaz, who backed away, tightening his grip protectively on Kelwyn.

"Don't worry, folks," Judy said. "This is just our robot. I suppose I should've told you about it, but it slipped my mind in all the excitement." She turned back to the robot. "Look, you go outside and stay close to the airlock. Watch for Dr. Smith—"

"*He* hasn't called me either," the robot volunteered, sounding seriously aggrieved.

"And I hope he doesn't! Now listen, Robot, quit interrupting. This is important. Watch for Dr. Smith. Accept no orders from him, not a one. Don't give him a chance to stick a control rod in you! Just grab him and hold him if you get the chance. But whatever you do, *don't let him into the* Jupiter!"

The robot seemed to take a moment to digest the orders. "As you wish," it rumbled, telescoping and folding everything that would telescope or fold, until it would fit through the airlock. "Is Dr. Smith in the doghouse again?"

"You might say that. I'll explain it all later. Just guard the door for now."

"As you wish, Dr. Robinson," it rumbled, generating a weird echo chamber effect as it eased its way through the airlock. "I will look forward to an informative chat on the subject at your earliest convenience."

Outside, it looked around at Zolkaz and the others. "You're as welcome as the floors in May," it said, mangling another cliché. "Any friend of Dr. Robinson is a friend of mine. Which I gather no longer includes Dr. Smith."

As the guards nervously sidled past the robot and into the ship, Judy took Kelwyn's almost wispy form from Zolkaz's arms, hurried with her to the medical bay, and placed the injured woman on the exam table. With Zolkaz looking on suspiciously, except for an occasional nervous glance over his shoulder in the general direction of the airlock and the robot beyond, she took a drop of blood for a DNA compatibility test. When it passed with flying colors, so to speak, she injected Kelwyn with a variety of antivirals and antibiotics and a powerful healing accelerant, then encased the area of the break with a feather-light spray-on cast. She even surprised herself by finding a pair of lightweight, fold-up crutches in the miscellaneous contingencies box.

"Don't put your full weight on it for the rest of the day," Judy told Kelwyn, "and don't stress it unduly for another couple of days. "It should be fine by then, and the cast will start to be absorbed in another day or so. It should be all gone in eight or ten days."

She turned to Zolkaz, who still looked both skeptical

and suspicious. "Now, I'd like to get back to my family as soon as possible so we can decide what to do about Smith. And then get back here to see if we can come up with a way of actually doing it."

Ordinarily she would have recommended that Don and the rest of the family hop into the *Jupiter* and leave Smith behind, but not on this world. It would be unconscionable to simply say, "Smith's your problem now, see you later." Especially if he had somehow tapped into that so-called defense system. It would be like making the survivors' descendants relive the Invasion. Or worse, considering what Smith was capable of.

"And will your mechanical man accompany us?" Zolkaz wondered uneasily.

Judy frowned. She would feel a lot safer with the robot accompanying her back to the others, but considering Smith's almost uncanny ability to find ways of taking it over, she wasn't sure it was a good idea for it to be out in the open where he would have an easier shot at it, especially now.

Grimacing, she ushered everyone outside, where the robot watched them politely while at the same time scanning the perimeter of the clearing. "Neither Dr. Smith nor his doghouse has approached," it said. "Now I believe you were going to tell me why he is currently in your bad graces."

She didn't want to take the time, but perhaps it was better if she did, particularly in light of Will's current AI program. The occasional petulance it produced was doubtless just part of the program, an over-the-top simulation, but there was no point in taking a chance on offending the robot when a minute or two of explanation would probably placate it.

Feeling only a little silly, she explained as simply and as quickly as possible. One of the robot's vision receptors nodded in simulated understanding.

"I see," it said when she'd finished. "You wish me to remain on guard here while you retrieve your family and Pilot West."

Judy shook her head. "I want you back inside the ship, where Smith will have less of a chance of getting at you. You do remember that he's managed to take you over and even reprogram you a number of times already?"

"Some of the experiences are available in my extended memory banks," it rumbled, "but I can assure you I am not the person I was when those embarrassing lapses occurred."

"I'm sure you're not," she said, resisting the impulse to tell it that it wasn't a person at all. Its AI program would probably take *that* the wrong way too, and there was no point in offending it, which might well make it all the more vulnerable to Smith's blandishments. "But I just don't want to take any more chances than absolutely necessary."

"As you wish," it rumbled. "You are, after all, the ranking canine in your father's absence."

"Top dog, you mean?" Judy couldn't suppress a grin.

"Isn't that what I just said?" the robot asked, puzzled.

"More or less. Now for the moment, you continue as you are. I'll let you know when to come inside."

Not waiting for a reply, she hurried back through the airlock to the bridge and the control consoles to add yet another layer of anti-Smith safeguards before beginning the trek back to her family.

Dr. Zachary Smith paused, only partially to catch his breath, and peeped through the concealing underbrush at what he hoped was the same building they had been held prisoner in. But now two guards stood near the wall where the door had appeared. Smith had been running—jogging, at least—almost steadily from the moment he'd recovered from the stresses of his escape, so he certainly deserved a brief rest and respite. But he also didn't want to take the next step, the step he had raced here to take. The results were far from certain, and he *still* didn't know precisely how he'd accomplish them.

But he had no choice, he told himself sharply. This was his chance, and he was going to take it.

Bracing himself, he once again let his mind return— be returned?—to those thousands of cruel deaths until, once again, he was surrounded by their grisly phantoms, as real to his tortured senses as the solid world plainly visible through their ever-shifting transparency.

Rising, he stepped out of his concealment toward the guards.

Minutes later—or had it been just seconds this time?—the nightmare faded from around and within him, and the guards, unconscious, sat slumped with their backs against the wall.

John Robinson looked up sharply as, without warning, the door to their collective cell appeared and opened. To everyone's surprise, one of the women who had questioned them the day before stood there, alone. No guards, no dart rifles, no knives.

"We are instructed to release you," she said, stepping back.

"It's about time!" Don West blustered, but Maureen Robinson gave him a "don't-push-it" look, and he subsided.

"What happened?" Maureen asked. "Has my daughter returned with your injured friend?"

The woman shook her head. "The one you call Dr. Smith has escaped, but Kelwyn has decided that the rest of you can be trusted."

John Robinson scowled. "Smith *escaped*? How? You sent six guards—"

"It is unclear at this point," the woman said. "Your daughter tried to stop him but was unsuccessful. They continued on to your ship, we are told, in order to prevent him from gaining access to it." She looked from face to face. "This is most puzzling. Is he not one of your group?"

Don West snorted. "Not by choice! On either side!"

Maureen tried to explain but faltered when the woman wanted to know why Smith had been allowed his freedom if he were indeed as treacherous as it appeared.

"It's a long story," John Robinson said, "and I don't fully understand it myself. We *thought* he was coming around, but . . . " He shook his head. "Apparently that was wishful thinking. Right now, I think we should join Judy at our ship. If you could return the equipment you took from us when you captured us, we can be on our way."

"Of course. I will take you to the room where it's being kept."

But the room, as featureless as all the others except for shelves along one wall, was empty. No communicators, no medkit—

No plasma rifle!

"You're sure this is the right place?" West asked, frowning. "I can't tell one room or one corridor from another."

But the young woman was already dashing away. Barely a dozen meters down the corridor, a door appeared and sunlight flooded in. Puzzled, the group hurried after the woman as she darted through the door.

Outside, they found the woman leaning low over one of two young men, apparently guards, both unconscious.

"Velthor?" she said loudly as she grabbed one man's arms and shook him.

For a moment there was no movement, and Don wondered if the man could be dead. But then, abruptly, Velthor's eyes popped open and he scrambled to his feet.

"I'm sorry," he stammered. "I don't know what happened! One of the strangers approached us—"

"Smith?" John Robinson asked, and before he could add a description, the man nodded.

"The one you call Smith, yes. He approached us, and that is all I remember." He looked anxiously toward the other guard.

Don snorted. "He must've grabbed one of the knockout guns when he escaped. And come straight back here!"

Velthor shook his head. "He was carrying nothing, and I was struck by nothing! Of that I am positive."

"Whatever," Don said. "I guess it doesn't matter. What matters is, Smith has everything we were carrying—including my plasma rifle. It's a good thing I put a voice-lock on it when I took it out."

"Don't count on that stopping Smith," Maureen said, more than a touch of sarcasm in her tone. "He's been known to find ways around that sort of thing."

"Dad!" Will broke in urgently. "Now we *really* have to get back to the *Jupiter*, fast! Before Smith can get there!"

John Robinson smiled indulgently, a look that would normally have infuriated the boy. This time he barely noticed. "And what makes you think Smith is heading for the *Jupiter*?" his father asked. "He knows he can't get inside without one of us being along. It would take him hours to get around all the safeguards your sister and I have set up."

"He doesn't have to get around them," Will said. "All he has to do is get the robot to let him in!"

"But the robot is programmed to not obey any orders Smith gives, not without one of us okaying it."

"Smith's got my remote *control*, Dad!" The boy lowered his eyes. "It's got a couple new features I was working on. And I'll bet it doesn't take him very long to realize it and figure out how to use them. Once he does, he'll be able to reprogram the robot to do whatever he wants, just like he did the first time!"

11

The silence seemed to stretch on for minutes, but in truth it was only two or three seconds before John Robinson turned to Velthor and the young woman who had come to announce their release. "Get your fastest runner and send him to our ship. Have him tell my daughter that Smith stole a remote control he can use to take over the robot. Tell her to pull the robot's power pack if that's the only way to immobilize it."

"And tell her to be careful!" Will added, glancing nervously at his father. "I programmed the robot to defend its power pack!"

His father scowled at him for an instant, then turned back to the interrogator. "Have your runner tell her that, too," he said. "Now go!"

John watched as the woman hurried off, then turned to Velthor, ignoring the second, still-sleeping guard a dozen meters away. "Now, unless you can tell us *very* clearly how to reach our ship, we're going to need a guide. Now is not the time to get lost!"

For a moment Dr. Zachary Smith thought he had success literally within his grasp in the form of the dear boy's remote control! Much more useful than the rifle, at least until he had time to reprogram the translator implant's voice simulator and use it to enable the weapon for his use.

But then, as he studied the remote and tried to recall precisely what he had overheard the spiteful child saying about it, he realized it might not be as valuable as he had first thought. Even assuming he could immediately activate it and contact the metal behemoth, it would take time—undisturbed time—to learn what was possible and what was not.

And time, let alone undisturbed time, was something that was in perilously short supply. Now that the entire clan and their pit bull of a pilot were free, they would doubtless all be on their way to the *Jupiter*.

But the one truly unfortunate fact, which he had only now taken the time to think about, was that the ungrateful Dr. Judy was almost certainly already there! Too weak in the immediate aftermath of his escape to stop them, he had watched from a distance as she sent the messengers back to warn the others of that escape. He could only assume that she had herself continued on to the ship with her mission of medical mercy.

Once there, she would undoubtedly have added to the already mazelike, anti-Smith security they took such petty joy in constructing. She would also, almost certainly, be keeping a close eye on the robot, and if it began to operate in an unacceptable way or merely in an unexpected way, she could—and would—snatch out its power pack, thanks to another of that child's hateful and shortsighted modifications. The metal creature was now

91

virtually helpless in the face of anyone who knew precisely where the power pack was located and how to grasp it. If he *did* manage to get control of it, that would be the *first* thing he would remedy. Warriors with easily accessible Off switches could find themselves at a serious disadvantage under battle conditions.

But for now, he had to reach the *Jupiter* as quickly as possible, *before* the entire Robinson clan descended on it. He was sure that Judy alone would not, at close range, present a problem. Even the remaining guards could likely be eliminated—*if* he had even a small amount of time. The entire herd, however, Robinsons and all, would, unless he grew vastly more proficient, present an insurmountable obstacle.

A heady mixture of uneasiness and anticipation gripping him, Dr. Zachary Smith set off for the *Jupiter* at a run.

Judy Robinson's stomach knotted as she read the sensor displays she had just called up.

She realized she'd been right all along. *Something* in that building the Rellkans called the Vault *had* been awakened. The energy being consumed now was almost an order of magnitude greater than the last time they checked it, nearly two days ago from orbit. If Smith was now controlling it, even ineptly—

She shuddered at the thought and wondered bleakly what she could possibly do about it.

The only solution that came to mind was: Capture Smith before he got *too* good at whatever he was doing.

The second solution, which forced its way into her

mind moments later, on the heels of nightmarish visions of what Smith was capable of, was to clear everyone out of the city, hoist the *Jupiter* into the air high above it, and proceed to obliterate the Vault altogether.

If it *could* be obliterated.

She hoped it didn't come to that, but if Smith *was* in control of it and *was* getting better, and if they *couldn't* capture and/or neutralize him in some way, they would have little choice but to try.

But before she could do anything, she had to tell her father and the others what she suspected might be happening. And she had to talk to Kelwyn and Zolkaz and try to learn more of what the Vault and its endless rows of cubicles actually *did*.

And if there was a way, short of total destruction, to shut it off.

Grimly, she wiped the sensor readings from the displays, made a last check of the safeguards she'd installed, and headed for the airlock, where Zolkaz and Kelwyn and the others were waiting to guide her back to her family.

John and Will Robinson and Don West were only ten minutes into their hurried trek back to the *Jupiter* when Velthor, who had insisted on making up for his earlier lapse by being their guide, lurched to a halt, his eyes caught by something half hidden in the dense vegetation alongside the "street bed" they were following.

"What is it?" John asked, his tone impatient even though a part of him welcomed the chance to catch his breath.

Before Velthor could reply, Don West pushed past him and leaned down, brushing aside the obscuring vines. "It's the runner we sent ahead," he said, hunkering down and feeling for a pulse. "He's out like a light—just like you were," he added, rising and turning to look at Velthor.

"A dart?" John wondered aloud.

"Not this time either," Don said, "not from what I can see, and we don't have time to waste looking for one. This is obviously Smith's doing, and all the more reason to make time getting back to the *Jupiter*. And to Judy. Whatever that traitor is up to, it can't be good!"

"Agreed," John said, breathing less heavily after the brief respite. "Let's get moving."

Velthor obediently wrenched his eyes away from the unconscious man and pointed himself again in the direction of the *Jupiter*. At least Smith apparently wasn't as homicidally inclined as he once had been, Robinson thought as they moved on. He hadn't killed the messenger—or Velthor, for that matter. It wasn't proof of a kinder, gentler Dr. Smith, but it appeared to be a step in the right direction.

Exhausted and sweating and completely out of breath from the fast pace he'd set for himself, Dr. Zachary Smith lurched and almost fell as he heard voices directly ahead. From the directions he'd forcibly extracted from the runner's mind, he still had to be at least a kilometer from the *Jupiter*.

Hastily, and as silently as he could manage in his

present weak-kneed, gasping-for-breath state, he moved well to the side of what trail there was. Crouching, he waited, trying not to breathe so loudly he could be overheard. The voices had fallen silent but the sound of their movement could still be heard, becoming more distinct moment by moment.

Then they were flickering in and out of sight as they picked their way past the point at which he'd left the trail. First, one of the guards he'd escaped from, then another, then—

The ungrateful Dr. Judy Robinson herself! Followed by an annoyed-looking Zolkaz still carrying Kelwyn, now sporting an almost invisible cast. And then—

Yes! The remainder of the guards but *not* the robot! It was still at the *Jupiter*, unprotected except for whatever safeguards had been programmed into it.

Smith's entire body went limp with a mixture of relief and exultation. The remaining kilometer—or however much it was—no longer needed to be covered at a lung-burning run. As soon as the last of the parade was out of earshot, he could proceed at a more leisurely pace, experimenting with the remote as he went.

As Smith waited, he inspected the remote. It had the usual deceptively rickety homemade look of most of the boy's contraptions, made as they all were from spare and cannibalized parts from totally unrelated items, all screwed and welded and lashed together. He recognized, in the very center, the standard controls that had been present on earlier incarnations, but around the periphery were two new touchpad keys, a miniature vision screen barely larger than the keys, and three holes in the frame, probably for more controls that the boy hadn't gotten around to adding yet.

Start with what you know, Smith thought, and work from there.

Breathing almost normally, he stood up as the sound of the last of the guards faded away. Back on the trail a few seconds later, he activated the remote control.

Almost immediately a tinny version of the robot's voice came from the remote. "Danger, Will Robinson," it said. "The execrable Dr. Smith has escaped and could pose a threat to all Robinsons everywhere."

Smith sighed, realizing the vocabulary segment of the creature's AI program must have been listening to him at some point. No one else in this group of Philistines would know what *execrable* meant, let alone be able to use it in a sentence.

"I *know* that, Robot," he said, trying to catch the boy's impatient inflection and hoping that the signals from the remote control were still inputted directly into the robot's audioneural network, bypassing the voice recognition circuits. The original remotes had been designed that way back on Earth as a cost-cutting measure, long before anyone worried about a remote getting into the wrong hands. "Is Judy there?"

"Your sister is on her way to join the rest of the Robinsons. Including you."

"Why would she do something dumb like that?" Smith asked, trying to stick with words and phrases the boy might normally use. The voice recognition circuits might be bypassed, but the AI program itself would likely pick up on grossly uncharacteristic speech patterns. "I mean, we're all already on our way to the *Jupiter*. Should be there in an hour or two. But why aren't *you* out there with her? If Dr. Smith is on the loose, my sister needs protection."

"I completely agree, Will."

"Then why *aren't* you out there with her?"

"There is nothing I'd like better, Will, but I have been instructed—I have been *ordered*—to remain within the *Jupiter*."

"But *why*? For Pete's sake, Robot, she needs you!"

"Perhaps, but those were her own instructions. She fears that were I to venture outside, the loathsome Dr. Smith might somehow gain control of me."

"What does *she* know? *I* programmed you, and that doofus Smith can't *touch* you, not without my say-so!"

"I understand, Will, but I have my orders."

"Well, *I* order you to get out there and protect her! What are you, a robot or a chicken?"

"For shame, Will Robinson. Insults are counterproductive. You of all people should know that. You designed my insult response algorithms yourself."

"You're the one who should be ashamed, Robot, letting my sister go out there by herself! If Smith catches her and hurts her, it's your fault! Or *kills* her!"

"I'm sorry you feel that way, Will, but I have no choice in the matter. I must respond as I have been programmed. I believe I should speak with your father now."

"He's not here. Dad's not in that good a shape, so I ran ahead."

"Lieutenant West, then. Surely you were not able to outrun *him* when your father sent him to fetch you back."

Smith cursed silently. The bucket of bolts was suspicious! "Not exactly, but outsmarting him wasn't hard. Now are you going to help or not?"

"You would seem to be in more danger that your sister, Will Robinson. The traitorous Dr. Smith did not harm her when he had the chance. In fact, he urged her to come with him when he escaped, and in the past he has professed to be considerably attracted to her. Do you really think he would harm her now?"

"Maybe, if he thought she'd turned on him. Anyway, how do *you* know all this?"

"Judy told me before she left, of course, while she was checking my programming. In fact, we had quite a nice chat."

This, Smith decided abruptly, was getting him nowhere. He couldn't even be certain that the creature's AI program wasn't on to him, just toying with him. Or keeping him occupied until Judy could be contacted. *Surely* she had taken a communicator with her.

"Okay, just forget it!" he said in what he hoped was a convincing display of childish petulance. "If you're going to be that way about it, see if I care! I'll look out for her myself!"

Without giving the robot a chance to reply, he shut off the remote and began to inspect it more closely. If he could get a look inside and see what those new buttons were connected to, *maybe* he could get some idea of what they were meant to accomplish.

12

Dr. Judy Robinson breathed a weary but heartfelt sigh of relief as she got the first glimpse of her father and Don West through more than fifty meters of trees and vines and undergrowth. Their captors must have turned them loose virtually the moment Kelwyn's messenger reached them and told of Kelwyn's decision to trust the Earthers.

But then, as the worried look on her father's face and their hurried pace became evident, a sinking feeling clutched at Judy's already leaden stomach. Had they somehow found out about the "awakened" Vault and Smith's probable connection to it?

And where were her mother and Penny and Will?

A small part of the sudden anxiety faded when Will, hidden until then by waist-high underbrush, appeared a dozen meters ahead of the others, rushing pellmell toward her. Out of breath and flushed, he lurched to a stop, almost running into her. "Where's the robot?" he asked urgently.

"In the *Jupiter*," she said. "After Smith escaped, I thought—"

"I have to get to him, fast! Smith's got the remote

control I was working on! If he figures out how to use it—" He broke off at her angry scowl, then lowered his eyes. "I never thought *Smith* would get hold of it! And if you hadn't let him get away, he never would've!"

"There'll be time enough later to determine responsibility," their father said irritably as he and the others, Maureen and Penny bringing up the rear, caught up with Will. "If we're lucky!"

"There's more to worry about than the robot," Judy said as they all headed back toward the ship, barely noticing that Zolkaz and Kelwyn and the Rellkans who had been accompanying them continued in the direction they'd been heading, away from the *Jupiter*. As the Robinsons and West half ran, half jogged behind Velthor, Judy told them about Smith and the seemingly awakened Vault.

When she'd finished, John, between gasps for breath, said, "As soon as Will gets the robot immunized against the remote Smith stole, finding out what that so-called Vault *does* had better become our top priority."

Finally, the clearing appeared in the near distance and Will once again raced ahead, despite his lungs aching from the unaccustomed, prolonged exertion. He knew, despite what he'd said to his sister, that the trouble with the robot *was* mostly his fault. Sure, he couldn't've known that Smith was going to steal it, but he should've known that he would at least try.

Not that he hadn't included safeguards, but if Smith figured out what the new buttons on the remote did . . . Once Smith got control of the robot, there was only one way of getting that control back, and it had to be done quickly, before Smith had time to hide the robot somewhere and work on it and hardwire out *all* the safeguards. There was enough stuff in the improvised tool kit Smith had stolen along with the remote and all the rest to do almost anything he wanted.

But as Will reached the edge of the clearing and the *Jupiter* came into full view, a sick feeling twisted at his gut. He was too late!

The *Jupiter*'s airlock was wide open. And the robot—

From the crushed underbrush, he could tell where it had left the clearing. Just barely audible over the rasping of his own breathing and pounding of his heart was the sound of something moving heavily through the forest.

Maybe there was still a chance!

"Dad!" he shouted. "Smith's got the robot, but maybe I can still get him back!"

His father, still more than fifty meters from the clearing, shouted back, "Will! Don't—"

But the boy was already racing across the clearing to where the robot had obviously gone.

"Robot!" he shouted as he ran, his words emerging in bursts between gasping breaths. "Can you hear me?"

"Danger, Will Robinson!" The words were like distant thunder, muffled and faint but perfectly clear. "The perfidious Dr. Smith has—"

Then silence.

"Robot!" Will shouted again, then fell silent as he thrashed through underbrush that seemed to grab at his legs and arms with every step. Behind him, he heard his father shouting at him again, and then Judy and even Major West.

But he didn't dare stop. He had to get close enough to—

Abruptly, he realized he couldn't hear the robot thrashing through the forest anymore. Had it stopped? Or—

Without warning, the robot loomed up directly in front of him, its modified pincer claws extended. As Will lurched to a stop, almost falling, the claws on one of the robot's arms closed painfully on his shoulder, then lifted him off the ground like a writhing feather and clasped him roughly to its metal torso.

"You wished to speak with me, child?" It was the robot's thunderous voice but Dr. Smith's precise diction and style.

As if to punctuate the words, the claws on the robot's other arm crackled with random electrical arcs, a form of energy leakage that indicated it was fully charged and ready to zap anything in its path.

Will flinched away from the energy display but could only wriggle in the robot's grip as its other, deadly arm swiveled about until it was pointed in the general direction from which Will's father and the others were noisily approaching. As Don West, charging ahead of the others, came in sight, a bolt crackled jaggedly from the robot's extended claw, incinerating a patch of underbrush only a few meters in front of the pilot.

Things were even worse than what he'd been afraid of, Will realized as Don skidded to a halt. Not only had Smith found out what the override button did, but he'd bypassed the circuit that should have kept the robot from jacking its firepower up to lethal levels.

But it didn't matter. All he had to do was calm down and catch his breath and—

Another energy bolt shot out, exploding a tree trunk to the pilot's left, uncomfortably close to where the rest of the group, John Robinson in the lead, had just appeared.

"For your own safety, stay back," the robot thundered. "I am unable to accurately direct this creature's firepower, and I wouldn't want a simple warning shot to prove fatal to any of you. It would, however, be but the work of a moment to crush this annoying child like the bothersome insect he is."

"He's right, Dad!" Will called out. "Just stay back. The screen on the remote is too small to get a good view of what the robot's seeing. All he can do is turn it until the—"

"Do be *quiet*, child!" the robot said in a less thunderous voice, simultaneously increasing the pressure on Will and unleashing another bolt of energy, this one leaving a small crater a dozen meters in front of the group. "You certainly don't want to give away *all* our little secrets."

"What the devil do you want, Smith?" John Robinson shouted.

"To be absolutely truthful, Professor, I don't know. I wasn't anticipating a situation so fraught with possibilities and yet so inherently unstable. I suggest we retire to neutral corners, so to speak, while I ponder the question."

"You've gone even more psycho than usual, Smith!" Don West volunteered loudly. "Just let the boy go and—"

"I believe this conversation is at an end," the robot said as Smith boosted the volume to an almost painful level.

"I'm the one you want, Smith." Judy Robinson stepped forward, past her father and Don. "You invited me along on your escape, remember?"

"I do indeed, but I also recall that you declined rather decisively, if unwisely."

"Trade me for Will," she said flatly. "I won't lie and say I like the idea, but I figure you're less likely to kill me than my brother. Or am I wrong?"

The robot was silent a moment, as if considering the proposition. "And your first act would be what? To make use of your longer arms to attempt to remove the creature's power pack?"

"Probably, if I thought I had a chance."

"I would expect nothing less. But I believe I will decline your generous offer, at least for the moment. There is, however, something you can do for me, Dr. Robinson. You can collect all the portable weapons aboard the *Jupiter* and bring them out where my metallic proxy can see them."

"What—"

"No more questions! I have just now come to a decision. The collection of weapons is the first step in implementing that decision. Once they have been disposed of to my satisfaction, I will make whatever other arrangements I determine are necessary to keep me safe from assassination when I return to do what I should have done long ago: Assume command of the *Jupiter*."

What a surprise! Will thought, still trying to relax. His lungs no longer hurt and he felt almost fully recovered from his multikilometer trek. Even the robot seemed to have relaxed its grip just enough to let him breathe normally, which meant, he hoped, that his voice would be back to normal. If it wasn't and the robot didn't recognize it instantly—

It was now or never.

"Robot," he said, "this is your captain speaking."

He waited nervously, but there was only silence for two or three seconds.

"Hey, Robot, I said—"

"What foolishness is this, child?" the robot demanded for Smith. At the same time, the robot's grip tightened.

Will froze. What was wrong? His voice was certainly close enough to normal that the robot's voice recognition circuits would accept it and—

Oh, no!

Suddenly, Will remembered. The last time he'd been working on the remote, just before that other ship had attacked the *Jupiter*, he'd changed the password!

But *what* had he changed it to?

13

Panic set in as Will realized he couldn't remember the new password. When he'd decided to do it, he'd been looking through some old twentieth century stuff in the computer—comics and cartoons and TV shows and—

"*Shazam!*" No, that wasn't it!

"My dear child—"

"Able to squash tall buildings with a single stomp!"

This time Smith didn't immediately respond, and Will wondered if he'd found the right password, then realized that he hadn't.

"Tell me what you are doing, child!" Smith demanded. As if to demonstrate his determination, he loosed another blast of energy, destroying several square meters of underbrush.

What had he changed the password *to*? Will's frantic efforts to remember seemed only to make his mind freeze up even more solidly. *Relax!* he told himself. Relax and *think*. He'd just been playing around, he knew, never dreaming it could come to this, with Smith actually stealing the remote and taking over the robot and—

That was it!

Takeover!

"Holy Takeover Scenario, Robotman!" he said, barely able to keep from shouting, which would've put his voice outside the robot's voice recognition parameters.

Instantly the robot's grip loosened, but the other set of claws remained enveloped in arcing electrical energy. "To the Robot Cave, Boy Wonder!" the robot thundered, then set Will carefully on the ground and held the other, still-arcing arm up in front of its own vision sensors as if to inspect it.

Abruptly, the arcing stopped. If a robot could blink, this one would have. "I don't know what got into me, Will Robinson," it said.

Will let out his breath in a huge whoosh of relief. "Don't worry about it, Robot. I know exactly what got into you—the scummy Dr. Smith."

The others, who had been watching with worried puzzlement from a distance, suddenly raced forward. Judy scooped Will up unceremoniously in her arms for a huge hug before setting him back down. "I don't know what you did, little brother, but I'm glad you did. I even forgive you," she added in a whisper, "for letting it happen in the first place."

Looking embarrassed, the boy turned to his father. "We can probably track Smith down. If you want to."

"It wouldn't be a bad idea," John Robinson said.

"He goes in the brig for good this time!" West said with a frown. "Right?"

"Most likely. If we can indeed track him down. Will?"

"Robot, find the remote."

"I will do my best, Will Robinson," the robot rumbled as it turned about and headed back the way it had been going before Will had interrupted it.

"And bring Smith back here if he's still anywhere near the remote when you find it," Will added.

"And be careful!" Judy called after it. "Remember what I warned you about before!"

"Of course, Dr. Robinson," the robot rumbled back. "I never forget unless I am instructed to do so. Or someone messes with my memory modules."

Judy looked down at Will. "Are you *sure* Smith can't take it over with that remote now?"

Will shook his head. "Not a chance. Until I cancel it, me personally, he'll respond only to my voice, nothing else, not even the remote. Or a control rod."

"Good work, son," John Robinson said, but turned to the pilot and added, "Don, you go with it, just to be safe."

"Dad!" The hurt was obvious in the single word and the look the boy gave his father.

"I'm sorry, Will. It's not that I don't trust your abilities, but I don't want to take *any* chances."

"Sending our hotshot pilot is not all that great an idea, Dad," Judy interrupted. "Remember what I said about Smith . . . *doing things* . . . to us. I still don't know what's going on, but sending one person, alone, out where Smith can get his hands on him is taking a much bigger chance than sending the robot."

Her father grimaced. "Perhaps you're right. What we have to do first is—"

"The tracking signal has ceased." The robot, less than a hundred meters away, had stopped abruptly, its visual sensors swiveling about as if looking for the missing signal.

Will closed his eyes for a second. He'd been afraid of this, but there was nothing he could've done about it. "Smith probably smashed the remote," he said. "He must've looked inside and figured out that the robot could track the remote, even if it *was* turned off."

"It's all right, son. You did as much as anyone could. We can talk to Kelwyn in the morning about sending out search parties." He looked around at the others as the robot began lumbering back in their direction. "Right now we had better all concentrate on the problem Judy outlined for us: finding out as much as we can about those cubicles—and what happened to Smith while he was in one."

Dr. Zachary Smith regretfully picked up the well-stomped remains of the remote control, checked to be certain its innards were indeed no longer functional, and tossed it into the deepest patch of underbrush in the area. Having control of the robot would have been both helpful and convenient, but it was far from essential. He would, in the end, prevail. Of that he was certain. It would just take more time. The first step, as he'd intended from the start, before he'd been distracted by the seemingly lucky accident of the child's remote control, was to make certain he *had* the time.

Opening the boy's tool kit, into which Smith had

hurriedly jammed all the confiscated equipment that would fit, he searched out the other remote, the one he himself had surreptitiously assembled from cannibalized parts during the long weeks of shipboard boredom. It wouldn't give him control over the robot or even entry into the *Jupiter*, but it *would* give him the time to achieve those goals and others.

Deliberately, he pressed the single button on the device, felt a faint subsonic hum as the signal was sent, and smiled as he envisioned their reactions, particularly that of their mesomorphic blockhead of a pilot, when they discovered that Dr. Zachary Smith was not as helpless as they had foolishly assumed.

The Robinsons started by talking to Velthor and any other Rellkans they could find or send for. First, they warned the Rellkans about Smith as best they could. Then they asked them to search their memories for anything and everything they had ever heard about the Vault and its role in the planet's defenses, no matter how insignificant or impossible it might seem.

Finally, they gathered on the bridge of the *Jupiter*, where they tried vainly to make sense of it all. On the viewscreens night soon fell, unnoticed, on the forest around them, and they continued talking.

But no matter how much they talked and speculated and argued, they somehow never arrived at any useful answers to the basic questions: What were the cubicles for? And what had happened to Smith during his extended stay inside one? Of course, John had been in a cubicle too, as he was quick to point out. But he'd been extricated more quickly than Smith, and thus presumably had not experienced what Smith had.

All speculation trails eventually led back to Judy's original, spur-of-the-moment idea that Smith had somehow become linked to the Vault, whatever *that* might mean. And that in turn led to the almost inevitable conclusion that the only way to find out what the Vault had done to Smith was for Don or John to undergo a similarly lengthy session of torture and "see what happened." That, however, was repeatedly rejected, not only for the obvious reason that no one was all that thrilled with the thought of undergoing several days of extremely realistic torture and thousands of deaths.

There was also the possibility that if Smith did indeed now have some kind of control over the Vault, whoever entered a cubicle could be completely at his mercy. For all they knew, Smith could, with nothing more than an errant thought, shut off the Vault's life support system and allow any cubicle occupants to be smothered by whatever it was that oozed out of the walls and enveloped them for the duration of their stay.

Not that their lack of success in coming up with definitive answers should have surprised them, considering what they had to work with. The oldest living Rellkan was still separated by more than a century from the actual events, and no one in living memory—until the arrival of the *Jupiter*—had defied the taboos that surrounded the Vault and actually entered one of the cubicles. No one had done *that* since a few years after the so-called Invasion, when the bodies that had littered the streets and homes had been absorbed but before the city itself began to sag and be reabsorbed. At that time, a few of the survivors, uneasily returning from their hiding places, had entered the Vault, presumably hoping to get some answers.

None, however, had ever emerged. It took only a few such disappearances before even the boldest—or most foolhardy—refused to go near the Vault, let alone enter it and stick his or her head into the lion's mouth of the cubicles.

But Smith had entered one of the cubicles.

And emerged.

And John Robinson had entered a cubicle and emerged.

But they had not been alone. If they *had* been, if the others had not been there to let them out, would *they* have ever emerged?

Was that what had happened to those long-ago victims? Had they entered the cubicles and found themselves trapped, dying thousands of times in their minds until their bodies finally broke under the stress?

Or simply died of dehydration or starvation?

Or, if the cubicles did indeed attend to all their bodies' needs indefinitely, could they have died only after tens of thousands of virtual years of torture—from old age?

But most importantly, what was it Smith might have awakened? The *Jupiter*'s instruments still showed the same level of energy usage that Judy had detected earlier, which was a thousand percent greater than their instruments had shown *before* John and Dr. Smith had entered the building.

And what, exactly, had Smith gained from that awakening? Had he, as Judy earlier feared, become linked to the building in some way? Could he command it to "do" things for him? Cause it to "interfere" with the functioning of people's bodies? Or their minds? Or was it on automatic pilot, so to speak, looking out for its own enigmatic interests, which occasionally just happened to coincide with Smith's?

In either case, based on what Judy had witnessed during Smith's escape and later, the one thing they needed to do whenever they left the ship was stick together. Whatever Smith could now do, he apparently had an easier time doing it with one or two people than with a group. At least so far. He could make one or two natives fall completely asleep and stay that way until someone shook the sleepers awake, but all he could do to a larger group—like the half-dozen guards and Judy herself—was affect their bodies, like making them trip over their own feet. And even that, if the tortured expression Judy had seen on Smith's face was any indication, was a serious strain.

Which meant, they concluded, that capturing Smith was more urgent than they'd first thought. If he could control whatever machinery lay buried in the Vault, and was getting better with practice, then their time was limited.

And Judy's earlier idea that they evacuate the city, take the *Jupiter* aloft, and destroy the Vault, went from being unthinkable to being a viable, even a preferable option.

"If you ask me," Don West said when she brought the idea up again, "we'd be doing these people a *favor* by getting rid of that thing. It's not as if it's ever done them any good, or ever will."

No one disagreed, but the discussion continued— pointlessly, as far as Don was concerned. A few minutes later he rolled his eyes at the umpteenth repetition of one argument or another and turned from the viewscreens to the navigation console. Here, he thought, was something he could understand, unlike the constant "maybe this, maybe that, maybe something else" he'd been drowned in for what seemed like forever.

Here, at the controls of a ship, you made a decision, sometimes logically and deliberately, sometimes instantaneously by pure instinct. And in any case, once the decision was made, you *did* something! You implemented the decision. You took off, you changed course, you fired a weapon, you retreated—you did something other than endlessly rethink and pointlessly debate. That way lay total paralysis.

It's no wonder Earth was in the shape it was in, he thought disgustedly, if its leaders all acted this way, turning every situation every which way and looking down its throat and peering up every other orifice until they decided what was the best or safest or most popular thing to do—while its enemies, like Dr. Smith, simply *acted*. The man was scum, but at least he was decisive scum.

Don's fingers brushed across the weapons controls, almost longingly, imagining Smith in his sights. And wondering, if they *did* capture him, would Professor Robinson display any more common sense than he had before? Or would he yet again let the doctor weasel his way off the hook and allow him to keep both his life and most of his freedom?

Don was pulling in a deep breath, reluctantly preparing to return to the discussion, when a tiny red light, pulsing in a corner of one of the navigation console screens, caught his eye.

Frowning, he leaned closer and saw that it was one of the engine status displays. The engines weren't on and neither should the light be, either pulsing red for malfunction or steady green for go.

But even as he watched, another half-dozen status lights on the same screen came on, all pulsing red. What the hell was going on?

"Hey, Professor!" he called, and John Robinson looked at him with a scowl. "Does this brainchild of yours run self-diagnostics even when it's turned off?"

Robinson nodded impatiently. "Of course it does. If you're going to find a malfunction, it's better to find it while the ship is still in the hangar, not when you're ten thousand feet straight up."

"Then you'd better take a look at this." Don stood back from the console while a frowning John Robinson left the group and came over to where the pilot was standing. His eyes widened as he saw not one single dot of pulsing light but nearly a dozen, all red.

"What the hell—" Robinson virtually leaped the last few meters to the navigation console, elbowing the pilot aside. His fingers darted across the controls, not the ones that West used to navigate the ship but a secondary maintenance panel.

Dozens of lights on various screens came on, along with at least as many readouts. At first, most of the new lights were green, but even as the two men watched, one after another faded to white and then brightened again, this time an ominous, pulsing red.

"Smith!" Judy Robinson's exclamation sounded more like a curse than a name.

"Very probably," her father admitted, wincing as the last of the screens' green lights turned red.

"You *can* fix it," West said. "Right, Professor? I mean, you designed this thing."

John nodded. "I assume the damage is repairable, yes. Even Smith couldn't be foolish enough to damage the ship beyond repair."

"Don't bet on it, Father," Judy said. "He was ready and able to help destroy all of Earth just for his own personal gain—"

"But that's just the point: personal gain. If the *Jupiter* is permanently disabled, we're not the only ones stuck on this planet for the rest of our lives. So is he. What's the gain in that?"

"How about total domination of the native population?" Judy asked angrily. "If he really is linked to whatever's in the Vault, and if he learns better how to use it . . . " She half shrugged, half shuddered. "A few thousand living, breathing puppets, us included, probably wouldn't be all that unattractive to our esteemed Dr. Smith."

14

Once again Judy Robinson was dreaming, but this time, surprisingly, the experience was pleasant. Even within the dream, she felt traces of bewilderment, a suspicion that things were not as they should be. She was not in an operating room or on an alien planet halfway across the galaxy from Earth. She was once again in college, a freshman, with no idea what lay ahead for her other than the bright hope of a medical degree.

At this particular moment in the dream, however, a medical degree was far from uppermost in her mind. Even the "surprise" anatomy quiz the teaching assistant had warned her about in return for a smile was below her mental radar. This moment and quite a few to come were reserved for decidedly unacademic thoughts.

Smitty was waiting in the park across the street from the dorm. She'd been waiting herself, looking out through the curtains of her second floor window between every paragraph in the text she had been trying to review ever since her roommate left on a date of her own an hour before.

And now he was there, stepping out of the shadows into the pale glow of the streetlight at the entrance to the park.

Closing her text without even tagging her place, she stood up, snatched her light jacket from the back of the chair where she'd draped it after returning from her last class of the day, and hurried out into the hallway and down the stairs to the front door.

Frowning, she saw that it was locked. But why should that surprise her? It always *was* locked after sundown.

But it didn't matter. She knew just what she had to do. First, the upper keypad: first her left index finger, then middle finger, then—

As if from a great distance, someone was calling her name, but instead of looking around to see who it was, she worked faster on the complicated dormitory lock.

Suddenly, unseen hands gripped her shoulders, pulling her away from the door no matter how hard she struggled to stay where she was. Screaming in frustration, she lashed out, but other hands caught her arms and—

The dormitory lobby vanished from around her. For an instant she *was* Smitty, looking out through his eyes at the building across the street from the park. But it *wasn't* a park she was in! It was a dense forest, and she was looking not at a college dormitory building but a strange metallic ship, circular and huge, sitting in a clearing in that forest.

And she realized that it wasn't Smitty through whose eyes she was looking but—

The scream of frustration turned to one of horror as she struggled to pull away, to disentangle herself from that *other* body she was somehow enveloped by, was actually a *part* of.

118

Abruptly, like the bursting of a gigantic, confining bubble, it released her, and everything vanished: the ship, the clearing, the dormitory, everything. As limp and helpless as a marionette whose strings had just been cut, she felt herself falling, crashing heavily onto a cold metal floor.

The impact seemed to jar her eyes open, but it took a conscious effort to keep them from flickering shut. It took an even greater effort to bring the wavering blur that surrounded her into focus, and yet another to focus her thoughts and realize that she was lying on the deck of the *Jupiter*, next to the airlock, and that the anxious face looming over her belonged to Don West.

"I never in my life thought I'd be saying this," she managed to mumble as her body finally began to feel as if it were solidly attached to her brain rather than on the other end of countless limp, rubbery control rods, "but I'm *really* glad to see you!"

Cursing silently, Dr. Zachary Smith hurried away through the starlit darkness of the forest. He'd been certain it would work!

And it would have, if those other busybodies hadn't interfered! Judy Robinson had been doing exactly as he wanted. She'd been halfway through opening the airlock when that blockhead West stopped her.

Stopped her and doomed her to live out the rest of her life in the same . . . *limited* . . . state she had heretofore endured.

Or perhaps not . . .

Perhaps, later, when all such crude resistance became utterly futile, he would give her a second chance. She *did* have a good mind, even a brilliant one, and that was more of a rarity than he had once liked to think. Unfortunately, it had been seriously corrupted by her upbringing, but soon he would be able to purge her mind of that corruption.

So perhaps . . . perhaps it had been for the best, this seeming setback.

Perhaps, just perhaps, he had been too impatient.

But still, the next step must be taken, and taken soon. He'd resisted the thought since it first occurred to him, but he could deny its validity no longer.

And in order to take that step, he needed someone to help him, as much as the thought galled him. He'd wanted it to be Judy Robinson. It would have been so fitting, so right. But it didn't need to be her. It could be anyone.

And considering the potential risk involved, it might be better if it *were* someone else, someone with less will, less obstinate contrariness—and less mental strength.

For a moment he smiled, thinking of West and the pleasure he would take from using the testosterone-laden pilot for this duty. But it would be too risky, not because West himself was dangerous, but because he would almost certainly never stray far from the Robinsons, particularly not now. The fool would think he was protecting his lady love, but in truth it was she who would be protecting him, she and the rest of the Robinson clan.

Pleased at the irony of the situation, Smith moved

on through the forest, toward a place where the helper he needed—for now—would undoubtedly be much easier to recruit.

"Whatever Smith did," Judy Robinson announced, looking up from the energy readouts she'd just called up on the *Jupiter*'s instruments, "it hasn't increased the energy the Vault is using. If anything, it looks as if it's beginning to decrease."

She was feeling almost normal again and was glad that the ruckus at the airlock had awakened only Will and not her mother and sister. As soon as she regained full control of her body, she'd done what she could to check herself out in the medical bay, while the others hovered anxiously. To everyone's relief, she found nothing out of the ordinary except for an understandable and presumably temporary jump in her blood pressure.

Her father, watching the Vault's energy readouts over her shoulder along with Will, frowned. "Decreasing? Are you certain?"

"Reasonably. But I imagine it's still in its 'awake' state, if there is such a thing. So if Smith really is using the Vault's so-called defense system, he's not using it for anything that requires more energy than before."

"Are you positive it was Smith who did this to you?" her father asked. "It couldn't have just been a dream? You *did* sleepwalk now and then when you were young."

She stood up sharply, irritated at his seemingly automatic questioning of her conclusions. Times like this made her sympathize with Will's complaints about their father's dismissive attitude. "It was Smith!" she snapped. "It was only a second or two, but I was *inside* his grimy little mind!" She shuddered, remembering. "But it wasn't *just* Smith. There was something else in there with us."

"One of the Rellkans—" her father began.

"None of the ones *I've* seen! Whatever it was, it wasn't even remotely human."

Abruptly, her father's expression switched from worried concern to something more urgent. He caught her shoulder and turned her to face him. "You *saw* this thing?"

She shook her head. "I *was* it! Just like I *was* Smith for a split second. I was *both* of them, at the same time!"

"What was it like, this thing you . . . became?" her father asked, both hands on her shoulders now as he peered intently into her eyes.

She shrugged uneasily, as much at her father's sudden, unsettling intensity as at the memory itself. "Indescribable," she said. "Alien. Revolting! Uglier than the ugliest thing you can imagine, with way too many slimy, hairy appendages, and I was *inside* it! I was *part of it*!" She grimaced and shivered as the horror seemed to envelop her all over again. It took her a few seconds to realize that her father was shivering as well.

"Dad?"

Swallowing, he reached out and hugged her. She could feel his heart pounding. "I'm okay, Dad, really. It was just—"

"It was the thing in the cubicle," he said, drawing in a breath and releasing her. "What you . . . experienced was what *I* experienced while I was in that cubicle, except you didn't get killed again and again. Did you?"

There was complete silence for several seconds as they just looked at each other. Finally, Judy said, "No, I wasn't killed, but my God, was *that* what happened to you in the cubicle? And you were in there—you said it seemed like half an hour! My God!"

He nodded. "And Smith was in longer than I was— much longer."

"So maybe the natives were right," Don volunteered in the ensuing silence. "Maybe Smith *was* 'possessed' the same way their ancestors were. And the thing that possessed him was trying to take *you* over, too, but we woke you up or forced you out of your trance or whatever before it got you."

John Robinson shook his head. "Are you suggesting that the Invaders took over the Vault two centuries ago and have been *living* in there ever since? And now they're popping out to possess people?"

Don shrugged. "How should I know? Maybe when they took it over, they put a hypergate in there somewhere, one that's hooked up to their home world—or their ship or their *something*. And they've been monitoring it and are reaching through, checking to see if there are any more victims to be had."

"Impossible!" Robinson snorted. "You saw the power readings Judy pulled up. Even if they jumped *another* thousand percent, it wouldn't be enough to operate even the most rudimentary hypergate."

Don shrugged again, grinning this time. "Remember that big one in orbit? You said it was way beyond anything Earth could build. Well, maybe the Invaders—or the Rellkans—had some other tricks up their sleeves. Maybe it's not a hypergate like yours but something that would only let 'immaterial' things through, like their minds. Anyway, say that what*ever* the Invaders were, they really did possess the Rellkans. And made them kill each other. When they ran out of victims, they just sat back and watched, waiting for someone to use the Vault again or wake it up or whatever. Which the two of you did."

West broke off, spreading his hands in a "who knows" gesture. "*Something* happened to Smith," he said. "You can't deny that."

"Then why didn't the same thing happen to *me*?" John asked irritably. "I was in there long enough to be killed a dozen times, so they should've had plenty of time to possess me, too."

"How can you be sure? I mean, I'm no scientist, but how long, scientifically speaking, does it take for an alien, immaterial *something* to possess a guy?"

John Robinson sighed. "You're right," he said with an edge of resigned sarcasm. "I'm sorry. There is no standard exposure time for immaterial alien somethings. But look, this isn't getting us anywhere. We may *never* find out what happened to Smith and why the same thing didn't happen to me. But as you said, we do know that something *did* happen to Smith, and now he's obviously more dangerous than ever before. And if what he did to Judy is any indication, he's getting more proficient at whatever it is that he's able to do. Therefore, whether he's been possessed and is getting along better with his possessor, or has somehow gotten some control over that machine, whatever the hell it is, we have to stop him."

He paused and looked around at the others. "While we still can."

15

The little girl's name was Frolyn, and she had no idea why she was suddenly awake. It was still completely dark outside, and the pallet she slept on, which grew out of the floor anew each night, seemed a little harder, a little less comfortable than it once had. The firefly glow that blotched the ceiling of her room had not yet begun to fade in expectation of dawn. There wasn't a sound, not anywhere.

Yet she was awake.

Someone, she slowly realized, had called to her. In a dream? Had she been dreaming? She did dream, sometimes, of when her family could go back to the village where her friends all were. It was nice here, but a little scary sometimes, living in these strange, constantly changing houses her grandfather said were "left over from before." It would be nicer to be back in their own village, in a regular house where the ceilings didn't have glowing spots on them and the walls and floors didn't now and then make funny, groaning noises as they changed color and shape and produced the daily array of furniture. Just some of the machines "left over from before," they told her. As long as anyone lived in a house, it kept working. If they moved out and no one else took their place, it would start to "relax," and within a few years it would be gone, just another indistinguishable part of the forest.

But even the houses the Watchers lived in, her grandfather said, were wearing out. Long ago the changes had been completely silent, but recently they had begun to make noises, like an old man's joints.

Maybe *that* was what had pulled her out of sleep— the walls making noise. They usually did it only during the day, particularly when the sun was especially bright, but they'd done it at night a few times too, when nothing anyone could see was changing, nothing being produced or absorbed.

She pushed the blanket down and sat up, listening.

But there was still no sound.

Except . . .

Outside?

With the thought came a feeling she'd never before experienced. A feeling, completely wordless, that someone needed her help.

Someone outside. A friend.

She blinked, startled, as, for just an instant, she could see the outside of the house, as if she were standing among the surrounding trees, watching her own window.

But then, as quickly as the image had come, it was gone, and she was climbing to her feet, slipping on her woven moccasins and walking softly to the door. She hesitated there, but just for a moment. Her grandfather had warned her about the strangers, warned her to stay inside and out of sight, but this was *different*. Someone *needed* her, and even if it *was* one of the strangers, it was also a friend, she simply *knew* it.

Outside, both tiny moons were high in a cloudless sky, giving just enough light for her to see an indistinct figure beckoning to her from the trail that, if you could follow it, led to the Vault.

With only a second's hesitation, she walked toward the figure. She knew her mother would be worried and angry if she woke up and found her gone, but Frolyn was certain she'd be back before her mother or anyone even noticed she was gone. And this newfound friend needed her so badly, she'd feel even worse if she didn't go with him to help.

For a moment she thought she heard the house sigh as a door opened and closed behind her, but she realized she couldn't have. Her mother was asleep, the way she always was at this time of night.

Moving faster now, a feeling of urgency beginning to grow within her, Frolyn reached the head of the trail and took the hand of her waiting friend. He *was* one of the strangers, she realized as soon as she saw his odd clothes and funny-looking beard, but it didn't make any difference. Without a backward glance, she let him lead her away.

It was only with the utmost difficulty that Dr. Zachary Smith kept from turning about and fleeing back into the night. Until he had actually entered the Vault's featureless white corridors, until he actually stood before one of the cubicle doors, looking down at the almost invisible protrusion that served as a handle for that door, his plan had been just that—a plan.

An abstraction, a calculated risk that the inexorable logic of self-interest dictated he take.

But now that he was confronted by the reality of the door he must step through, all the horrors he'd experienced the first time forced their way back into his mind and literally took his breath away. His heart was pounding and every inch of his body tingled with a hypersensitivity so great that even the touch of his clothes on his skin was as painful as the scrape of sandpaper.

And once he stepped through that all-too-real door . . .

He shook his head stiffly, almost spasmodically. Whatever happened beyond that door *wasn't real*, he told himself firmly. Every injury that had been inflicted upon him was inflicted not upon his real, physical body but on a virtual body created by the same "machinery" that kept his real body safe and unharmed throughout the entire process. As before, that body would be waiting, unharmed, when the process ended.

Everything that happened to him happened *only in his mind*. And his mind, he told himself confidently, had the strength and discipline to take it all in stride, to survive the ordeal and emerge unharmed and even more powerful than before.

Powerful enough to make the rest of his life—his *real* life—unlike anything even *he* had ever imagined.

And all because of the Robinsons and their sadistic pilot.

Even now Smith found himself smiling mentally at the irony of the situation. If West hadn't casually forced him into the cubicle and left him there to undergo hundreds of subjective hours of all-too-real pain and thousands of terror-laden deaths, he would never have been forced to uncover—to *begin* to uncover—the power that had hitherto lain dormant in the deepest recesses of his mind.

The fact that it would soon result in West's enslavement to his every whim only added to the delightful irony.

But first, before he could grind the Robinsons' faces in the dirt with his mental boots . . .

Like a first-time skydiver edging closer to the slipstream waiting to drag him from the plane, he reached out and touched the handle, but did not turn it. Instead he pulled his hand back and stood to one side, motioning the child forward.

After only a moment's blank-eyed hesitation, she stepped up, took the handle in both of her tiny hands, pushed and twisted at it for a second, then pulled it easily open.

He breathed a sigh of relief. She was physically capable of the required act. And, unlike every adult he'd come in contact with, she still showed no sign whatsoever of resisting his "suggestions." And for this particular operation, that was absolutely essential. If, sometime in the next few hours, she were distracted—

Shuddering inwardly, he drove the possibility from his mind. It's now or never, he thought, angered by his own hesitations. If he lost his nerve now, he would never regain it. And he would be doomed to this "in between" state, knowing just enough to sense what he would be missing if he didn't follow through. If he didn't take the chance *now*, he never would, and he would never attain the . . . *exalted* state that he knew was possible—and was rightfully his.

No matter what, precisely, that state proved to be.

With a last shuddering intake of breath, Dr. Zachary Smith entered the cubicle and forced himself to wait silently for the girl to close the door behind him.

Unable to sleep after Judy's almost-kidnapping, John Robinson spent much of the rest of the night attempting to undo whatever Smith had managed to do to the *Jupiter*'s controls. When the obvious diagnostic routines netted him nothing, he began pulling panels. Smith had almost certainly caused the disruptions by remote control, which meant there had to be something within the equipment itself to respond to the signals Smith had sent.

But there was nothing—nothing he could find, at least. And if he—he *had* designed it, after all—couldn't find it, then it likely wasn't there.

And still the red lights pulsed accusingly. Was it possible, he wondered uneasily, that whatever power had enabled Smith to tamper with Judy's mind—albeit a sleeping mind—a few hours earlier also enabled him to tamper directly with the control circuits or the computer that drove them? Was some kind of telekinesis any less likely than the other powers that Smith had proven he either possessed or controlled?

As the first traces of dawn began to appear on the viewscreens, a loud pounding on the airlock jolted him out of his uneasy reverie of speculation.

A glance at the viewscreens showed him it was an angry Zolkaz. A dozen other natives were clustered behind him, most carrying the same dart rifles John and the others were all too familiar with.

Frowning, John activated the external speakers. He had intended, once it was full light, to search out the natives in hopes of instigating a full-scale search for Smith, but none of them looked to be in all that cooperative a mood.

"What can we do for you, Zolkaz?" he asked. Behind him, Judy and Maureen and then the rest of the crew emerged onto the bridge. No one, with the exception of Don West, looked as if they'd gotten a lot of sleep.

"Have you found the one called Smith?" Zolkaz demanded without preamble, glaring at the loud but diffuse source of John's words.

"We believe he was here last night, outside our ship," John said, wondering what Smith had been up to that prompted the question. "We also believe he tried to trick my daughter into coming outside, so he could kidnap her."

"But he failed?" Zolkaz scowled suspiciously.

"He failed, but only because the rest of us worked together to stop him."

"With my granddaughter, he did not fail," Zolkaz said angrily.

A sick feeling gripped John as he wondered what

Smith—or the creature that seemed to be coexisting within him—could possibly want with the child.

"When did this happen?" John asked, setting the airlock to opening as he spoke.

"Last night, not long after midnight," Zolkaz said, scowling at the belated gesture of trust. "My daughter can tell you what happened."

At his gesture, a distraught-looking young woman stepped forward out of the cluster that had been following Zolkaz. "I thought she was sleepwalking, but when I called to her, she kept on going, as if she hadn't even heard me, and when I tried to run after her, I *couldn't*! I couldn't move! All I could do was watch! And this man Smith was waiting for her outside. They just—just walked away. He was holding her hand, but I couldn't run after them or wake anyone else up or *anything*. All I could do was watch, and then I passed out, and when I awoke it was almost morning."

Judy pushed through the airlock past the others and took the woman's hand. It was trembling and her cheeks were streaked with tears. "We'll find her," she said, sounding far more confident than she felt. "Which way did they go?"

"That way," the woman said, pointing with her free hand, "toward the Vault."

Judy stiffened, remembering, realizing the woman was right.

Last night, swamped with the horror of the creature she had found temporarily sharing her mind, it had not registered, but now, suddenly, the information bobbed to the surface of her memories. In that brief moment in which she had *been* both Smith and that other nightmarish creature, there had been a destination somewhere in the amalgam of minds, a destination the thought of which was tinged with both anticipation and terror.

The Vault.

The cubicles.

Without a word, Judy dropped the woman's hand and raced back inside the *Jupiter*, leaving the others gaping, puzzled. Frowning, her father hurried after her. Within seconds she had the displays she wanted on the ship's instruments. She almost collided with her father as she started back toward the airlock.

Looking up at him, she said, "The energy readings are up another hundred percent. I can't be sure, but I'd bet anything that Smith's gone back to the Vault, back to the cubicles."

16

With the kidnapped girl's mother in the lead, followed by Zolkaz, flanked by West and a native of similar size, they made good time. At Don's urging, John had offered them all a choice from the *Jupiter*'s weapons store, but even Zolkaz had turned them down, insisting on keeping his familiar and less-than-deadly tranquilizer rifle. The thought of using deadly force, even against the kidnapper of his granddaughter, still made him uneasy.

To Don's annoyance, both Judy and her mother had come down on the side of the tranquilizer rifle. "For one thing," Judy said patiently, "we don't know what Smith is capable of yet. And if there's any chance he can zap us long enough to steal our weapons, I'd a lot sooner they were knockout guns than plasma rifles. Besides, he already has *one* of those things."

She looked around at the others. "And don't tell me that you wouldn't be just a *little* more hesitant to fire if all you had was something that turned the target into charcoal. Especially if we get a chance to sneak up on him."

No one disagreed but West, who said with a purposely evil grin, "A charcoal Smith sounds pretty good to me."

As they walked, Zolkaz demanded to know why Smith had taken the girl to the Vault, of all places, but Judy could only profess, as sincerely as she could manage, that she had no idea. She wasn't about to share the wild suspicions her own mind had insisted on manufacturing once she'd accepted the possibility that both Smith and the long-dead Rellkans had indeed been possessed.

Inwardly, however, she couldn't help but wonder if it wasn't a chain reaction of some sort. Smith, already possessed, might be simply bringing another victim to the Vault to be "fed upon" or to be possessed, perhaps in order to, in effect, restart the Invasion. The creature doing the possessing obviously wasn't physically real, living in the machine—the computer?—that powered and controlled the cubicles. It would have to be a virtual, technological monster of some kind, unless there really was a grain of truth in Don West's off-the-wall suggestion that the Vault contained an impossibly low-powered hypergate. But the exact nature of the Vault would make little difference to anyone who was forced into a cubicle to be fed upon or possessed or just tortured.

Suppressing a shudder, Judy continued to half run, half walk, hoping her wild imaginings were just that.

They were still at least a kilometer from the Vault, not far past the point at which only two days before the entire crew of the *Jupiter* had been stunned and captured, when a young girl of eight or nine lurched into view fifty meters ahead. Her face was smudged and tearstained, her hair tangled. The moment she saw her mother, she broke into an eager run. Her mother did the same, summoning up a reserve of strength to lunge forward, thrashing through the grasping underbrush until the two figures literally collided. The woman snatched the girl up in her arms, hugging her tightly, assuring her over and over that she was safe while the girl herself simply clung, her arms tightly wrapped around the mother's neck.

As the group caught up and clustered around the pair, the girl blinked and seemed to shiver. A moment later her eyes fastened on John Robinson's bearded, haggard face, and her expression went blank. Her entire demeanor changed as well. Gone were the frightened eyes, the silent sobs, the gasps for breath. Her arms, clamped so tightly around her mother's neck, loosened but did not drop.

She smiled—not the smile of a child, but the sardonic smile of an adult. Her eyes shifted to Judy briefly, then went back to John Robinson.

"Professor Robinson, I presume," the girl said, her high-pitched voice producing the eerily recognizable phrasing and intonations of Dr. Zachary Smith. "Dr. Smith expects you will be pleased to learn that the *Jupiter* will soon have a new master, one who knows how to make proper use of its capabilities. If you so desire, of course, he will be more than happy to consider signing any or all of you on as his crew."

Stunned into silence by the girl's words, the Robinsons could only watch as, her speech apparently completed, she blinked as if awakening from a short nap. For an instant a new look of fright darted across her features, but then she apparently realized she was still in her mother's arms and her own arms tightened again around her mother's neck, though not as spasmodically as before. The woman, with a dark glance at the Robinsons, turned and walked determinedly back the way they had come, followed closely by Zolkaz and the others.

"What the hell just happened here?" West asked with a scowl. "Was it my imagination, or did that child sound like Smith?"

Judy nodded, grimacing. "It was from Smith, obviously. He was using the girl as a messenger. It's also pretty obvious that he's getting better at whatever it is he's doing. Unless just being closer to whatever's in those cubicles makes it easier for him. Makes the connection stronger, if that's what it is. But at least he didn't use her to 'feed' whatever's behind those cubicles." She watched the natives' retreating backs for another moment, then sucked in her breath with another grimace.

"I've got to talk to that girl," Judy said, "and find out what the devil *really* happened to her! Maybe it'll give us *some* idea of what we're up against. Come on, let's get a move on!" She glanced at the others. "Unless one of you has a better idea?"

No one did.

They trailed after the native group, Judy making entreaties that she be allowed to talk to the kidnapped girl, to no avail. The group was almost back to their homes, however, when Maureen Robinson's patient persistence, one mother to another, prevailed where Judy's impatience and John's attempts to reason with her logically had all failed. She was allowed to question the girl, albeit only under the once again suspicion-filled eyes of Zolkaz.

But once the gentle questioning started, the story came out quickly. The girl remembered virtually everything and actually seemed relieved, even grateful, to be asked to tell someone about it.

To everyone's surprise, particularly Judy's, the kidnapping hadn't frightened the girl at all, nor had the trek to the Vault. She had known—and still knew—that the man leading her there was her friend, and had felt perfectly safe and comfortable with him. Smith had obviously gotten into her mind even before the girl ever saw him, Judy concluded. The same way he'd gotten into hers a few hours earlier, invading her dreams and trying to trick her into coming out of the *Jupiter*.

Even when Smith had taken the girl inside the Vault, which her parents had warned her over and over was extremely dangerous, she hadn't been upset or worried, only anxious that she might not be able to help her new friend the way he wanted her to.

"What *did* he want you to do?" Maureen asked softly when the girl hesitated, for the first time displaying signs of uneasiness.

"He wanted me to let him out."

"Let him out? Of what?"

"The little room. He went inside and I closed the door, and then when the sun came up I let him out. Just like he told me to."

A stunned silence greeted the child's words as their seemingly impossible meaning came clear: Smith had reentered one of the cubicles, willingly subjecting himself to countless more hours of the worst torture any of them could imagine.

17

With what struck him as a superhuman effort, Dr. Zachary Smith forced himself to his feet and pick up the plasma rifle from where he'd left it leaning against the wall next to the cubicle door. He didn't know how long he had lain twitching on the corridor floor, his body recovering—divorcing itself—from the weeks or months of horrors that had been perpetrated on its virtual counterpart in the last few hours. All he knew for certain was that *nothing* would get him back inside one of those cubicles again. He would die first. Literally, not virtually.

The very act of standing up, however, made him feel better, as if the motion itself broke some of the bonds that still linked him to that virtual body that had been tortured and killed so many times. Even the hellish phantom images that seemed to flicker in and out of existence with the firing of his synapses faded until the stark white corridor around him came into sharp focus and he could see where, only three or four meters down, it intersected the radial corridor, which would lead to the outside.

Still, the journey was a long one. As he walked, vivid memories of the tortures that had been inflicted countless times upon his virtual body swamped his senses anew, as if they weren't yet finished with him, as if they were trying to drag him back in, to force him to relive it all. The featureless white walls around him seemed to act like an all-encompassing movie screen on which the nightmare images were projected, swooping in and out of focus with each step until, finally, he lurched through the door onto the lawn that surrounded the building.

For a long moment nothing changed, but then the real world all around him—the oasis of perfectly manicured lawn, the dense forest that surrounded it, the clouds whispering across the blue sky—began to provide him something to focus on, something to compete with the horrendous images still bubbling over from his memory into his subjective reality.

Eventually—he had no idea how long it took—he was able to blot out the remembered nightmare world, even to suppress, to a degree, the remembered pain that went with the terrifying images.

And to see that it was at least an hour after sunrise, perhaps two.

The girl, he realized uneasily, was nowhere in sight. She was probably back with her parents by now. If he was lucky. If he wasn't and she had somehow come face-to-face with John Robinson—

For once in his life Dr. Zachary Smith regretted his tendency toward overconfidence—"arrogance," the Robinsons would almost certainly call it. But how could he have known that instead of being incapacitated for a few moments, as he had been after his first emergence from a cubicle, he would be totally helpless for at least an hour? By all rights, it should have been just the opposite. Knowing what to expect when he'd entered should have prepared him, should have made his recovery all the quicker, as should the certain knowledge that it was only an imagined, virtual body that had been tortured and killed again and again, not his actual physical body. It, he told himself firmly again and again, was totally unharmed.

But in the long run the unexpected delay wouldn't matter. He hadn't been found and killed while he lay helpless, and that was all that counted. Not that any of the Robinsons would have had the courage and common sense to slay an unconscious man. No, his success, all but certain a dozen hours before, was utterly inevitable now. He had survived his second—and final!—little cubicle adventure, and soon . . .

Still, there was no need to take chances, even tiny ones.

Looking around, he located the guard they had encountered on their arrival. He was still seated on the ground a dozen meters to one side of the door, his back against the wall, his sleeping face vacant.

For several seconds Smith stood looking down at the man. With a faint shudder, he let the memories that still clamored around him become more solid, more real, stirring other, related memories of things that only days before he could not have imagined.

With the memories to guide him—surely, these excruciating "crutches" would soon become unnecessary and he would be able to stand on his own mental feet—he found himself sliding *into* the man's mind.

He began to work.

Suddenly, as the little girl revealed how Smith had purposely reentered one of the Vault's torture cubicles, everything fell into place in Will Robinson's mind. It was like when the solution to one of his hacker problems just *appeared* out of nowhere, converting what had been a dozen unrelated pieces into a single, coherent, blindingly obvious pattern.

Restraining the impulse to shout out his discovery, Will forced himself to think it through logically, to make sure his solution was the right one, that there were no huge, gaping holes in it. His subconscious wasn't infallible, he knew. More than once he'd jumped feet first into one of his "blindingly obvious" hacker solutions, only to find, when he tried to implement it, that there was an equally obvious flaw, the hacker equivalent of discovering you'd just divided by zero in solving a math problem.

But not this time, he decided as he half listened to the girl's increasingly agitated account of how her "friend" had fallen to the floor and just lay there when she opened the door to let him out, how he'd been shaking and moaning while she herself, suddenly terrified, ran from the building.

As the girl finished and her mother took her protectively in her arms, Will turned to his father, and saw him being practically dragged to one side by Don West.

"Let's go!" West was saying excitedly when Will caught up with them.

"Go?" Robinson scowled at him, puzzled. "Go where?"

West frowned, as if he couldn't believe Robinson could be so dense. "To get Smith, of course! This is our chance! Don't you remember how he was when we let him out the first time? He practically fainted! From what that girl says, the second time was worse—a lot worse. If he hasn't pulled himself together yet, we can *get* him!"

"It's been more than two hours! Do you really think—"

"Dad!" Will broke in, nearly shouting as he grabbed at his father's sleeve to get his attention. "He'll be gone by the time you can get there, and even if he *was* still there, it would be worse! The only way we'll ever beat him now is if *we* can get into those cubicles ourselves!"

His words caused even more of a stunned silence than the girl's revelation of what Smith had done. Both men looked down at him, his father with a frown, West with the beginnings of a disbelieving grin.

"You want *us* to go in there and get ourselves killed a few hundred times?" the pilot snorted. "Are you *nuts*, Will?"

"No! I know what those cubicles *are*!"

West blinked, then laughed. "Just like that? I don't suppose you'd care to tell us *how* you know?"

"Weren't you listening? The girl said Smith went back inside—intentionally!"

"So? Smith's crazy. We all know that."

"Crazy like a fox! He went back inside because he wanted more of what he got the first time! Those cubicles aren't torture chambers, they're *training rooms!*"

"Training in what, kid? How to die?"

Will shook his head angrily. *Kid!* Just because he wasn't a grown-up, no one wanted to listen to him, no matter how right he was! "Training in how *not* to die!" he said. "It's simple! Look, you all *said* Dr. Smith has some kind of power now, something he never had before, right?"

"And it's probably a result of being trapped in that torture cubicle and developing some kind of link with the Vault," Judy said, coming up unseen behind Will. "I figured out that much myself, remember? We discussed it for hours last night! So maybe he thought he could get a better connection the second time around."

Will shook his head again. "That's not what happened! That doesn't even make *sense!* What happened is, Dr. Smith was *trained* in there. He was trained in how to control people—with his mind. Like he did with that little girl. Like he almost did with you last night when you were trying to go outside to him until we stopped you."

"I still don't see how being tortured and killed over and over—" West began irritably.

"It's like what you said when you activated the hypergate to jump us here, remember? 'Sink or swim!' you said."

"It was just a figure of speech, kid! Besides, what the hell does *that* have to do with *this?*"

"In those cubicles, it *isn't* 'just a figure of speech.' It's what really happens to you!" Will turned back to his father. "*You* must see it, Dad! You were *in* there! You said you were killed a dozen times! Dr. Smith must've been killed hundreds of times, or maybe thousands—until he figured out how *not* to be killed. *He figured out how to control whatever it was that was killing him!"*

John Robinson blinked, forcing himself to think back to the horrors he'd been trying hard *not* to think about. The nightmarish creature advancing on him—not quickly but slowly, inexorably, like the mummy in those hundred-year-old vids. It was as if it knew the victim couldn't escape and was taking its time—

Or it was giving the *victim* all the time *he* needed to *do* something? Not to escape, but to somehow stop the creature's advance?

Every time it had been the same, John realized uneasily. Every time there was the slow, deliberate approach followed by a tortured death.

The boy could be right! If—and it was a huge *if*—you assumed that humans had latent mental powers that only needed the right circumstances—the right *push*—to emerge. Like a hundred-pound woman lifting a five-hundred-pound girder to free her child. Filled with panic and adrenaline, humans could perform seemingly miraculous physical feats.

So why not miraculous mental feats? The brain—the *physical* brain, with its synapses and ganglia and specialized areas—had been mapped and described to a fare-thee-well in the last hundred years. But the *mind*—which *lived* in the brain but was *not* the brain—was still largely a mystery. Maybe the ultimate mystery.

So it was at least *possible* that Will was right, John

thought with a grimace. The cubicles might indeed be training rooms—training rooms equipped with the ultimate in virtual reality equipment. It would be like teaching someone to swim by throwing him in the deep end of the pool.

In real life it would never work, of course. The trainee would drown nine times out of ten or ninety-nine times out of a hundred. But there, in those cubicles, trainees could be thrown in not once but thousands of times. Eventually, after one drowning or a hundred or a thousand, the trainee would figure out—or, more likely, accidentally stumble across—a way to keep afloat.

Learn by doing, by trial and error, John Robinson thought. It could be a very effective procedure, something you would never ever forget—provided you were able to survive all the virtual deaths without being driven insane.

"You may be right, son," he said, a faint glow of pride evident in his thoughts if not his words. "That *would* explain why these people thought this was a defense system. It trains people not to *kill* their enemies but to control them."

"Except," Don pointed out, "it apparently didn't work all that well two hundred years ago. Virtually everyone was killed by these Invaders. So even if the kid's right, what makes you think it's working any better now?"

John shrugged. "For one thing, we don't know what sort of enemy they were up against back there."

"Look," Will said, fidgeting with impatience, "it's *already* worked on Smith! That's why he's able to do—

whatever he's been doing! Now one of us has to go in there and get the same treatment!"

"Major West and I will go," his father said abruptly, apparently dispensing with his usual internal debate and coming to a quick decision. "The rest of you go back—"

"It was *my* idea!" Will protested.

"And we appreciate it," his father said. "But there's no way I'll allow you into one of those cubicles. I was *in* one, and I know what they're like! You'd never survive."

"It's not *real*, Dad! It—"

"It's not debatable, son! All you're doing is holding us up." John Robinson turned to West. "Let's go, Major. If *you* want to debate which of us goes in, we can do it on the way."

And they were gone, leaving Will to stare after them in irritated frustration.

Gratefully, Dr.Zachary Smith withdrew from the man's mind.

Despite the fact that immersing himself in the other's mind seemed to cushion him against the physical pain triggered by the persistent memories of his training ordeal, it was not a pleasant trade-off: minimized physical discomfort in return for having to wallow in cloying and counterproductive sentimentality.

The man's name was Corvalus, and Smith couldn't imagine how he'd managed to survive as long as he had. He had only the barest spark of real self-interest, but what could you expect from people whose ammunition of choice was a tranquilizer dart? In certain circumstances,

Smith could understand their use. On the crew of the *Jupiter* for instance. They had been, after all, a set of total strangers who might conceivably be of more use alive than dead.

But the darts were the *only* ammunition for the *only* weapons this lot had managed to preserve out of everything their pre-Invasion ancestors had presumably possessed. Originally, according to the spotty and likely faulty history Corvalus had been exposed to, the dart rifles had been used in much the same way similar tranquilizer guns had been used on old Earth—to capture panicked or dangerous animals that needed either medical treatment or a safe return to captivity.

And now the so-called Watchers carried them in case the Invaders ever reappeared. Why they would wish to be so gentle and nonlethal with the people who had destroyed their world was beyond Smith's ability to comprehend, but there it was.

Not that he was overly interested in the answer. The only answer he was truly interested in at the moment was to the question of whether he'd been successful in his attempt to convert Corvalus into an effective guard, which is to say, one who would obey his implanted instructions to make practical use of a plasma rifle if anyone other than Smith himself tried to enter the building.

1 8

"Come *on*, Professor!" Major Don West scowled in exasperation as he and John Robinson pressed on toward the central building at double-quick time. "You *know* I'm the one who should do this! For one thing, this situation with Smith is starting to look very much like a war, and I'm the military arm of this expedition."

"If this were a process that enhanced the body, I'd agree, Major, but it *isn't*. This 'war,' as you call it, will be fought with the mind, not the body."

West snorted as he jogged on. "You think the military trains you only physically, not *mentally*? I may not know as many equations as you do, Professor, but I'll match my knowledge of tactics with yours any day!"

"As far as I know, Major, there are no training courses for wars like this, between minds. We'll be making it up as we go."

"And you think I can't improvise? There may not be any training courses for this specific situation, Professor, but there are plenty that teach you to think on your feet, under pressure. *Deadly* pressure. To think—*and* to act! And that's one place where all the brainpower in the galaxy won't help you. You can come up with the most brilliant plan anyone ever thought of, but it won't do you one damn bit of good if you can't execute it. Fast!"

West looked back at the heavily breathing Robinson and the obstinately professorial look that dominated his sweat-streaked features even now. "If you hesitate to pull a trigger even a fraction of a second," the pilot continued forcefully, shifting the plasma rifle slung over his shoulder, "you're dead! And you can't tell me that *Smith* would hesitate even a microsecond if he had the chance to finish you off."

"This isn't a quick draw contest, Major, physical *or* mental. And I doubt that there will be all that many tactics involved, nor that much need for mental agility. If Judy's experience is any example, or the little girl's, it will be a matter of which mind is *stronger*, which mind can take the most advantage of this so-called training."

"Then we should *both* do this! Together—"

"And who would let us out? No, this is *my* decision, Major. In any event, it may all have become academic by the time we get there." Robinson glanced around as they continued to jog heavily along. "In fact, I'm surprised that Smith hasn't already stopped us. I would suggest we not waste any more breath on pointless debate."

Don West covered the last fifty meters to the edge of the parklike area at a run, plasma rifle in hand rather than slung across his shoulder. At the edge, he halted, peering out from a position of relative concealment at the huge, circular building. John Robinson, laser pistol gripped clumsily and uncomfortably in his right hand, joined him after a few seconds.

As before, the only sounds, other than Robinson's labored breathing, were from unseen animals in the forest and occasional chirps and squawks of birds. Unlike the first time they'd looked out at the building, the entrance gaped open invitingly.

There was no sign of Smith.

A faint hope flickered through Robinson's mind. Could Smith be inside after all, still incapacitated by his ordeal? If not, why was the entrance still open?

Looking through the plasma rifle's optics, West scanned the opening. "All clear."

Robinson snorted as best he could, considering his shortness of breath. "You expected him to stand in the doorway to give us a good shot at him? Is that what you learn in your tactics classes?"

"I don't *expect anything*," West snapped, "but I'm *prepared*. Now you stay back here while I take a closer look."

Without waiting for a reply, the pilot plunged out of the forest. Crouching low, he zigged and zagged as he darted from one cover to another, pausing momentarily in the lee of a bench, then a tree, then a statue. With a burst of speed that John Robinson realized he couldn't come close to matching, West sprinted across the last open area and flattened himself against the wall a dozen meters to the right of the entrance. Cautiously, he moved toward the opening.

He'd covered no more than half the distance when a sizzling bolt of energy from a plasma rifle erupted from the door at a sharp angle, scorching a long stripe of grass less than a meter from his feet.

West froze, his back pressed tightly against the wall.

"Don't come any closer!" A tense, almost trembling voice emerged from the opening. It sounded more frightened than threatening.

And it didn't sound anything like Smith.

"Why not? We don't mean you any harm."

"It doesn't matter. I cannot allow it! I cannot allow *anyone* to enter."

"Is Smith in there with you?"

"No one is here but myself. Just go away! Please! I do not *want* to kill you, but I will not be able to stop myself if you do not leave!"

"Major West!" John Robinson shouted from the edge of forest a hundred meters away. "Stay out of—"

Robinson's words were cut off by another sizzling bolt of plasma energy erupting from the opening, charring another stripe of grass, this one stopping just short of Robinson's place of concealment.

There was a moment of total silence before the tiny communicator clipped to West's belt vibrated. The pilot, his back still pressed tightly against the wall, snatched the device up and held it to his ear with his free hand. The other kept his plasma rifle centered on the opening in the wall.

"Major West . . . " John Robinson's whispered voice came faintly from the communicator. "Just listen! Don't say anything. Just stay out of sight of that door and get back here. I'll meet you—"

"I think I can take him, Professor," West interrupted, whispering into the communicator himself. "He's obviously a lousy shot and his heart isn't in it, so—"

"That is precisely why you will *not* 'take him,' as you euphemistically put it! He's obviously under Smith's control. He's not responsible for his actions, and I don't want him killed because of what Smith is forcing him to do! Is that understood?"

"Yes, but how will we get inside unless—"

"Just get the hell out of there, Major!" Robinson hissed. "I don't particularly want *either* of you to get killed! If nothing else, I wouldn't want to have to explain something like that to Kelwyn or Zolkaz. We're likely to need their help before this is over, and killing one of their friends, no matter what the reason, is not the best way to gain their cooperation. We'll figure out a way to get in there—*without* killing an innocent bystander."

Sighing silently, West listened while Robinson officiously told him which point of the clearing perimeter to head for, since he couldn't retrace his original path without getting in range of the plasma rifle.

"I'll meet you there," Robinson finished unnecessarily. With a terse acknowledgment, Don began easing himself back the way he'd come along the wall, repeatedly checking the door as long as it remained in view. Orders or no orders, if that guy came out of his shell and still had the rifle in his hands . . .

John Robinson backed away into the underbrush until he was sure he couldn't be seen by the shooter and began making his way around the perimeter toward the meeting point.

So this was how it was going to be, he thought: Smith

implanting orders in natives' minds like posthypnotic suggestions, and keeping out of the line of fire himself. Not that he should have been surprised. Courage was not Smith's strong point, especially when trickery and hiding behind someone else's skirts was a possibility.

In any event, what he and Major West had found here did indicate, if not quite prove, that Will's idea about the true nature of the torture cubicles was correct. They were indeed training rooms of some sort, and Smith didn't want him or anyone else from the *Jupiter* to get in there.

The situation was not yet hopeless, however. For one thing, Smith must not have come out of his session as all-powerful as he'd hoped. If he had, he would've wasted no time searching out and taking control of the *Jupiter* crew. Instead, Smith had merely taken control—and only partial control, at that—of this one native and left him as a guard. The guard's own will was obviously still operating, still resisting Smith's orders. Otherwise he would have blasted Don rather than warning him off.

Second, the fact that Smith had left someone to guard the building proved that he didn't want anyone else to receive the same . . . treatment? Which made it all the more imperative that someone *did* get in there.

As he continued to move toward the meeting point with West, John Robinson keyed another code into the communicator.

Will had returned to the *Jupiter* only grudgingly. It just wasn't right that he didn't get to go along with his father and Major West. After all, *he* was the one who'd figured out what those cubicles really were! Without him, they wouldn't have a clue.

Not that *that* was anything new!

It wasn't long, however, before the boy was engrossed in another problem: the apparent malfunctions in the *Jupiter*'s control systems that everyone assumed Smith was responsible for.

His father had been poking around in the consoles half the night but still hadn't come up with anything. Probably because he was looking in the wrong places, Will thought. He might be a brilliant physicist—he *had* developed the hypergate, after all—but that didn't make him a brilliant everything else. Einstein had come up with the theory of relativity, but half the time he'd forgotten to put his socks on.

And computers weren't hypergates. They *controlled* the hypergates, just like they controlled virtually everything else in the *Jupiter*—and all over Earth, for that matter. If Earth still existed, that is. In order for the hypergates to operate, his father had long ago given the computers all the necessary information, all the formulas, and in effect told the computers which ones to use, what order to use them in, all that sort of thing. That way, when it was time for the hypergate to be turned on, all you needed to do was turn the two keys simultaneously and push a few buttons. The computers then did what they had long ago been told to do when this happened. They performed countless essential calculations and used the results of those calculations to activate the hypergate by sending

157

the right types and amounts of power to the right places at the right times, all the while making thousands of adjustments every microsecond to make sure that the hypergate utilized that power correctly and functioned the way it was designed to function. The way his father had *designed* it to function.

His father, obviously, understood hypergates. He also understood how to tell the computers what they had to do in order for the equipment to perform its proper function.

But John Robinson didn't understand computers themselves or how they operated. He didn't have to. All he had to do was use them, which the people who *did* understand computers, after decades of jargon and obfuscation, had finally made it very easy to do. By the mid-twenty-first century it was, in some ways, like using your own brain. You didn't have to understand its inner workings—or be able to perform surgery on it—in order to use it.

Will, on the other hand, understood computers, *really* understood computers, and had been performing "surgery" on them for years. And one thing this understanding told him was: *Any* computer, any*where*, can be hacked into by anyone who *really* understands computers and *really* wants to hack in.

Common sense told him that Dr. Smith would have *really* wanted to hack into the *Jupiter*'s computer. All he had to find out now was, did Dr. Smith understand computers well enough to do it?

It took Will approximately ten minutes of scanning screens full of messages and codes to find the answer.

Yes.

The *Jupiter* computer's security had been breached, not once but several times. Smith had probably had to do his work a bit at a time so as not to get caught.

And what Smith had done, Will had to admit, was very smooth. The malfunction lights—the first one Will investigated, anyway—was giving a false indication. Independent checks showed that the circuit that the light *said* was out of order was, in fact, functioning perfectly.

But only as long as no one tried to actually *use* the circuit. When that happened, the circuit in question would fail. At least for the duration of the attempt.

It was like booby-trapping the fuel gauge on a car. It was rigged to show "Empty," but if you looked in the tank, you could see it was full. However, if you ignored the gauge reading and started the car, the gauge itself would siphon all the fuel out of the tank so that then it really *would* be empty.

To get around the booby trap, Will knew he'd have to undo whatever Smith had done, and do it very carefully, avoiding whatever digital trip wires and minefields Smith had included.

By the time Will had safely defused the first of the traps and had the first of the lights glowing green, he'd developed a grudging respect for Smith's talents. Smith might be a creep—*was* a creep!—but he was a smart creep. And if he ever got back inside the *Jupiter*, he could deactivate all his booby traps, probably in a matter of seconds, and the ship would be ready to go.

With or without any of the Robinson clan on board.

Sauce for the goose, Will thought with a grin as he

did a little booby-trapping of his own with the first circuit.

And then the second.

And the third . . .

There were only three red lights still pulsing when both his own communicator and the *Jupiter*'s comm system came to life.

"Will? Are you there?"

"Dad? Is that you?"

"It looks like you were right about the cubicles, son," his father said without elaboration. "Smith is gone, and he left a guard behind—with the plasma rifle he stole when he escaped. The guard is apparently under Smith's control, so we'll need the robot to get us into the cubicles without killing him. It *does* have nonlethal capabilities now, doesn't it?"

"Sure, Dad, but I'm not sure how it'll hold up against a plasma rifle. Those things are nasty."

"Just so it holds up long enough to disable the guard without killing him. Or to destroy the rifle. I'm sure you'll be able to repair whatever damage the robot may suffer. Now get it ready while I talk to Judy and your mother."

Sighing, Will glanced at the three remaining malfunction lights, stowed his hacker's deck and headed for the robot bay, not even glancing sideways at his mother and sisters and the half-dozen Rellkans who had been huddling together ever since they arrived. Dad was right, Will thought grudgingly. Anything a plasma rifle could do to the robot could be repaired. Even so, he couldn't help but feel guilty about it. It wasn't as if the robot was just a *machine* . . .

1 9

"John, are you all right?" Maureen Robinson asked from the *Jupiter* comm unit, sounding concerned but not anxious. "You said someone is guarding the building with a plasma rifle?"

"We're fine," John said, giving her a brief "shots fired" summary. "Major West and I will just stay out of range of the entrance until Will gets here with the robot."

"Then you still plan to go into a cubicle yourself?"

"You heard what I told Will before we left. It looks very much as if the boy was right. These things probably *are* training devices. Considering the obvious advantages Smith has gotten from his sessions, I can't see that we have any choice."

"And what if Smith comes back while you're still inside? Do you have any idea where he went? Or why?"

"I don't know any more than you do, just what the girl told us. Smith was in a pretty bad way when she let him out, so my guess is, he's lying low somewhere until he recovers."

"With any luck," Judy put in, "he *won't* recover!"

"And with the kind of luck we've been having lately," Penny said, "Smith *will* recover and Father won't!"

"Don't even *joke* about something like that!" Maureen flared. "If you don't have anything positive to contribute, you can go to your room!"

"Sure, like it's *my* fault we're here!" the girl groused, turning and stomping off the bridge, adding, just as the access doors closed behind her, "If Smith takes over, maybe we'll at least go somewhere *interesting*."

"Penny!"

But the girl was already gone.

"Don't be too hard on her," John said over the comm system. "She didn't mean it. She's just venting. Now, have you found anything useful on how Smith's newfound abilities may work?"

Maureen shook her head, though she knew he couldn't see her. "Nothing that seems to have any relevance to the situation here. We haven't had time to read every article we've turned up in the computer's database, but it doesn't look promising. The only reliable information seems to be Rhineian studies of one kind or another. They have a century and a half of data, but it's virtually all statistical analyses of card runs and attempts to manipulate feather-light objects under laboratory conditions. Stories of anything more substantial are just that—stories. Anecdotal evidence. And even there, the only things even remotely like what Smith appears to have stumbled into are possession and out-of-body experiences. And we haven't found anything at all that even *suggests* a scientific physiological basis for such phenomena."

"What about Zolkaz and the others? Has this given

them any new insights into what might have happened to their ancestors?"

"Nothing beyond the obvious, that the Defenders were so traumatized by the training that they were unable to make use of it and were overrun. From what Zolkaz says, prior to the Invasion they were very peaceful, even pacifistic. I know it's hard to believe, but he says there had been no wars of any kind on the planet itself for thousands of years. And very little crime."

John sighed. "The rose-colored glasses of ancestor worship, I imagine, at least to some extent. In any event, it probably isn't relevant to the present situation anyway. But keep at it. And Judy, you come with Will and the robot. Bring your medkit. Just in case things don't go as smoothly as we hope and the guard is injured."

"Sure, Dad, I was planning to come along anyway. I'm not accomplishing much around here."

At that point the robot emerged from the robot bay and made for the airlock, trailed closely by Will. A moment later they were on their way.

Returning to her cell, the Space Captive, aka Penny Robinson in her less bitter moments, was feeling hopeful for the first time since they'd left Earth. Unlike the others, she wasn't horrified at the thought of Smith getting his brain boosted and taking over the *Jupiter*. Actually, she *liked* the idea.

As long as she wasn't left behind.

Sure, he had tried to kill them all, but it hadn't been *personal*. Some nutsos had offered him all the money in the world to sabotage the *Jupiter*, and he'd tried. She knew that if someone had offered *her* that kind of money—and promised her she'd be able to stay on Earth and spend it!—she would've been tempted herself.

Maybe.

Anyway, if Smith took over, they'd have a better chance of finding their way back to Earth, which, as far as she was concerned, was priority number one. For one thing, unlike her ultracautious parents, he wouldn't make such a big deal out of jumping through the hypergate. For another, if the brain boost business really worked, he'd be able to get the information he wanted from anyone he ran into. Fast. Just get a grip on someone's mind, give it a good squeeze, and all the information you'd ever want would pop out.

If the information existed, of course.

But whether it did or not, a brain-boosted Smith would be able to find out—quickly. And if it didn't exist on a particular world, he'd move on. Another jump, another world.

He'd be away from this one in a flash, given the chance, no matter what Judy thought. The Space Captive laughed at her sister's completely nutsy idea that Smith might decide to use his brain boost to become this world's dictator.

Sure he would!

After all, who could resist the lure of being the unquestioned ruler of a few thousand guys with two-hundred-year-old dart rifles and houses that started melting if you didn't pay attention to them—and not a single shopping mall on the whole stupid planet! It was every would-be tyrant's dream! At best, maybe—just maybe—he'd take it over for practice, but that probably wouldn't take long.

And before you knew it, the *Jupiter*'d be on its way, hop-scotching across the galaxy until they found someone with a map. Or at least a road sign. No more of the plodding "should-we-or-shouldn't-we, what-if-something-goes-wrong" school of space exploration as practiced by the Space Captive's hopelessly wimpy captors. Use the hypergate only in life-threatening emergencies, they insisted.

"There's no way of knowing where we'll come out," they said. As if that meant anything! After that first jump—to keep from getting burned up when they fell into the sun—they were as lost as it was possible to get. No identifiable stars, nothing! They could be a hundred light-years from Earth or a hundred thousand, for all they knew. They might even be in another galaxy altogether. Nothing in the rules against it. So how could they get any *more* lost, for Pete's sake?

"There's a very real danger that we'd come out somewhere totally disastrous, like inside a star!" they also said.

"*Life* is a risk!" the Space Captive said, and so did Smith.

Probably.

Besides, what were the actual odds? Had anyone done a series of test runs and counted how many times you ended up safely out in space somewhere and how many times you ended up inside a star? Or even *dangerously close* to a star?

No!

The *Jupiter* was the first and only ship of its kind. The only test run was the one they were on right now! And they hadn't even come *close* to a star! Do the math. One hundred percent safe arrivals. Those were pretty good odds.

Smith would have the good sense to *see* that.

And he'd see that playing it safe and being trapped on the *Jupiter*—or on this stupid planet they were on now!—for the next hundred years wasn't a life at all. It was a prison sentence!

With a faint smile, the Space Captive stretched out on her bunk and dreamed of Liberation.

And of shopping malls.

Dr. Zachary Smith watched Major West as best he could from a point of relative safety and concealment at the far side of the central clearing. He'd been out of the cubicle almost three hours, and there were still times when he felt as if he'd been flayed alive and left out to dry. But it wasn't nearly all the time now, as it had been the first few minutes, when all he could do was lie on the floor and writhe in agony, though he knew that he was simply trapped in the persistently vivid memories of the horrors he'd experienced in the cubicle. But they were memories that were more than memories. They assaulted not just the cells and synapses of his brain, but the very nerves in every part of his body. In effect, he wasn't just *remembering* the tortures his virtual body had been subjected to. His *real* body was being forced to *relive* them.

He was, however, growing more confident in the knowledge that the memories themselves, no matter how vivid and painful, were of things that had happened not to him, not to his physical body. Rather, they had happened to a series of grotesque imaginary bodies that existed only in his mind. They'd had no real, physical effect on him, either then or now. His *real* body, his *human* body, as he could see by simply looking down any time he wished, was totally untouched, totally unharmed.

And as Smith gradually came to accept that reality, he became more capable of suppressing the memorized pain itself. Gradually, it was losing its power over him. As a result, his concentration was returning and he was able to dredge up the *useful* memories—the ones that showed him how to make use of the talents that had been tortured out of the hidden corners of his subconscious where they had lain, unknown and untapped, all his life.

And now he knew he had to exercise those powers. It would have been better to wait another hour, another ten, while he found other weak-willed guinea pigs like Corvalus to practice on. But he didn't have the time. The robot would be here in little more than an hour, he suspected. The rest of the Robinson clan, as well as a number of dart-bearing natives, couldn't be far behind.

He knew he wasn't fully prepared, wasn't fully comfortable with his newfound powers yet, but he had no choice. As he found himself saying more and more often lately, it was now or never. At least approximately.

Smith focused on West's distant figure as it moved out of the shadow of the Vault and clumped across the lawn. The world wavered around Smith as his mind reached out like an invisible hand. After a moment, he *felt* it touch West's mind. Before, with Corvalus and the others, his touch had been so light, the actual "feel" of the contact had been smothered by the myriad other, vastly more powerful sensations that had still clung to him from his time in the cubicle. It had been like trying to taste a culinary delicacy with a tongue scorched into insensitivity by a barrage of red hot spices, he thought. The meals had been "consumed," but without a hint of their true taste.

But now . . .

Now he was enveloped by a sensation he could not have *imagined* forty-eight hours before and even now couldn't accurately describe. An all-over, inside-and-out *feeling*; not really an electrical tingle nor a physical vibration, but something *like* both, coupled with a sensation that was, impossibly, a combination of taste and scent that pulsed throughout his body.

Like a spherical sphincter, Smith's mind *closed* around West's . . . and *squeezed*.

And Smith found himself looking out through the pilot's eyes, the image confusingly superimposed on the image formed on his own retinas.

Abruptly, before the wavering double image twisted his stomach into a knot of nausea, Smith closed his own eyes.

He felt West's throat muscles tighten, his mouth begin to open.

As if West's muscles were his own, Smith stopped the words before they could be uttered. He felt sudden panic erupting in the pilot, the sort of panic West could apparently feel but would never exhibit openly, choosing instead to conceal it beneath his grotesquely macho exterior.

For a moment Smith let himself enjoy this gratifying display of cowardice and hypocrisy, contrasting the *real* Major West with the shallow, heroic facade he presented to the world. Then, with an effort so slight it startled him, Smith quashed the other's panic.

And turned him about, facing toward Smith's place of concealment two hundred meters distant, and set him walking.

He was definitely getting better at this, Smith thought with a smug mental smile. Although, caution warned him a moment later, it wouldn't do to get overconfident—again.

He mustn't let himself forget that controlling a mind of West's caliber doubtless presented far fewer problems than he would encounter when going after even the least of the Robinsons. They might be moralistic, self-righteous fools, but their minds, while woefully misguided, were far from weak. Even during the brief and highly limited contacts he'd had with Judy Robinson's mind, he had, he now realized, felt its strength. At the time, stumbling around blindly, he hadn't recognized the feel of that strength for what it was. He'd only been frustrated by it. But now—

Suddenly, West was resisting, violently. Angry curses

bubbled up in his mind but could not get past his throat as Smith instinctively *squeezed* once again.

And Smith realized two things simultaneously. It had been his own thoughts of Judy Robinson that prompted West's sudden efforts to break free. And West's memories, his very thoughts, were an open book to him.

But it was a book he did *not* want to read, Smith realized as, one after another, nauseating images of macho posturing and preening whipped through his mind. The man was even more puerile than he'd imagined. The very thought that Judy Robinson could be anything other than contemptuous of a boorish oaf like this—

Squeezing even more tightly, Smith was able, without knowing exactly how, to silence West's rebellious thoughts, his every effort at resistance, until it was almost as if he were walking his own body, completely and unquestionably in control.

Smiling mentally—wondering idly if his own body was smiling as well—Smith felt his confidence completely restored, and he began to look forward to the next step in this little game more with anticipation than with apprehension.

20

John Robinson looked around irritably. Where the hell *was* West? How difficult could it be for a thoroughly trained military mind to cross two or three hundred meters of grass and show up where he was supposed to?

Tapping West's code into the communicator, he waited, scowling. "Major West! Respond!"

Nothing.

Wondering if West could have drifted—purposely?—into the line of sight of the reluctant sniper, Robinson moved a few meters back the way he'd come, to where the door to the building was visible, and peered out into the clearing.

No body, upright or prone.

He was keying the communicator again when he saw West in the distance, halfway around the building, walking in his direction. What the devil was he doing back there?

Hurrying out of the sniper's line of sight, Robinson clipped his communicator to his belt as he emerged into the clearing. Scowling, he stood waiting for West, who gave no indication of being in a hurry. In fact, he plodded along as if he were carrying a full pack, including a tent, on his back.

Suddenly, Robinson's head started started *itching*.

Inside.

What the hell—

Instinctively, he reached for his communicator, not his holstered laser pistol. But even as his fingers were closing on the device, almost touching it, they refused to move the final few millimeters.

Instead they opened.

Against his will, his fingers opened!

It was Smith! It had to be!

The itching inside his head abruptly became worse, as if thousands of microscopic insects were packed inside his skull, the entire swarm squirming frantically as its individual members raced back and forth in all directions.

John Robinson felt fear then, real and immediate. Until now, the idea that Smith might be able to control someone else's mind or body had had an academic tinge of unreality about it. He'd accepted—intellectually— that Smith had a certain, ill-defined power. He had even seen the results of that power—on natives who'd been forced by Smith to sleep for a few hours, and in the invasion of his daughter's dreams and the attempt to draw her, sleepwalking, out of the *Jupiter*.

But Judy had awakened and been fine, as had the natives, and the emotional reality of what Smith had done to them had not been driven home to him.

But now . . .

He was wide awake, in broad daylight, and Smith was *in* his mind, not just prodding it from the outside!

Desperately, Robinson tried to close his fingers over the communicator. Instead, his arm dropped limply to his side, as if it were no longer a part of him.

And it *wasn't*, he realized.

It was a part of Smith—or whatever Smith had become.

His vision flickered. For an instant he saw himself a good fifty meters away, standing like a blank-faced automaton, the image superimposed on the image his own eyes had of Major West.

As if, for just an instant, he was seeing through two sets of eyes.

Just as abruptly as it had begun, the itching subsided. His body was once again his own.

Grabbing the laser pistol, he almost dropped it as he jerked it free of its clip. At the same time, his heart pounding, he darted looks in all directions. If he could spot Smith before he lost control of his body once again—

In the distance, Major West collapsed to the ground and lay in a disjointed heap.

As quickly as John Robinson had regained control of his body, he lost it. Once again he almost dropped the laser pistol, this time as his hand, completely against his will, clumsily forced it back onto its clip holster.

"Smith!" he began, but further words froze in his throat as the returning swarm of microscopic insects began to not only itch, but to sting. He thought he heard a laugh, but couldn't tell if he heard it with his ears or his mind.

173

Beyond West's motionless body, Robinson saw Smith emerge into the far side of the clearing and walk toward him. John's fingers twitched once as he strained to reach for the laser pistol, but he couldn't move.

As Smith passed West's body, John could see the smile on his face.

A moment later he almost blacked out as the itching inside his skull reached a crescendo—and vanished, replaced by an even more frightening numbness, as if everything behind his eyes had suddenly faded out of existence.

He felt his hand move and realized he couldn't resist it. He could only watch, a helpless passenger in his own body, as it picked up the communicator and punched in the code that would connect it to all the other communicators as well as the *Jupiter* itself.

"I must say," the robot thundered, "it's a lovely day for a stroll."

"If you say so," Judy said, giving Will a look. "At least no one's taken a shot at us. Yet."

"There's always a first time," the robot responded jovially.

"Will!"

"Don't yell at *me*!" the boy said. "*I* didn't say it."

"You programmed it! To be 'spontaneous,' I think you said. I don't think your program has quite figured out the distinction between 'spontaneous' and 'stupid.'"

"And *people* always *do*? If you think you can do any better—"

174

Further discussion was cut off when both their communicators came to life.

"I think we can all relax just a little bit," they heard their father saying a moment later. "We found Smith, and there's nothing to worry about."

"He's dead?" Judy asked.

"Nothing like that. He's just unconscious. I assume—"

"If he isn't dead, I wouldn't recommend assuming anything. I certainly wouldn't suggest relaxing!"

"Nor would I, John," Maureen Robinson added forcefully from the distant *Jupiter*. "Are you sure it isn't a trick? What, precisely, happened to him?"

"As I was about to say," John said, his tinny voice sounding aggravated, "I *assume* that his second training session was too much for him. For his mind, at any rate. Aside from the fact that he's unconscious, he *appears* to be in good physical health. Judy, did you think to bring your medkit?"

"Of course, Dad. For the guard, remember?"

A brief silence, then: "That's right." He half laughed, half snorted. "Slipped my mind, like most everything else the last few minutes. All I can think about is how relieved I am I won't have to go back inside the Vault. Believe me, that is not something I was looking forward to."

Judy shuddered. "I can imagine. Just getting a secondhand glimpse last night when that bastard Smith was sliming around in my mind was more than enough for *this* lifetime."

"Where'd you find Smith, anyway?" Will asked.

"Last time, you said you thought he was lying low somewhere, recovering."

"He was trying, I imagine. Major West found him on the edge of the forest, on the opposite side from the Vault's door. He looked as if he'd gotten that far and passed out. Remember, the little girl said he was in terrible shape when she let him out. And he was in that cubicle for at least four hours this time. I can't even imagine what he must've gone through. I'm surprised he's even alive."

"What about the guard? Since you're not going to have to get into the building now, do you still need the robot to get him out?"

Another silence, this one a little longer. "All things considered, it's probably better to leave the man alone, at least for the time being. Without Smith reinforcing the suggestion every so often, I'd think he would be coming out of it pretty soon without any help from us."

"And what about Smith?"

"What about him?" John Robinson asked when Will didn't continue.

"What if he wakes up? Couldn't he do the same thing to you he did to that guard?"

"Not likely. Frankly, I think he burned himself out in that second session. He may *never* come out of it."

"I hope you're right," Judy said. "But just to play it safe, I'll give him a shot of something as soon as we get there. It'll keep him out of mischief for as long as we want. And give us time to figure out what to do when he *does* wake up." She shook her head. "*If* we want to even *let* him wake up. The more I think about this, the less I like it."

"I'm sure you're worrying needlessly," her father said. "In any event, we can't keep him sedated *forever*."

"And what's the alternative? If there's the slightest chance that he could take one or more of us over when he wakes up—you *know* that's a chance we can't take. Not just for our sakes, but for everyone's. Can you even imagine what he would do if he took command of the *Jupiter* the way he planned to and then actually managed to find a civilized world to land on?"

There was an even longer silence this time. Finally John Robinson's voice came over the communicators again. "You're right, of course. We can't take the chance. Get here as quickly as you can. I assume you have a suitable sedative in your medkit?"

"Something that'll do the job. I'll be there as soon as I can," she finished, snapping off her communicator. "Let's go, little brother."

"You go ahead," Will said, pulling his latest hacker's deck from its pouch. "We'll catch up. I've got to talk to the robot a second."

Judy gave him a brief frown, then shrugged and moved out at a determined jog. After a dozen meters, as an image of Smith waking up before she could get there with the sedative flashed through her mind, she increased her pace to a run.

Even with the robot breaking trail for him, Will's short legs simply couldn't carry him fast enough to catch up to his sister before she reached the Vault. At least he'd seen no sign of her yet, and the edge of the clearing was just ahead.

With a last burst of speed, he passed the robot in the final dozen meters and lurched to a halt at the very edge of the clearing. Anxiously, he peered out through the concealing cloak of foliage.

The clearing was empty, the door to the building closed. Behind him the robot lumbered to a halt.

"Do *you* see anything, Robot?"

"As a matter of fact I do, Will Robinson."

"What?" the boy asked exasperatedly when the robot didn't elaborate.

"The building of cubicles, called the Vault, and—"

"You know what I mean, Robot! Do you see any sign of Judy or my father? Or Smith or Major West?"

"Of course I see them."

A chill shot up the boy's spine as he darted looks in all directions and still saw only the empty parklike area with its barren paths and unoccupied benches, and the huge, sterile-looking circular building. "Where? Where do you see them?"

"You're joshing me, Will Robinson," the robot said after an uncharacteristic hesitation. "But I must admit, I do not understand your motive for doing so at this particular time."

"Robot, I'm not kidding around! Where are they?"

The robot swiveled its sensors toward the boy, as if to inspect him more closely. "You truly do not see them?

This is not a pop quiz designed to uncover faults in my programming?"

"*Where are they?*"

The robot raised its sensors and then one of its arms, its pincerlike claws closed. "They are there," it said, pointing as best it could without fingers, "approximately eleven-point-six meters directly in front of you."

Even as the robot spoke, the air wavered in front of them, distorting an area of the building beyond like a fun-house mirror. And someone laughed, someone who sounded a lot like Dr. Smith. Someone who couldn't be any farther away than the wavering air.

Shivering, the boy took a step backward, bumping against the robot.

In the blink of an eye—literally—the wavering, now translucent air was replaced by a laughing Dr. Smith. Behind him on the grass lay his sister Judy, his father, and Major West. Like the Rellkan guards the day before, they were asleep.

Will very much hoped.

"Welcome, child," Smith said, smiling as broadly as Will had ever seen him smile. "Won't you step into my parlor and join your compatriots?"

2 1

"Robot!" Will began, but before he could get a second word out, his every muscle froze and he *itched* all over, inside and out, but especially in his head. The itching in his head, he realized belatedly, was not new. It had started, very lightly, when he first reached the clearing, but he'd been concentrating so much on other things—like wondering where his sister had disappeared to and what Smith was up to—that he hadn't noticed.

"Now, now, child," Smith continued, wagging a finger in the air, "don't be more bothersome than you have already been. Your metal friend can't help you. However, he *can* help *me*, so I would be eternally grateful if you would turn him over to my control. And cancel any of the ingenious little booby traps you're so fond of. Not that you have any choice in the matter."

Smith took a step closer. The itching in Will's head got even worse, as if his skull were filled with an undulating swarm of tiny, tickling feathers. For an instant his own image—as seen by Dr. Smith?—flashed across his retinas. He could see the forest and the robot standing behind him.

And then—

Will heard Smith laugh again, sounding less amused this time. "I didn't *think* you would be particularly cooperative, child. But no matter. Resistance is an exercise in futility—and a considerable source of discomfort for you."

Will's headful of nanofeathers went from itching to painful for a moment, and he found himself remembering the last work he'd done on the robot's program. Then he felt his lips and tongue and jaw move, no matter how hard he tried to keep them still. And he heard himself say, "Robotman, cancel program Smith-is-a-dastardly-pusillanimous-recreant."

"Not very flattering, child," Smith said, "nor imaginative. But it will do, I suppose. Robot, you will—"

"No, I will not!" the robot thundered. Without warning, it lunged forward, a halo of energy discharges enveloping one set of claws, which it thrust in Smith's direction while with the other set it snatched Will up unceremoniously and clasped him to its metal chest.

Doing a fast one-eighty, the robot crashed full speed back in the direction it had come.

Will felt himself struggling to escape, although escape from the robot was the last thing he wanted. Luckily, the robot's grip could not be broken. Will's head continued to itch furiously, with occasional stabs of pain intermixed, as if a growing number of the nanofeathers had grown needle-sharp points.

Until—

Suddenly, his body stopped struggling. A moment later the itching and the needle pricks were gone from his head.

Was it over? Was he out of Smith's range?

A moment of elation rippled through him at the thought, but it left him almost instantly, as he realized he had to warn his mother and Penny!

"Keep going, Robot!" he shouted, managing to wriggle one arm free of the metallic grip and get his hand on his communicator. He was just punching in the code for the *Jupiter* when the horde of nanofeathers invaded his head once again. Before he could finish the code, his body froze, as it had when Smith first appeared before him.

Except this time . . .

This time it wasn't completely frozen. He could still move, but only with molasseslike slowness, as if his muscles were fighting against each other.

But the resistance was diminishing with every meter the robot put between himself and Smith. Whatever power Smith had, Will thought, it was subject to the inverse square law.

He managed to key another digit in. Only one more to go! At the rate the resistance to his movements was fading, he would be out of Smith's range in another minute or two. If he could just—

All at once, the needles in his head seemed to explode in all directions, and he flinched. His fingers flew open, releasing the communicator, which clattered against the robot's restraining arm and fell, disappearing into the brush through which the robot was carrying him.

"Robot—" Will began, but cut himself off. There was no point in even trying to communicate with him until they were totally out of Smith's range. And even then . . .

He began to see some holes in the spur-of-the-moment plan and the instructions he'd hastily formulated for the robot before taking off after Judy. For one thing, how would either he or the robot know for sure when they were out of Smith's range and it was safe for the robot to start obeying his own commands again? Even if Smith did have to actually *see* someone in order to establish control for the first time, it was now obvious that he didn't have to *remain* in visual contact for his influence to continue.

Will grimaced as the mixture of needles and nanofeathers indulged in a new flurry of activity. But still, overall, they were fading with time and distance. Another minute, another hundred meters, and—

Abruptly, his eyelids were heavy, his senses dulled, as if he'd been enclosed in a soft, sensationless cocoon. An image of his father and sister and Major West, lying asleep in the clearing, flashed through his mind, but it had no effect on him. The adrenaline surge he'd gotten when he first saw them didn't return. Instead, a wave of sleepiness spread over him. Even the sounds of the robot, still crashing through the underbrush, were muffled, as if someone had put an insulating bag over his head, and the constant, repeated impact of his own body against the robot's chest had no effect. It was as if it was all happening to someone else, not him—a vid that he was watching, but one so dull that he could barely stay awake.

He tried shaking himself in the robot's grip, tried

shouting at himself at the top of his lungs, tried pinching himself until he was afraid he'd draw blood, but nothing helped. His eyelids kept growing heavier by the second, as if some unseen force was dragging them down.

He knew it was Smith doing it, of course. It was probably the same thing Smith had done to his father and sister and to Major West and the Rellkan guards.

But knowing didn't help. The lead weights attached to his eyelids continued to grow heavier and heavier, until —

With what seemed an almost audible thump, his eyes closed. No matter how hard he struggled, he couldn't reopen them. The lead weights had been replaced by glue, and the molasseslike thickness he'd felt before was now spreading back through his brain, slowing his thought processes until his mind — not Will Robinson, but his mind — surrendered and allowed sleep to close in.

The Space Captive sat at the terminal in her cell contemplating the dozens of choices, each of which lead to dozens of other choices, each of which in turn led to still other choices.

All of which she was terminally bored with.

She had long ago tried every game, every programthat even *looked* interesting, and discovered that most of them weren't. And the few that *were* interesting when she first tried them had long ago plummeted to the Depths of Dullness.

Because they weren't *real*.

No matter what she won, no matter how many

points or credits or kingdoms, she couldn't ignore the depressing fact that it was nothing more than minuscule electrical currents running through a bunch of nanocircuits. No matter who or what she met in the course of her "adventures," no matter who she befriended or rescued, she couldn't extract them from the computer and take them to her room or to a shopping mall or a vidshow. Or do anything at all that she was able to do with *real* people.

Or, more accurately, anything she *had once* been able to do with real people, back in the prehistoric days when she'd lived on a world where things like shopping malls—and real people—existed. There were moments—particularly after awakening from a dream of those ancient times—when the Space Captive wished the memories themselves would go away. That way she could simply forget that Earth had ever existed. It would be easier, less painful. She wouldn't be constantly reminded of what she no longer had. Of what she would never have again.

Ever.

Closing her eyes, the Space Captive tapped the screen at random, waited a moment, tapped it again, blindly, waited another moment, tapped it yet again. After at least five taps, she opened her eyes.

And laughed for the first time in days. Not because she was happy at what she saw, but because, even in her dark mood, the game her random tapping had accessed struck her as ludicrously appropriate: solitaire. The cards were already dealt and distributed in lifeless piles across the screen. Just the thing for a person sentenced, to all intents and purposes, to a lifetime of solitary confinement.

Which was all that she had to look forward to, now that Smith's brain boost had turned out to be a bust. For an hour or two she'd actually believed that Smith would take over the *Jupiter* and find a way back to Earth, but then her father had called with the news. Her hopes had vanished along with Smith's powers.

She was back where she'd started, all hope for a normal life gone.

Glumly, the Space Captive ordered the ten of clubs onto the jack of diamonds.

Will Robinson came awake slowly, wondering where he was and why he was lying flat on his back in a tangle of flattened weeds.

"You are awake, Will Robinson!" The deafening voice of the robot, obviously nearby, sent the boy scrambling to his feet as adrenaline flooded his bloodstream. Shaking from the shock, the boy looked around.

The robot was standing hip-deep in weeds itself. It must have stomped a patch of them down to give him a more comfortable—or rather, less *un*comfortable— place to sleep off . . .

. . . whatever it was he'd just slept off.

Suddenly it all came back to him.

Smith!

A new burst of adrenaline made Will's body prickle as he spun around, looking in all directions. "Where's Smith?" he asked. "Did we get away from him?"

"Apparently so. But you would know better than I. Do you feel his influence in any way?"

Will shook his head. "Not a thing. How far did you take me?"

"Approximately three kilometers. You slept like a baby the last two."

"How long was I out?"

"More than two hours. You left no instructions for that eventuality, so I had to improvise. I tried to wake you every few minutes, but you didn't respond. Were my actions satisfactory?"

"Don't fish for compliments, Robot. What happened to everyone else?"

"How would I know, Will Robinson? I was busy aiding and abetting in your escape."

"You're a big help!"

"Indeed I am. Were it not for me, you would be in Dr. Smith's clutches at this very moment."

Will sighed. He still hadn't figured out a way to get the robot's still-somewhat-literal AI to recognize sarcasm. Not that it was a prime concern at the moment. "So you have no idea where Smith went or what he's doing?"

"No more than you, I would imagine. If I *could* imagine, that is. However, having no imagination, as you nonrobots define the term, I can only deduce that he has returned to the *Jupiter* in order to take it over. And quite possibly abandon us all. Is that scenario compatible with your imaginings?"

Will grimaced. "I'm afraid it is," he said, remembering the warning that Smith had programmed the little girl to deliver. "And that guard is probably still at the door to the Vault, ready to blast anyone who comes near."

"Can I assume, then, that you plan to come near? And enter one of the infamous cubicles?"

"I *have* to," Will said, realizing even as he said it that it was the truth.

At the same time, he realized that he *really* didn't want to. Any more than he'd want to have all his teeth pulled without an anesthetic. But now that Smith had control of everyone else, Will knew he was the only one who left who *could* do it, with or without a guard taking shots at him.

"Then times a-wastin', Will Robinson," the robot thundered, extending one of its multiclawed arms. "You will doubtless make better time if you allow me to once again provide transportation."

Reluctantly, Will nodded in agreement despite the stomach-churning fear—panic, almost—that he felt. And then he was clasped once again to the robot's smooth metallic chest as the behemoth thudded and crashed its way back toward the clearing.

Dr. Zachary Smith and his *Jupiter*-bound caravan of automatons—two Robinsons and one West—had gone less than a kilometer when they were blocked by Zolkaz and a cluster of a dozen natives, armed with their omnipresent dart rifles. All were watching Smith suspiciously.

"Professor Robinson," Zolkaz said, his eyes flickering back and forth between John and Smith, "your wife gave us to understand that Dr. Smith had been incapacitated by his recent experience."

For a moment Smith considered answering through Robinson, but only for a moment. He was getting better each time he made use of his power, but under these circumstances, with the plasma rifle and the laser pistol in hands other than his own, he knew he couldn't afford a slipup, a loss of concentration, for even a second.

"I was incapacitated," Smith said, leaving the others on automatic pilot and speaking through his own lips, "but it was only temporary. Dr. Judy was able to bring me around. I'm feeling much better now."

But even as he spoke, Smith saw that Zolkaz wasn't buying it. The man's eyes continued to dart back and forth between himself and John Robinson. He was virtually radiating skepticism. Unless one of the Robinsons spoke, confirming what he had said—

So be it! Smith decided. His natural preference was for guile and deception, but he was not so wedded to the concept that he couldn't bring himself to take direct action when it was both safer and easier.

2 2

Before even the quickest of the natives could do more than raise a dart rifle, Smith sent the entire, unsuspecting group tumbling into unconsciousness. Both Robinsons twitched, an indication that their latest "orders" were beginning to wear off. Sighing, Smith reached out to each individually and *squeezed*, reinforcing the commands he'd given them earlier. West, not surprisingly, gave no indication of recovery. The dolt was virtually an automaton even when nominally awake, driven not by rational thought but by a distasteful collection of instincts and reflexes. If everyone's conscious mind served up as little resistance as West's, he thought, this business of mind control would be a great deal easier.

Alas, such was not the case. For one thing, no matter how hard he tried, he couldn't directly control more than one person at a time — in real time, so to speak — not even when one of them was West. Once he had complete control of one subject and was, essentially, looking at the world through the subject's eyes and using that subject's body and mind as his own, he couldn't take over another. He could keep his own body operating, at least enough to do simple tasks like walking and chewing gum, but in order to reach out and grasp a second subject, he had to relinquish his hold on the first and further loosen his hold on his own body.

Luckily, he was able to implant commands—relatively simple ones, at least—in any number of subjects, one after the other, like the native he'd set to guarding the cubicles. And like the little group he was now shepherding back in the direction of the *Jupiter*.

Not quite so luckily, those commands had a limited half-life, particularly when they involved a continuous physical action—like walking—and even more particularly when, like the wretched Robinsons, the subjects were automatically and unalterably opposed to any suggestion he might make.

As a result, he had to constantly boost the commands in order to keep them from simply fading away, which would free the subjects to do whatever they felt like. At this point, that would doubtless involve some form of mayhem directed at their putative captor. It reminded Smith of a prehistoric entertainment vid he'd once seen—the *Elvis Sullivan Show*? Something like that. One of the acts had been a plate spinner. The man began with an armload of plates and several slender poles standing upright on stage. To frantically paced music, the man spun the plates on the poles, one after the other, like a series of tops. Once he got eight or ten of them going, the first one would start wobbling and he'd have to go back and give it a boost before he could start another new one spinning. Before the act was over, the man was darting around like a madman amid a forest of spinning plates, giving each one a boost when it slowed and began to wobble, all the while trying to find a spare second to get yet another new one going.

Smith, with only one West and two Robinson "plates" spinning, hadn't gotten to that stage yet, but he knew that trying to bring Zolkaz and his friends under his influence would almost certainly have taken him to that point or beyond. So he'd resorted to the easiest and quickest of the tricks he had been tortured into learning in the Vault cubicle.

He'd put them to sleep.

Instead of attempting to keep the plates spinning, he had, in effect, grabbed them off their poles and stacked them safely on the floor, where they wouldn't require any further attention for hours.

And now, for all the attention he'd had to give them, he wondered if he shouldn't have taken the same route with West and the two Robinsons.

Or perhaps he should have gone with his first impulse and simply disposed of them. Permanently. With plasma rifle and laser pistol at hand, it would have been both easy and logical to do so. It was not as if there were any practical reasons to keep them alive. He could have returned, unhindered, to the *Jupiter*, and taken it over from the remaining Robinsons and had all the time in the world to root out and repair the sabotage committed by the precocious and insufferable boy.

But he hadn't, and he wasn't completely sure why.

Before he'd started this little caravan, he invaded their minds, one at a time, and dug out all the information he needed to take over the *Jupiter*. He even tiptoed gingerly through the swamps they called their lives and decided, logically enough, that he would be doing them a favor by killing them.

Particularly West, who was the most obnoxious of the lot and sometimes seemed to be actively *searching* for death, although the fool obviously saw things differently. West saw his actions—like the insane risks he'd taken to save various comrades in arms—as "heroic," of all things. Such acts were utterly beyond Smith's comprehension. "Hero," in Smith's dictionary, was defined as someone who was both incredibly foolhardy and incredibly lucky, which certainly fit West.

But there was no point in killing them now, he told himself placidly. There was always the chance he would find a use for them. Besides, he'd brought them this far, so he might as well continue. And by the time Zolkaz and the rest regained consciousness, he would be in the *Jupiter* and, most likely, on his way to another, hopefully more useful, world. There was, therefore, no advantage to be gained by getting rid of them. And killing simply for the fun of it had never been his cup of tea.

Sighing, he reassembled his automatons into a line and resumed his trek to the *Jupiter*.

Major Don West might not have the kind of brainpower required to solve differential equations in his head, but he *was* a good observer—under any and all conditions. His training and his subsequent military career had made sure of that. If you were unobservant during training, you flamed out and didn't survive to graduate. If you were unobservant later, in the real world, you flamed out in spades and didn't survive—period!

He was *very* good at surviving.

During the first part of the forced march, he observed.

Everything.

For one thing, he observed that the pace Smith set made it more of a stroll than a march. The man would never have qualified for the Brownie scouts, let alone the infantry, he thought contemptuously.

Unfortunately, the pilot couldn't *do* anything but follow Smith and John and Judy Robinson, bringing up the tail end of the short, single-file column. No matter what his conscious mind tried to force his legs to do, they ignored him and kept on walking. And his hands ignored all his mental commands too, no matter how desperately he wanted to unsling the plasma rifle from his shoulder and fry Smith.

The situation, he soon realized, was very different from his first encounter with Smith, just outside the Vault. That time, he'd felt Smith in his mind, controlling his every move, as if his body was Smith's own. Which, essentially, it had been, since it was Smith moving its arms and legs, and even speaking through its mouth. In addition, West found himself remembering things that had never happened to him, things that he was now certain had happened to Zachary Smith, not to him. From moment to moment he'd actually been aware of Smith's thoughts, of Smith's utter contempt for him and his almost equal contempt for the Robinsons.

But now, while being forced to walk where he didn't want to go, West could see that he wasn't under the same complete control. Smith wasn't *in* his mind this time. Smith had been in there, but only to give a few orders and leave, like a master sergeant ordering a misbehaving recruit to "Give me twenty laps!" and then retiring to the canteen for a brew or two while the recruit sweated it out around the track.

West assumed it was the same process Smith had used on Corvalus to turn him into a guard. In that case, West recalled, Smith's control had not been complete, for when he himself had approached, Corvalus had been able to fire a warning shot and then to verbally warn him and John Robinson away. Which meant that the guard at least had a modest amount of free will he could exercise. Therefore, West realized, he himself would probably soon have the same limited freedom.

And then he observed something else.

He observed that if he tried very hard, he could consciously move his arms and fingers, at least a little. At the start of the stroll, he hadn't been able to. His left hand had flopped at his side as if it wasn't a part of him, while his right kept a loose grip on the butt of the plasma rifle to keep it from shifting position or jarring against his back as he walked. Both arms did react reflexively—grabbing at something to keep from falling, for instance—but that was all. Scratching his nose or wiping sweat from his forehead, anything that required a conscious command from his brain to his muscles, had been impossible.

And it was the same with the Robinsons, he suspected. What he observed was that, after ten or fifteen
minutes, the hands of both Robinsons began to move,
just a little, not much more than twitches. But then, during the confrontation with Zolkaz and the other natives,
those twitches became more pronounced. At which
point Smith noticed the movement. From the momentary stare he'd directed at the Robinsons and the subsequent total motionlessness of their hands, West assumed
that Smith had strengthened his hold on them, or had
done something to rob them of the slight freedom they
had briefly regained. He himself had played possum,
remaining utterly motionless, without a single twitch that
wasn't part of the program. His hope had been that that
Smith, with his overwhelming contempt for his mental
abilities, would not bother to quell him as he had the
Robinsons.

To his relieved surprise, Smith hadn't. Instead, the
good doctor had given him a brief, contemptuous glance
and turned away, as if certain that someone as dim as
Don West could not possibly break free.

As he had for several minutes before the encounter
with the natives, Don watched Smith's back, observing
his every move. Smith was more of a creature of habit
than he would like to admit, and by now the pilot was
sure he could predict when the doctor was about to turn
his head and look back. Every time he did so, a split second before his head turned, his balance shifted slightly
and his shoulders made a slight hunching motion. That
split second of warning was all Don needed to make his

arms motionless. Between Smith's darting looks, then, with his legs still operating largely on autopilot, he was able to test his hands, not with large movements but with small ones, wiggling his fingers one at a time and in various combinations. He didn't move his arms, however, since he wasn't sure he could get them back into position fast enough. He decided he would have to take the chance that when he was able to make his fingers move singly and together, without hesitation, he'd be able to make his arms move just as quickly and reliably.

It took another twenty minutes before he was satisfied. By then his legs were moving largely at his conscious direction rather than at the behest of the orders Smith had planted in his mind. And at the same time, he saw that the Robinsons' hands were showing signs of movement again.

This time, Don was certain, Smith would include him in whatever it was he did to the Robinsons. The man would have to be an utter idiot to let his contempt color his judgment *that* much.

So it was now or never. The trouble was, the Robinsons were directly in the line of fire. If he could simply unsling the plasma rifle and fire, Smith would be dead in an instant. But he would have to move out of line to get a clear shot, and that might give Smith enough time to stop him.

But it was the best chance he had, the best chance they *all* had. If Smith remained in control and took over the *Jupiter*, he could—he *would*—use the Robinsons as his personal slaves, assuming he didn't kill them once he tired of gloating and demonstrating his "superiority." And there was Judy Robinson . . .

Now or never! he repeated in his mind. Silently and precisely, he bent his fingers one at a time, waiting patiently but nervously while Smith once more glanced back at those following him. The moment Smith turned his head to the front again, Don eased his hands up and gripped the plasma rifle, relieved that his arms did indeed move almost normally, as he'd hoped they would.

In a move he hadn't had occasion to use since basic training—pilots rarely engaged in ground combat—he shrugged the rifle's sling off his shoulder with only a whisper of sound, then leaped sideways—only to discover that a remnant of the command that had kept him walking forward all this time still remained, or just enough to tangle his feet and send him lurching to the ground.

Even as he was falling, he brought the rifle around, bringing it to bear on Smith. He pressed the firing stud as he hit the ground on his side, hard, sending the deadly flare wide of its mark, incinerating several meters of vegetation.

Smith was already spinning around to face him by the time the plasma bolt crackled past, and for a moment his look of annoyed arrogance turned to fear. Don knew that, if the past was any indication, it would take Smith at least two or three seconds to reassert his mind-controlling commands, time enough for him to bring the rifle to bear on Smith again and get off a second shot.

In fact, he did manage to whip the rifle's muzzle in Smith's direction. But in the fraction of a second that it took the nerve impulses to race from his brain to the finger that would press the firing stud, his entire body went limp. Every muscle instantaneously relaxed, turning him into a two-hundred-pound rag doll that flopped lifelessly to the ground, the rifle dropping from his spaghetti-limp fingers.

A flash of anger shot through West then, followed an instant later by panic as a sharp pain erupted in his chest and pinpoints of light appeared out of nowhere, whirling and flashing, almost obliterating his already fading vision.

He remained conscious just long enough to wonder what the hell was happening—and to realize that, no matter how much his chest hurt, his heart was no longer beating.

2 3

"Wait up, Robot!" Will shouted, pounding on the behemoth's metal chest.

"I was under the impression you had a positive hankering to reach—"

"Just stop, Robotman! Now!"

Obediently and suddenly, it stopped. "As you wish, little master. May I inquire as to the reason?"

"There's the reason," Will said, pointing a dozen meters ahead and to one side, where he could see two natives sprawled in the underbrush. "Now put me down. And you stay right here. Unless I call you."

Hurrying ahead, Will saw more bodies scattered around. Dr. Smith's work, he was almost certain.

Hastily, Will dropped to his knees next to the first man. He was breathing, so at least Smith hadn't killed him.

Not so gently, Will shook the man's shoulder. And again. The fourth or fifth time, the man blinked and half sat up, almost bumping into the boy.

"Are you all right?" Will asked. "Did Dr. Smith—"

From a few meters away, someone else groaned and sat up. It was Zolkaz, and he'd already spotted Will and the robot in the near distance. Frowning, the older man struggled to his feet, looking around at the others. When they didn't all immediately revive, he looked accusingly at Will.

"The one you call Smith did this."

"I know," Will said. "He did the same thing to me a while before. But where did he go? Do you have any idea? To our ship? And what about my dad and my sister? Were they with him?" Or were they still unconscious back at the Vault? he wondered, but did not ask.

Zolkaz nodded. "They and Major West were with him. And under his control, if I am not mistaken. Or under the control of whatever now has control of this Smith!"

Will shook his head. "It's just Smith being Smith," he said, then went on to explain, as fast as he could, how Smith had come to be traveling with them and how there was virtually nothing he wouldn't do if he thought it was in his own best interests.

"It looks like the only chance we've got against him," he finished, "is for one of us to go into one of the cubicles and get a dose of whatever Smith got. Dad and Major West were going to, but Smith got them, so I guess it's up to me."

Zolkaz's eyes widened. "But you are just a child! Surely—"

"Don't *you* start! You sound like my dad! He just—" Will broke off, realizing he was wasting time. He'd already wasted precious minutes waking these people up and explaining things to them.

"Unless you've got some other ideas," he went on, still angry, "it's the only chance I've got to save my folks!" As he spoke, glaring at Zolkaz, the reality of what he was saying finally hit him like a blow to the stomach. If he didn't do *something*, he might never see his folks or his sisters again, and even if he did, they'd all be Smith's slaves!

And the more time he wasted here, the more likely Smith would discover what he was planning and stop him.

Turning, he gestured to the robot, which immediately lumbered forward. "If you want to help," he said to Zolkaz, his voice shaking, now that the danger posed by Smith had become more real to him, "go back there and climb in yourselves and get some training of your own. Help me gang up on Smith!"

Then the robot snatched Will up, pressing him against its metal chest, and moved quickly away, leaving Zolkaz and the others staring after him.

For one terrifying moment Dr. Zachary Smith was certain he was going to die.

He'd heard the rustle of sudden movement behind him and spun around to see which of his automatons was ready for another booster shot when a bolt from Major West's plasma rifle sizzled past him, missing him by less than a meter. West was on the ground, struggling spasmodically to get the rifle pointed at him for a second shot, and Smith realized that in the moments before that shot could be loosed, he did not have time to exercise any of the mental controls that had been tortured into him.

Sheer panic set in as he lunged mentally for the pilot's mind, hoping against hope that the steady improvement in power and speed he'd been experiencing since his second emergence from the cubicle would suddenly undergo a quantum jump, enabling him to shut his attacker down before he could fire again.

A moment later, before he had a chance to actually take the action he'd intended, it was as if his desperate wish had been granted. Like a puppet whose strings had been cut, West collapsed and sprawled on the ground, the rifle falling from his limp fingers.

Instinctively, Smith leaped forward, snatched up the rifle, and backed away, sweeping the weapon's muzzle back and forth between the two Robinsons, who had dutifully come to a halt. Hastily, the rifle still scanning them, he reached out with his mind and *squeezed*, renewing their automaton status.

He breathed an uncertain sigh of relief as he turned to look more closely at West.

The man wasn't breathing!

Dropping the plasma rifle to the ground, Smith knelt next to West. He felt for a pulse and found none.

What the hell had happened here? He hadn't had time to grasp West's mind, either to take it over or to drive it into unconsciousnss. And yet West had collapsed and, apparently, died.

Concentrating, he tried to reconstruct precisely what he'd done and thought during the moments after he heard movement behind him. First, he'd turned sharply around. As he turned, the plasma bolt had sent his heart into his throat, and he instantly knew there was not enough time to stop West from firing a second shot. Nevertheless, perhaps reflexively, he'd reached out with his mind, just as he had before, with the native and with West himself.

But this time . . .

This time, he realized, he'd done something differently. Instead of clasping a mental hand *around* West's mind, he'd driven headlong *into* it, penetrating like a needle-sharp arrow, apparently homing in on a specific part and *impaling* it.

Paralyzing it.

He didn't have the words to describe the process. He only knew the result: instant and total paralysis of all muscles, including those that drove the heart and lungs. It was something he'd done countless times in the virtual world of the cubicle. Something he had been *taught* in the cubicle.

Something that, now that he was aware of its existence, he could do again, at will.

Easily.

Far more easily than any of the other things he'd learned.

Why hadn't he been aware of it before? he wondered. It was by far the most effective weapon in his mental arsenal. Instead of straining to control someone directly or to implant suggestions in their mind, you simply commanded them to do what you wanted, and if they resisted, you demonstrated your power over them.

Although, if the first demonstration killed them . . .

With this new insight into his abilities, Smith reached once again into what remained of West's mind.

And found that it was still alive. But not for long.

His first impulse was to withdraw and leave the posturing fool to finish dying.

His second impulse, a more considered one, was to reverse the procedure, to remove the block that was causing the paralysis and allow the pilot to return fully to life. Dead, the man would be nothing more than a minor annoyance removed. Alive, who knew how he might come in handy? Despite his other shortcomings, West *was* a good pilot. And would doubtless make a good slave, Smith thought, smiling, not to mention a living testimony to his power.

Suddenly, West was gasping for breath.

Smith waited patiently, watching as the pilot's eyes cleared and color returned to his face.

"Welcome back to the land of the living, Major," Smith said, smiling. "I trust you won't give me cause to regret my decision to allow you to return."

Maureen Robinson frowned at the viewscreens as she watched Kelwyn and the half-dozen natives—Watchers— leave the clearing, some turning back for a last glimpse of the *Jupiter*'s forbidding presence. What she needed to be, she thought, was not a xenobiologist, but a combination xenopsychologist and xenohistorian. Then perhaps she'd have a better idea what had really happened on this world two hundred years ago—which of the natives' multigenerational memories were literally true, which were distorted, and which were simply made up by the survivors or their descendants to try to make sense of the destruction of their world. It might also give her a better idea what her husband or Don West might be getting themselves into when one of them entered the cubicles two centuries later.

Even if Will's theory that the cubicles were virtual reality training devices was correct, it raised more questions than it answered. For instance, if everyone who entered a cubicle got the kind of power that Smith now apparently enjoyed, how could the natives possibly have failed? From the number of cubicles available, it could have produced thousands of Smiths every day, millions every year. How could any Invaders stand up against that?

Unless the Invaders themselves already possessed this same ability, only to a greater degree. That would account for the belief by some that the Defenders were possessed by the Invaders. But not for the fact that virtually everyone, worldwide, had died or been killed.

Unless that was what the Invaders had in mind all along: extinction, not conquest. Could they have turned the tables on the defenders and possessed—or simply controlled—them, forcing them to kill themselves or each other? If the Invaders had come through the gate just before it was destroyed, if they then found themselves stranded here, perhaps, in a frenzy of vengeance, they had possessed and killed everyone not immune to their power.

And left.

Hopefully never to return.

Turning from the viewscreens to the computer displays, Maureen resumed her journey through the forest of anecdotal evidence of mental powers. There was, of course, nothing useful. As she had told John earlier, the legitimate studies were all on distance viewing, psychometry, precognition, and the like, where success was measured by the percentage by which a subject beat the odds. The closest any came to actually controlling a subject's mind was when someone looking at a photo or a drawing in one room tried to impress the image on the mind of a subject in a second room. Even when successful, that was several orders of magnitude removed from what Smith was doing, the difference between changing the course of a falling feather and demolishing a stone-and-steel building.

She'd been at it for several minutes when she felt an itch where none should be possible, a place where the tactile sense did not exist: inside her brain.

She looked up and around abruptly, her eyes drawn to the exterior viewscreens. Smith emerged into the clearing a moment later, followed by John and Judy and, finally, Major West.

And no one else.

Activating the external speakers, she hurried to the airlock. "John," she called, "where's Will?"

But her husband didn't answer, didn't even appear to have heard her. Smith, however, smiled at her.

The itching increased, and Maureen Robinson realized she couldn't move.

● ● ●

The Space Captive glanced at her watch as the remnants of the last solitaire game dissolved on the screen and the cards were redealt.

At least, she thought, they would be moving on from this dreary world whether Smith took over or not. Once her folks got Smith under control, made sure he couldn't cause any more problems, there was no reason for them to remain here. And maybe the next world—

"Penny, come to the bridge."

The Space Captive frowned in the general direction of the intercom speaker. Her mother's voice sounded odd. "What is it, Mom?"

"Just come to the bridge. Don't argue!"

Sighing loudly enough for the intercom to pick up the sound, the Space Captive donned her most long-suffering expression and moped her way up to the bridge. Her eyes glued sullenly to the floor not far in front of her toes, she stopped just far enough inside the doorway she'd just entered to allow the door to hiss shut behind her.

"Well?" she demanded, knowing there was no point in looking up, where she'd be forced to see the same depressing scene of endless vegetation on the view-screens.

"Your rebelliousness has a certain charm when directed against others," Dr. Smith's unmistakable voice informed her, "but directed against me, it wears thin very quickly."

While Smith spoke, her head began to itch. Inside.

She looked up—or attempted to—as she tried to bring her hands up to scratch at her scalp.

"Just a precaution, child," Smith said, "so no one will do anything foolish before my demonstration is finished."

When he finished speaking, whatever had been keeping her from lifting her head disappeared. The itching forgotten, along with all thoughts of the Space Captive, Penny finally looked up.

Her mother and father, her sister Judy, and Major West all stood together on the far side of the bridge, not far from the airlock, their faces expressionless, their eyes staring past her at the bulkhead. Behind them, just inside the airlock, stood Dr. Smith, plasma rifle cradled in one arm. She tried to run toward her parents, but her legs barely twitched.

Mom! Dad! What's going on? Her mind shouted the words, but her lips were motionless.

The itching increased, and memories not her own darted through her mind.

Smith laughed. "Can't you see, you lucky child?" He looked at her for a long moment, beaming mockingly. "Your fondest dream has just come true. *I* am now master of the *Jupiter*. Or I will be, as soon as my little demonstration is complete." He turned his smile on the others. "Now if you will all be so kind as to join the self-styled Space Captive, we can get under way."

2 4

Peering out into the central clearing, Will saw no evidence of either Smith or a guard.

But there was little evidence of a door either. It had not simply been closed and locked, Will discovered as he inspected the spot where the door had been.

It had been closed and *fused*.

He could see the remains of the almost invisible break where the edge of the door had once been. The result of a plasma rifle, he thought angrily, with maybe a little help from a laser pistol, all at very close range, the range at which the surface layers of human flesh were not charred but vaporized. However advanced the designers of this building had been, they hadn't been a match for humanity's gift for destruction.

"Can you get me in there, Robot?"

"Just stand back, pardner," the robot said, apparently still in the country-western mode it had fallen into after the rescue. Will wondered what database it might've picked *that* from and hoped it wasn't one that included music. He could just imagine the robot bellowing out a bluegrass version of "Whistle While You Work" as its claws extended and began arcing and sparking vigorously.

It took several minutes to produce a molten hole large enough to accommodate the robot. Will had wanted to take a running jump through the slag-lined hole when it was half that size, but the robot, sensibly, had blocked him. Even now it insisted on preceding him and checking to be sure the temperature of the floor just inside the torched door wasn't dangerously hot. "You know the rules about harm and inaction," the robot explained with what Will took to be self-satisfaction.

With a last look around for any sign that Zolkaz or any of his friends had decided to follow him, Will leaped through the curtain of heat, the robot ready and waiting to keep him from stumbling or falling backward. Without hesitation, Will raced to the nearest cubicle door, then changed his mind and ran to one of the cross corridors, turned right and didn't stop until he'd gone at least a quarter of the way around. If Smith *did* show up, at least it would take him a few minutes or hours to find this particular cubicle. Provided he couldn't figure out a way of getting the information out of the robot.

When the robot appeared around the bend in the circular corridor, Will grasped the almost invisible handle. The door opened smoothly and in total silence, revealing the same featureless white interior he'd seen in the others.

"Just so you'll know this is the one, Robot. But once I'm in there, you go back to the front door. Just come back here to let me out."

"And when should I set my alarm for?" the robot rumbled. "How long do you wish to immerse yourself?"

"Smith was in there for four hours altogether, so maybe I should stay in for five."

"Are you positive, Will Robinson?"

Will shivered. "I have to be. It's our only chance."

"I see."

"And whatever you do, if Smith *does* show up—or sends somebody—don't let him know which one I'm in! Understand?"

"Of course. I may be a robot, but I'm not stupid. Unless someone shuts off the AI module you installed."

Will managed a nervous laugh, wondering even now which of the robot's internal databases its AI was drawing on for its conversation.

Will turned back to the cubicle's open door.

And hesitated.

Now that his goal was right in front of him, literally a step away, he hesitated. His stomach, he realized, had abruptly tied itself into a massive, aching knot about a thousand times worse than when his father hadn't shown up for one of his schoo'sl science awards. Or for his birthday. The seriousness of the situation had finally closed in on him, emotionally as well as intellectually. It almost made him physically bend over, it was so tight, so intense.

No matter what he told the robot, he really didn't want to do this. He was just a kid, for crying out loud! As everyone liked to tell him, every chance they got! Maybe if Zolkaz and his crew showed up, they really *could* get a quick boost and then gang up on Smith, and he'd never have to—

He shook his head sharply. He was just procrastinating. He really didn't have a choice here. He had to go in. If he gave up now, he would be letting Smith have everything his way. And with Smith in charge, the absolute best-case scenario was a lifetime of being forced to do whatever Smith wanted! He didn't even want to guess as to what a worst-case scenario might be. Being left behind on this world? Being killed for real and forever, not virtually and temporarily?

No, he told himself yet again, he absolutely *had* to go ahead with this. If he was going to have even a small chance to save his family and himself, he had to step inside the cubicle and let his virtual self be tortured and killed, not once, but hundreds or even thousands of times.

If he could just force himself to step through the door.

"Robot," he said abruptly, the words coming out in a headlong rush, "let's get this show on the road! Shove me inside this thing! Now!"

"If you really don't want to do this—" the robot rumbled.

"Do it! Now!" Will shouted. "That's an order, Robotman! It's for my own good!"

"Have it your way, pardner," the robot said, then grasped the boy with one set of claws and forced him—as gently as possible for several hundred pounds of metal— into the open cubicle. Will couldn't keep from struggling, a series of automatic but ineffective twitches, really, but he did manage enough control to keep his mouth clamped shut so hard his jaw muscles hurt and he wasn't able to countermand his last order. As the door closed silently behind him, the last words he heard were, "Happy trails, buckaroo."

The graying inner wall, already bulging out to engulf him, cut off anything else the robot had to say.

For Dr. Zachary Smith, the demonstration went swimmingly. He enjoyed it to no end. The only blot on an otherwise perfect few minutes was the absence of that insufferable child and his metal pet.

Except for Major West—who had already been treated to *his* demonstration—everyone, predictably, resisted, which merely made the experience all the more delectable.

First, he walked them all across the bridge and lined them up with Penny, still restrained just in front of the elevator, while he remained near the airlock and pointed the plasma rifle in their general direction.

Next, he released both Judy and her father and had her attach her stethoscope sensor to her father's chest and set the tiny video monitor from her medkit directly in front of the group. Everyone could then see the line that crawled across the screen, pulsing and beeping in perfect unison with the sound of Robinson's heart in Judy's earpiece.

Without a word, Smith stopped John Robinson's heart. Instantly. During the hour since he had inadvertently—and quite fortuitously—stopped Major West's heart, he'd learned how to limit the collateral damage, so to speak. Instead of relaxing *all* the muscles in the subject's body, he'd discovered—"remembered"—how to narrow his focus and relax only those muscles controlled by the autonomic nervous system, primarily the heart and lungs. The result was an instantaneous halting of both heartbeat and breathing.

Robinson's eyes widened as he grimaced and clutched at his chest. Judy's earpiece fell silent, as did the minivideo, which abruptly went flat-line.

Smugly, Smith waited, watching as John Robinson's eyes began to glaze over. His body slumped backward against the elevator door and slid jerkily toward the floor as his muscles went flacid, and the display continued to flat-line.

As Robinson's posterior hit the floor and his upper body tilted sideways, Smith smiled and gave his heart back to him. For another moment there was silence as the display continued to flat-line. Then, simultaneously, the sounds and the display started up, the pulse racing at almost double the previous rate. John Robinson gasped in a lungful of air, as if a stopper had been removed from his throat, and jerked spasmodically into an upright seated position, his back pressed hard against the elevator door.

Still smiling, Smith looked around at the group. "I believe we understand each other now," he said softly. "However, if any of you would like your own personal demonstration, I would be most pleased to oblige."

It was late afternoon when the four who had decided, against all common sense, to follow the boy, arrived at the clearing around the Vault. The remaining problem was to work up the nerve to follow him into a cubicle—

assuming he'd arrived before them and had indeed entered one. Each step they took across the clearing made the images that filled their mind more vivid, images of the madness that had overtaken their bolder, more foolhardy, ancestors when *they* had entered the building.

Uneasily, they approached the shadowy opening they assumed was the building's door, only to find it was now an uneven hole in the outer wall. Congealed blobs of once-molten material formed an uneven step below the opening. There was only the faintest evidence of "healing" around the perimeter of the opening.

They were still several meters from the building when the robot appeared with a muffled thud, literally filling the opening. Electrical discharges arced and crackled demonstratively between the claws on one of its arms.

"Gentlemen," it rumbled, "may I be of service?"

Raban, their default leader only because he was oldest, managed to keep his voice steady as he replied, "We have come as the boy suggested, to obtain the training needed to help him gang up on the one you call Smith."

The arcing increased in intensity for a few moments as the robot appeared to consider the statement. Then it faded to a sputter and finally to silence. The robot stepped back, leaving the opening clear.

"Step right in, gentlemen, and name your pleasure. How long a lesson does each of you desire?"

Virtually wading through the ever more horrific images of his maddened ancestors, Raban lead the way through the opening and began to explain to the metal monster what they had decided.

Dr. Zachary Smith scowled at the *Jupiter*'s flight controls. It had taken him only a few moments to clear the three booby-trapped malfunction indicator lights that someone—the ubiquitous child, Smith was certain—had not gotten around to defusing.

But the row of green lights he so easily resurrected had vanished almost as quickly. All that remained were the three he had just cleared himself. They weren't replaced by red ones either, they just went out. And stayed out.

Just to be certain, Smith tried reclearing the lights that Will had already cleared. Beyond that, he checked for the presence of the viruslike programs he himself had hidden one by one over the long shipboard months, deep in the computer's own programs. They were, indeed, gone, cleaned out as if they had never existed. No trace of their existence or of their removal remained. The boy *was* good, Smith admitted reluctantly.

But still the flight controls were dead. Which could mean only one thing: that insufferable child had substituted booby traps of his own.

Not that it surprised him. In truth, Smith would have been amazed if the boy had not done something of the sort. Still, it was annoying. He had no doubt that he could root them all out, but the process would be time-consuming. The less time he had to spend on this primitive backwater world, the sooner he'd be on his way to a world on which his newfound talents could be put to real use.

A *civilized* world. A world worth the trouble of taking over.

All of which meant that, if he wanted to save time, he would have to find the boy and bring him back. Which meant finding the robot, which was almost certainly still with the boy, somewhere in the ruins or the surrounding forest. Glancing at his watch, he wondered if the boy had regained consciousness yet. He'd been at the very edge of Smith's range of influence, so it was impossible to gauge just how deeply he had been able to put the boy under.

But asleep or awake, Smith knew he'd be with the robot, which would be easy enough to find, provided the creature's built-in locator beacon hadn't been abandoned during one of the boy's many redesigns. More likely, the boy had improved and upgraded the device, just to be absolutely sure the metallic behemoth would never get lost. It often seemed that the boy considered the lumbering creature his best—perhaps his only—friend, and he'd never do anything that would make it easier for the creature to get beyond his reach.

Abandoning the flight controls, Smith made his way to the robot bay, where he tapped the Find code into the bay's control panel. A small screen lit up obediently, displaying an approximate distance and direction.

Smith's eyebrows arched as he overlaid the figures on the mental map he had long since constructed of the area. Barring a major memory lapse on his part—an unlikely possibility at best—the robot, and hence the boy, was in or near the Vault.

Could the child actually be foolhardy enough to try to *enter* one of the cubicles? Was he misguided enough to believe it would bestow the mental wherewithal to challenge him? The robot probably would be able to gain the boy entry—there was little it couldn't break or burn its way through—but what then? It was laughable to think that a mere child, even an admittedly bright one, could survive enough of the lessons to become anything other than a minor nuisance. More likely, he would simply go mad or shut down entirely when the repeated horrors and deaths overwhelmed his mind. For a moment Smith found himself feeling sorry for Will, but he brushed the unaccustomed thought away like the errant and unwelcome wisp of fog that it was.

Returning to the bridge, Smith activated the ship's intercom to talk to his "crew," all still confined to quarters. "Professor Robinson," he said, "is it possible your son would be foolish enough to attempt to avail himself of the training you and Major West were vying for?"

"Would he enter one of the cubicles, you mean?" Robinson shot back.

"Exactly, Professor. Would he?"

"I suspect he would. In fact, I'm damned sure he would. Are you saying he *has*?"

"I wouldn't know. All I know is, the robot is in the vicinity of the Vault."

"Check the power usage," Judy broke in. "Or let me out of my room and *I'll* do it."

"As you wish, my dear," Smith said, reaching briefly into her mind and removing the compulsion, already weakening noticeably, that kept her from crossing the threshold of her own room. He could sense her recoiling at his mental touch, but he'd long since resigned himself to that, annoying as it might be.

Moments later she appeared on the bridge and leaned over the console. She couldn't entirely repress a gasp as she brought up the readings.

"Is there something I should know?" Smith asked sharply, coming quickly to look over her shoulder.

"*Something* is going on," she said, her voice betraying her uneasiness. "The power drain is at least double what it was during *your* little session."

Smith scowled. "And this means what? That he *has* gone inside?"

"You tell me," Judy said, still watching the readouts. "You have more cubicle time than anyone else, so you're the closest thing we have to an expert."

For just an instant Smith found himself again imagining what the boy must be going through, but he quickly pushed the roiling images aside. "Perhaps a native or two accompanied him," he suggested, but before anyone could respond, Maureen Robinson's voice crackled from the intercom.

"You have to let us get him out!"

"She's right," John Robinson agreed, an edge of emotion evident even in his tightly controlled voice.

"My thought precisely," Smith said, "although my motive may be slightly at variance from that of your helpmate."

He reached out with his mind and released Major

West from the same fading compulsion he had released Judy from minutes before.

"Major West," he said, "your house arrest is terminated. Pick up a control rod from the robot bay and come to the bridge. I have an assignment for you."

2 5

Major Don West fingered the control rod in the pocket of his leather battle uniform and wondered if it was going to be as useless as he expected it to be. He tried to remember what Will had said about the programming changes he'd made that would cause the robot to try to block anyone who attempted to insert a control rod. Had he programmed it to use lethal force, for instance? Since Will had been thinking about the robot defending itself against Smith, it was possible.

Don couldn't remember how many versions of the robot, complete and incomplete, Will had produced since the first one was left behind on the *Proteus*, but one thing they all had in common was the ability to be lethal if they set their minds to it. Or even if they didn't: they'd also all been capable of being lethal purely by accident.

But there was no point in worrying about the robot, he told himself. What he should be worrying about was Smith, although that wasn't likely to be much more productive. Or it hadn't been so far. He'd spent the first two kilometers of his current errand wondering how to overcome an opponent who could not only get inside your head at will, but put you to sleep or stop your heart on an instant's notice. Especially if he never left the *Jupiter*, which the new, improved Smith had so far shown no inclination to do. If he ever *did* decide to step outside, a dozen or so natives hiding in the bushes with dart rifles *might* work.

If such a group of volunteers could be assembled, that is. As far as Don could tell, Smith wasn't able to read minds casually, nor did he seem to have any kind of mental radar that would allow him to detect unseen enemies waiting in ambush. As a result, he might not spot the would-be ambushers from the safety of the ship, and therefore might not be able to reach out and put them to sleep or kill them before going out to confiscate their weapons.

He *might* not.

On the other hand, for all he knew, Smith might very well be capable of doing exactly that. Or, more likely, considering Smith's justifiable paranoid streak, the doctor might climb into his enemies' minds every so often just to see what they were up to, and learn about any planned ambush *that* way. And happily wipe out the natives, the instigator, and maybe the Robinsons too, just for the hell of it.

No, when someone had the kind of power Smith had developed, not to mention the vicious temperament he'd *always* had, it was both pointless and counterproductive to take chances like that, where the odds were at least ten to one that you'd fail and that *everyone* would end up worse off than before.

Or dead.

Taking chances with your own life, even with long odds, even when you screwed up—as he had when he'd tried to take down Smith a few hours ago—was one thing. Taking chances with the lives of others—particularly those you had a responsibility to protect—was another. Under the present circumstances, all Don could think to do was to be constantly alert and ready to take advantage of the first opportunity that arose.

And then not screw up—again.

It was something.

Not much, but something.

When he reached the spot where Smith had zapped Zolkaz and the others, he paused and looked around. He was relieved to see that they were gone. They must've awakened and—

Abruptly, the familiar itching invaded his head. Scowling, he glanced at his watch. He'd just checked in with Smith, for God's sake! He still had ten minutes before his next quarter-hourly call was due, so what the hell did Smith want? Maybe just a test to see how far his influence reached? Not surprising, the paranoid bastard!

Taking his communicator from its belt clip, he started to activate it.

And stopped halfway through the code. Screw it! Screw *Smith*! Better that he *not* know just how far his influence reached.

Replacing the communicator on its clip, he—

—blinked.

For just an instant the itching hit a peak and the world seemed to flicker around him, going in and out of focus like a badly made immersion vid. What the hell was Smith up to? Dialing up the power?

Then everything steadied. The itching disappeared.

Puzzled and angry, Don pushed on through the wilderness that had once been a city, but after a few hundred meters found himself thinking about the technology that had produced it, a technology that could have saved Earth from at least one of its major curses: pollution. With something like that, and the common sense to use it, Earth might not've gone terminal and the *Jupiter* wouldn't have been sent out to look for a lifeboat world and Smith wouldn't have sabotaged it and they wouldn't all be stuck out here beyond the back of nowhere—

But the Rellkans had once had the technology, he thought, and look what it had gotten them.

If one thing doesn't get you, another will. Life is a terminal condition. Maybe civilization is too.

The communicator interrupted his uncharacteristically philosophical mental meanderings. Scowling, he snatched it up. Smith's voice came through immediately.

"I wouldn't want you to think me a stickler, Major, but you *did* agree to relieve my concerns for your continued safety by checking in every fifteen minutes."

"Which I have done," Don snapped, "and will continue to do!"

"Indeed? Then how is it that more than twenty minutes have elapsed since your last communication?"

"Check your watch again, Doctor! I checked mine not more than two minutes ago, and—" Don broke off as, automatically, he darted a glance at his watch.

And saw that Smith was right.

Impossible!

Turning, he looked back. The spot where Zolkaz had lain was barely a hundred meters behind, two or three minutes at most. And that was where Smith had poked at his head and he'd checked his watch and—

"Yes, Major?" Smith's voice interrupted the pilot's confused reverie.

Don blinked, as if hoping the action could activate a reset button in his head or his eyes, but the time on the watch remained the same, clicking inexorably ahead.

"My mistake," he said, though he didn't really believe it. He made mistakes, but there was no way he could have misjudged the time that badly. Unless something had happened when Smith had been poking at his mind back there. In which case there was no reason to let Smith know that he suspected something. "Was there anything else you wanted?"

"Not at the moment, Major. Continue on your errand," Smith said in patronizing tones.

"Of course," Don replied, clicking the communicator off and taking another confirming glance at his watch.

Scowling, half in anger, half in puzzlement, he pushed on, wondering just what it was Smith had done to him back there. And why. What had the man hoped to accomplish, other than keeping one of his opponents guessing? But maybe for Smith that was enough. And the principle was sound, strategically. The more uncertain your enemy is, the more likely he is to be distracted, and the better your chances are to take him by surprise.

Stepping up his pace to a steady jog, he let himself wonder just what was happening to Will Robinson, if he really *was* in one of the torture/training cubicles. As Judy Robinson had discovered with the *Jupiter*'s instruments, *something* was going on. The building's power usage had been even higher than when Smith himself had been in there, but Don had no idea what, if anything, that meant. The only even semilogical possibility that occurred to him was that perhaps some Rellkans—Zolkaz and his group?—had entered the cubicles in hopes of getting what Smith had gotten out of his stay. Being rendered instantly unconscious by Smith might well have provided the Rellkans with just the right impetus to take that kind of chance.

But Rellkans aside, the more he thought about it, the more certain he was that at least Will himself had entered one of the cubicles. The boy had been upset, even angry, when his father refused to let him accompany them to the building.

And if the boy really *was* in one of the cubicles . . . Don shook his head. Will was just a kid, no matter how bright he was, and nothing could have prepared him for what he'd find in there.

Nothing.

From what Professor Robinson had said about his own brief experience in a cubicle, Don imagined it would be like throwing the boy into the middle of a Space Marine basic training program during a live ammunition obstacle course. The cubicle might keep his body alive, but his mind . . .

Grimacing, Don stepped up his pace yet another notch.

Dr. Zachary Smith scowled at the latest set of diagnostic readouts on the screen. He could've sworn he had located the offending set of instructions, the ones that triggered the digital booby traps, but the moment he'd tried to excise them, they vanished, replaced by standard programs he'd seen a hundred times. It was like starting to surgically remove a cancerous tumor only to have it magically transform itself into normal, healthy tissue, wholly benign, right before your eyes.

"Trouble, Doctor?"

John Robinson, watching from the edge of the Robinson exclusion zone Smith had established on the bridge, smiled infuriatingly.

"Nothing that concerns you, Professor," Smith said, turning toward Robinson. "Unless you have more insight into the workings of your son's mind than you have thus far admitted. I don't suppose," he added, his look turning speculative, "you would care to alter your earlier professions of ignorance."

John shrugged. "Should I? You've been inside my head, so you should know as well as I what I do and don't know."

If only it were so, Smith thought, wondering if it would be worth the time and effort to take Robinson over once again, this time actively seeking out his memories rather than deliberately isolating himself as much as possible from the man's cluttered mind and often saccharine and guilt-ridden thoughts.

Probably not, he quickly decided, his decision spurred by those very same unsavory thoughts as they bobbed disconcertingly to the surface of his own mind. In any event, Robinson's son was the only one in the family with any real understanding of a computer's inner workings.

And the child would be here soon enough, once West found him and his infernal robot. Assuming the boy survived his encounter with the cubicles, that is. Once again, to his surprise, Smith found himself feeling sorry for the boy, and once again he quickly overcame the momentary weakness. The boy deserved whatever he got, and more.

And Smith knew he didn't need him in order to undo the sabotage. It would take longer without him, but he had no doubt that he would eventually succeed.

Turning back to the console, he began a new search, not for the triggering mechanism he'd found—and lost—but for the next layer of the booby trap, the layer that, apparently, could snatch the triggering mechanism itself out of one program and immediately hide it somewhere else.

It was a cyber variation of the shell game, he thought with a reluctantly admiring smile. You find which shell the pea is under, but before you can lift the shell and reveal the pea, the game's sleight-of-hand operator slips the pea under another shell or up his own sleeve, and you have to start all over again. What he had to do, cybernetically speaking, was find the operator and immobilize or destroy *it*. And then find the pea again.

As Smith began the search, he barely noticed the

faint itching somewhere beneath his scalp, and when he did, he absently assumed it was simply a side effect of his newfound powers. According to Robinson and the others, his intrusions made their minds itch, so how surprising could it be that his mind now and then felt as if it were itching as well?

Even that minor awareness faded as he suddenly saw, buried in the midst of the hundreds of lines of instructions that scrolled across the screen every few seconds, something that looked suspiciously like precisely the sort of thing he was looking for. With a flick of his finger he reversed the flow across the screen.

And froze the display.

And saw that he was right.

Cautiously, half expecting this set of instructions to go the way of the previous set, Smith began to systematically delete it, line by line.

When the last line vanished from the screen, he laughed. He didn't need the insufferable child at *all* now.

The robot, however, might come in handy. . . .

One part of Don's speculation was confirmed the moment he stepped into the central clearing. Apparently, the Rellkans *had* proceeded here after they awakened from the coma Smith had put them in. He could see four of them, and from the look of it, they had probably tried to make use of the so-called training cubicles—and were dropped into another coma for their trouble. The four lay motionless and silent on the neatly manicured grass not far from what used to be the door to the Vault. Only the slow rise and fall of their chests gave any indication that they were alive. The robot hovered over them, although Don couldn't tell if its manner was protective or threatening. Protective, he hoped, since there were no electrical discharges arcing between various parts of its limbs.

Its sensors shifted toward Don the moment he emerged into the clearing.

"Mazel tov, kimosabe!" it rumbled. "You might want to summon Dr. Judy and her medkit for our Rellkan friends, here."

"In a minute. What happened? Did this lot crawl into some cubicles and find out they couldn't take it?"

"Something like that. But—"

"Where's Will? Is *he* in there?"

"I believe these men need medical attention, Major West."

"I'm sure they do! But *is* Will in there?"

"I saw him enter a cubicle, and I have not yet released him."

"Then let's get cracking! Which cubicle? *I'll* let him out!"

The robot's sensors wobbled back and forth, almost as if it was shaking its head. "That is impossible. I have my orders. Will Robinson specifically commanded me to leave him inside for at least as long as the nefarious Dr. Smith was inside."

"Damn it, Robot! *I* command you to take me to the cubicle Will is in! Now!"

"I'm sorry, Don, but I can't do that. And I don't think you can make me."

"We'll see about that!" Snatching the control rod from his pocket, Don darted around the robot. But the robot turned with him, trundling backward until its back, and the slot that took the control rod, was against the building's wall.

"Robot! Do you have any idea what you're *doing*? You're *killing Will*, that's what! Look what happened to those guys," Don pleaded, gesturing at the still-comatose Rellkans. "What makes you think a little kid can survive in there if it does something like that to grown men?"

"Do not worry, kimosabe. I have it on good authority that Will Robinson is not in danger at the present time. He will not come a cropper in his cubicle."

"*What* good authority? That Will told you not to worry when he went in? He didn't know what he was letting himself in for! Can't you see—"

Don broke off, shaking his head. He was arguing with a damn robot! As if it could do anything that Will hadn't programmed it to do! And Will, filled with more confidence than common sense, had probably programmed it to resist all attempts to get him out of the cubicle before the time was up!

Making up his mind and acting virtually simultaneously, Don lunged for the opening and dived through. To his surprise and relief, the robot didn't follow. Now if he could just locate the right cubicle, if he could spot the slightly darker handle that indicated the cubicle was occupied—

Before he could start his race down the first corridor, his communicator sounded. Damn! In the rush to find

Will, he'd forgotten about Smith and his check-in times.

The moment he clicked it on, Smith's voice came through. "Forget about the boy. I don't need him. The *Jupiter* is operational and will be landing just outside the Vault in a few minutes. I suggest you stay out of the way while I clear a landing area."

The communicator went dead. When Don tried to call Smith back, the call was ignored. Cursing, Don looked down the first circumferential corridor and realized that he wouldn't have time to race around more than a single corridor before Smith arrived, and there was no guarantee that even if Will *was* in one of that first corridor's cubicles, he would be able to spot the light gray handle as he ran past, the only thing that would distinguish it from the hundreds of others.

And the Rellkans—they were still laying on the ground outside.

Sticking his head out through the opening, he shouted at the robot, still backed against the wall a few meters away. "Get the Rellkans inside! Smith's going to be landing the *Jupiter* on the front lawn in—"

One of the trees a hundred meters distant, in the middle of the parklike area, burst into flames as the ravaging beam of a laser cannon lanced down out of the darkness.

"—in a few seconds, from the look of it," Don finished as he sprinted toward the Rellkans himself.

26

A mixture of relief and terror washed over Zolkaz as he and the three-score Rellkan Watchers looked up to see the huge alien machine slide silently overhead, a house-sized circular shadow that could crush—or incinerate— his entire group in an instant if its masters chose to do so.

"Perhaps they are leaving," Zolkaz said.

"And perhaps they are not," Kelwyn replied, continuing to watch the metal behemoth, calculating its direction. "If I am not mistaken, it is moving directly toward the Vault."

Zolkaz grimaced, knowing he was on the losing end of the discussion, as he almost always was with Kelwyn. As he had been when he made the mistake of telling Kelwyn about the new powers Smith appeared to have developed.

"We should just steer clear of the strangers altogether," Zolkaz had said, as firmly as he could manage. "Stay out of their way and let them kill each other."

"In good conscience, we can't, Zolkaz," she had protested. "We're responsible for what Smith has become. We should have stopped them—or at least *approached* them—*before* they reached the Vault rather

234

than waiting until they were returning to their craft, the damage already begun. In any event, if it weren't for the existence of the Vault—"

"We didn't force anyone to enter it! On the contrary, Smith forced his way in the second time—and kidnapped my granddaughter in the process! And before you tell me how the others are innocent victims, remember that the one called West is the one who forced Smith inside in the first place! None of that—*none!*—is our responsibility!"

"Nonetheless, if the Vault itself did not exist—"

"My God, Kelwyn! Even *you* can't say that *we* are to blame for what our ancestors of two hundred years ago did! Or for what a thief and trespasser like Smith is doing now!"

And so it had gone, but not for long. Zolkaz, as he always did, eventually acquiesced. He also helped round up over sixty Watchers, armed with their dart rifles, and set out for the *Jupiter*. Their only plan, other than prayer, was to conceal themselves in the forest facing the craft's entrance and wait for the one called Smith to emerge.

As far as Zolkaz was concerned, it was a terrible plan, because it relied not on known facts but on guesses and hope—hope that Smith's powers didn't include the ability to detect them as they lay in wait. Hope that their darts would hit the target and would act rapidly enough to keep Smith from slamming them all into unconsciousness—or death!—before he himself succumbed. But most of all, hope that he *would* emerge from the craft at some point, at least giving them a chance at him.

And now . . .

Now even that almost-certain-to-fail plan was lost to them. And if Kelwyn was proven right about the craft's destination, the plan was about to be resurrected in an even more ungainly and dangerous form.

With the robot finally deciding to help, the four unconscious Rellkans were taken safely inside the Vault—if *anywhere* was safe now—by the time Smith's laser cannons had finished clearing a spot for the *Jupiter* to land, demolishing a dozen trees and twice as many benches and statues in the process.

Don debated further attempts to get the control rod into the robot but decided against it. For one thing, all it did was allow you to control the robot's physical movements. It did nothing to access its memories. Besides, for all he knew, Will had programmed it to develop total amnesia the moment a control rod was inserted.

In any event, either Smith would allow them time to search out Will's cubicle or he wouldn't. And Don knew that his having the robot directly under his control meant nothing, since Smith could control him or anyone else he wanted to and order the robot around that way, by proxy, if necessary.

And maybe, just maybe, whatever Will had programmed into the robot before going into the cubicle was something that would throw a monkey wrench into Smith's plans. And give everyone else a chance. Don knew that all he could do was wait and watch and hope.

• • •

With a massive effort, Maureen Robinson managed to get one foot through the open door of her cabin and into the hallway.

"This is insane!" she grated through clenched teeth for at least the tenth time in as many minutes. She *knew* there was no real, physical reason she should not simply step through the door and have done with it.

No reason whatsoever except for what Smith had done when he last invaded her mind.

Like a hypnotist giving her a posthypnotic suggestion while she was wide-awake, he'd implanted a command that turned the threshold of her cabin into an invisible, seemingly impenetrable barrier. But at the same time, in telling her—almost taunting her—that he would most likely leave Will locked forever in his cubicle in the Vault, Smith had inadvertently given her the strength and determination to penetrate that barrier.

If the effort didn't kill her, as she was beginning suspect it might.

Heart racing at least triple speed, breath coming in aching gasps, every limb trembling as muscle fought muscle, she remained frozen, straddling the threshold, for at least a minute, until—

As if pulling a vacuum-sealed plunger free, she lifted her other foot and forced it into the hall, her whole body shaking with the effort.

The moment her entire body was out of the cabin and into the hall, the muscles that had been straining to force her body across the threshold were suddenly unopposed. Her body hurtled forward, crashing into the far wall.

She was free.

Pausing only a few seconds to control her breathing and let the reeling world begin to stabilize around her, she staggered and lurched down the hall. After a dozen meters, the stabilization was complete and she was able to race the rest of the way to the weapons storage locker. Thumbing it open, she snatched out a laser pistol and keyed it to fire only for her. Then she was running back the way she'd come, locating the rarely used stairs that led up to the bridge. As silently as she could, she crept up the bare metal steps.

Opening the door at the top of the stairs a tiny crack, she peered through to the bridge. As she'd assumed from the sounds and vibrations that had filtered down to her cabin, the *Jupiter* was in flight. Smith, of course, was at the controls. His back was to the door she stood behind. John stood five or six meters beyond, toward the airlock, facing the external viewscreens, but from the blank-eyed expression on his face, she doubted that he was actually seeing them.

Easing the door open another fraction of an inch, she raised the laser pistol and wished ardently that she'd spent more time in target practice. And that, if she were lucky enough to bring Smith down, the laser wouldn't also put a hole in the control panel he was seated at. It would take more than a little reprogramming to repair *that*.

But the alternative, being forever a slave to Smith's every whim, not being allowed to extract Will from—

Forcing the image of her trapped son from her mind,

Maureen took in a silent, steadying breath, held the door ajar with her left hand, held the laser pistol in her right, and sighted meticulously.

Her finger tightened on the trigger—just as she felt an itch, faint but unmistakable, deep inside her skull.

The *Jupiter* touched down just as Dr. Zachary Smith became aware of the itch inside his skull. Spinning around, he saw the slight opening of the door to the stairs that led down to the cabins.

Knowing there should be no one there, he reached out blindly, closing a mental fist tightly around—

Maureen Robinson? Impossible! She couldn't have gotten free of her cabin *this* soon! The strictures he'd imposed on her mind should have been good for several hours yet! Unless she was developing an "immunity," a resistance to his commands.

Or unless he'd underestimated her, he thought with a sinking feeling, the same way he had underestimated Major West earlier—and almost gotten himself killed in the process.

Retaining his paralyzing grip on her, he hurried across the bridge and opened the door the rest of the way. And found himself staring into the emitter portal of a laser pistol, held in a hand that trembled with the same tension that made the tendons stand out on its back like wires.

Despite the sudden rib-rattling thumping of his heart, Smith managed to retain his surface composure, even assemble a "tsk-tsk" smile as he reached out with his left hand and gently diverted the pistol's aim to one side. When it was no longer pointing at him, the woman's fingers relaxed, the tendons absorbed by the flesh, the pistol drooping.

Maintaining his smile despite knees that trembled and threatened to buckle, he took the pistol from her unresisting fingers.

And sent her to stand, blank-eyed, next to her equally blank-eyed husband while he worked to get himself once more completely under control.

Third time's the charm? he wondered.

First West almost took him out, failing only because the pilot's feet had gotten tangled at the critical moment. And now Maureen Robinson! Who was the next would-be assassin? Judy? *That* certainly wouldn't surprise him.

Uneasily, he reached out with his mind and touched Judy and then Penny. But they were still in their cabins. There were no signs that the strictures he'd placed on them needed renewing yet.

And John Robinson—he too was still fully under control, essentially paralyzed, as far as any kind of voluntary action was concerned.

And yet his wife had broken free.

Seating himself in as comfortable and stable a position as he could in the navigator's chair, Smith closed his eyes and reached out to grasp Maureen Robinson's mind. Carefully, he *squeezed*.

To his surprise, there was resistance, something he hadn't encountered before. Though that might have been because, previously, the minds he'd invaded had not been aware of what he was doing, not even aware, at first, of his presence. Maureen Robinson, on the other hand, seemed to be fully aware of his presence and his purpose. And was doing all in her power to thwart him.

But her untrained mind was no match for his.

With no attempt at gentleness, Smith increased the pressure until, abruptly, he felt the resistance crumbling and found himself looking out through Maureen Robinson's eyes.

2 7

Experimentally, Dr. Zachary Smith moved Maureen Robinson's fingers, her hands, her arms. Whatever resistance there had been to his entry into her mind, it had no residual effect on his control of her body. Physically, he could make her do whatever he wanted.

But no physical act he could force her to do would get him what he wanted: her memories of how she had been able to do what she'd done. For that, he would have to let down his own defenses, let his mind virtually blend with hers.

Bracing himself, taking the mental equivalent of a deep breath, he lowered every barrier that he had, almost automatically, erected.

All at once, he was drowned in a flood of terror and love and dogged determination and—

—hatred!

Hatred above all else, hatred for the creature that sat in the navigation chair a dozen meters away.

Himself!

No surprise, he thought, as he saw the figure in the chair flinch, though he was not aware of causing his body to move.

Ignoring the stomach-churning hatred as much as he was able, Smith moved backward through her memories until—

For a moment he—*they*—were trapped in the remembered terror of her laborious escape from the cabin. In that same instant, however, he got what he wanted.

He realized *how* she'd overcome his commands and escaped. He *recognized* what had happened to her.

Because it was, in a way, the same thing that had happened to him in the Vault.

After being threatened with death hundreds or thousands of times, he'd eventually dredged up powers buried so deep within his mind that until then he had no idea they even existed. Maureen Robinson hadn't been threatened with death again and again, but she *had* been threatened with what, to her, was even more horrifying: the death of her son. Smith had virtually taunted her with it.

Instead of dredging up a deeply buried mental power that allowed her to control her attacker, she'd dredged up something more down to earth: mental *strength*, more sheer willpower than he'd imagined could exist in one person.

Maureen Robinson had always had that kind of strength, he realized with an uncomfortable mixture of scorn and envy as other memories assaulted his mind. Without it, she would never have been able to cope with the endless pressures and crises of what had for decades been her everyday life—a demanding profession and an even more demanding family, not to mention the years of continuous crisis that had been the *Jupiter* project itself.

But a few minutes ago . . .

A few minutes ago she'd outdone even herself.

Like the anecdotal hundred-pound woman whose adrenaline-enhanced muscles allow her to lift several times her own body weight in order to save a loved one, Maureen Robinson had forced her way through what, for any normal person, would have been an impenetrable barrier.

Abruptly, having gotten what he came for, Smith pulled back, trying to disentangle himself—and found the same resistance he had encountered before, when it had tried to keep him *out* of her mind.

This time it was clinging to him like a leech, refusing to let him go.

Trying to control *him*!

Through Maureen Robinson's eyes, he saw his body twitch in the navigator's chair, then jerk forward, one arm outstretched, reaching—

—for the laser pistol!

In her mind there suddenly appeared the image of his own hand grasping the pistol and turning it on himself!

Frantically, Smith pulled back, thrashing violently, trying to free himself from her mental grip. His body jerked in the navigator's chair, slamming hard against the back of the chair and—

He was free!

In his own body and his own body alone, his heart threatened to erupt from his chest.

Forcing his own eyes to open, he saw that Maureen Robinson had slumped to the floor, her body limp, and he realized that as he'd spasmodically withdrawn from her mind, he simultaneously sent her into a deep sleep, almost a coma.

Despite her almost superhuman willpower, she hadn't been able to stop him. He shuddered to think what she would be capable of, however, if she subjected herself to a few hours in the Vault.

Abruptly, the debate that had been simmering in the back of his mind all day was resolved.

The Vault had to be destroyed.

Now!

He almost certainly could not bring himself to enter for a third time, no matter what the potential rewards might be.

But others could. And would.

Left intact, the Vault would be a constant threat. What it had done for him, it could do for others.

For Maureen Robinson.

Even, perhaps, for her infernal son, who was *in* the Vault even now, had been in it almost as long as he himself.

Smith doubted that the boy was still alive and sane, let alone ready to emerge and provide a serious challenge. But he'd also doubted the capabilities of both Major West and Maureen Robinson, and it had been a mistake.

He wasn't about to underestimate his enemies yet again.

The Vault had to be destroyed—*before* Will Robinson emerged.

John Robinson crumpled, asleep before he hit the floor next to his already unconscious wife. Then Judy and Penny collapsed in their cabins, also asleep. Outside, Major West, who had spent the last few minutes repeatedly attempting to get Smith to respond to his communicator, and trying to override the lockout Smith had apparently placed on the airlock, pitched to the grass next to the robot, whose sensors swiveled apprehensively toward the fallen man.

"What's wrong, kimosabe?" it rumbled.

But there was no reply.

A plasma rifle under one arm, a control rod in an easily accessible pocket, Dr. Zachary Smith walked quickly across the perfectly manicured grass to where the robot stood uncertainly over the fallen Major West.

"Take the major into the *Jupiter*," Smith ordered.

To his surprise, the robot scooped West up without hesitation or question.

Smith was debating whether to try to slip up behind the robot and insert the control rod when the frighteningly familiar itch deep inside his skull returned, even more strongly than when Maureen had been about to attack him. He knew, at that moment, that dozens of Rellkans were gathering in the darkness at the edge of the clearing, ready to strike him down. With their dart rifles, undoubtedly, but under the circumstances, that would be enough. At least one of his charges, most likely

Maureen Robinson, would awaken before he did.

In which case it was unlikely he would ever awaken again.

Hastily, not questioning how he was suddenly able to pinpoint the location of the hidden Rellkans, Smith reached out, as he had before. But this time, without quite knowing how he did it, he formed not a grasping hand but a mental *net*, flung wide to cover every Rellkan. It was as if his mind itself was that net, and he could sense it falling on every one of the hidden Rellkans, could sense their surprise as he pulled the net tight, virtually strangling their consciousness.

Most fell without a sound, though a few managed to get off a shot. A half-dozen darts whizzed past him, some thudding into the ground, some clattering harmlessly against the side of the *Jupiter*, one glancing off the back of the robot as it entered the airlock with Major West.

Following the robot inside, Smith cycled the airlock shut. Once again he silently debated the advisability of trying to get the control rod into the robot.

And once again decided against it. For one thing, the robot was obeying his commands without question, so why rock the boat? Besides, there was nothing he needed the robot for, not for the short time he was planning to remain on this world. Later, on other worlds, it would be a different matter altogether.

"Robot," Smith commanded, "return to the bay and place yourself on standby status."

For three or four seconds the robot didn't respond, and Smith wondered nervously if it was going to protest.

Or simply refuse. His grip tightened on the plasma rifle as the robot's sensors swiveled from the pilot's unconscious form to Smith's face.

"As you wish, Dr. Smith," it rumbled, then turned its back on him and lumbered away. "If you need me, you know where to find me."

And it was gone, leaving Smith gratified but still puzzled. The boy in the Vault would be counting on the robot to let him out. And he surely would have programmed the robot to resist his own attempts to take command. Surely—

Don't look a gift horse in the mouth! he told himself sharply, turning back to the navigation console. He'd been considering checking the Vault's energy usage, but now he couldn't remember why. In any event, what was the point? In just a few minutes none of this would make any difference.

The Vault—and the boy—would be gone, incinerated by the same laser cannon that had cleared a place for the *Jupiter* to land.

Seating himself at the console, Smith took a last look at the image of the building on the viewscreens.

And lifted off.

At two kilometers he stopped. From this height the Vault and the cleared area around it was a circle of light disfigured by the destruction that had created the landing field.

For a moment an image of Will's face invaded his mind, but he shoved it aside. It was, he told himself firmly, just the result of his encounter with the boy's mother. He had been *in* her mind, sharing her thoughts, her memories. It was inevitable that bits and pieces would stick to him. The same had happened when he was in West's mind and then in John Robinson's.

But he knew which were his own memories, his own feelings, and which were the loathsomely emotional rubbish he'd tracked in from outside and which now clung to his mental shoes like mud. He would be able to purge them, he told himself; maybe not immediately, but eventually.

For now, it would have to be enough just to ignore them as best he could, to overwhelm them with logic and common sense.

And to get on with what he had to do.

With a grimace, Smith returned his full attention to the Vault, a huge, well-lighted bull's-eye in the midst of the darkness below. Still half expecting the robot to come thundering back to the bridge, he activated the laser cannon. The image on the viewscreens wavered then, as if distorted by the sudden power drain caused by the cannon.

But then all was crystal clear again as the laser began to eat into the pristine white of the Vault roof.

The entire process took less than five minutes, Smith noted with pleasure, far less than he'd anticipated.

28

Blinking, the Space Captive came awake.

And realized with a sinking feeling that, now, she really *was* a Space Captive. Along with her entire family.

That creep Smith had double-crossed her! He had said that the first thing he'd do once he took over the *Jupiter* was start a *real* search for Earth, no more of this "don't use the hyperdrive or we might hurt ourselves!" Or he'd at least *implied* it. But what he'd really done was go off the deep end on some kind of power trip. He'd started poking around inside everyone's head, making them act like *zombies*, even the one and only *original* Space Captive herself! She'd been on his side, for Pete's sake, and he'd treated her just like everyone else! If he thought—

"I regret to inform you," the cabin intercom announced in Smith's unmistakable tones, "that I have determined I have no choice but to continue my journey unaccompanied except for the robot. Therefore, you each have one hour to assemble whatever you wish to take with you to the planet's surface. If any of you have questions, you are welcome to come to the bridge and discuss them, but you should be warned that you will be wasting time that could better be spent in making your selections."

The intercom fell silent, and no amount of angrily shouted questions could restore it to life. With no alternative, Penny thumbed open the cabin door and tentatively extended a toe across the threshold.

No resistance. Last time she'd tried to even approach it, she was tied up in knots by the time she got within half a meter.

She was stepping into the corridor when Judy came hurrying up from the direction of her own cabin. "Are you okay, Penny?"

"How okay can I be? You have any idea what's going on?"

Judy shook her head. "We better get up to the bridge and find out," she said, grabbing Penny's hand and heading down the hall again, her sister trailing after her. "All I know is what we both just heard: Smith's going bananas."

"He wouldn't *really* strand us here!" Penny was suddenly more scared than ticked. "Would he?"

"Are you kidding? In case you've managed to forget, this is the guy who's already tried to *kill* the whole lot of us. Like you're always saying, little sister, do the math!"

"But if he leaves us all behind, how'll he work the hyperdrive? He'll need *someone* to turn the second key!"

"The robot, I suppose. Or a tame Rellkan. Besides, it won't take him long to figure out how to override the safety circuits. If he hasn't already."

Penny shuddered. She thought she'd felt bad when she was forced to leave everything behind on Earth, but to be stuck on *this* planet, with no chance of going *anywhere*!

Ever!

Compared to that, even being killed didn't sound all that bad.

The rest of the trek to the bridge was a mind-spinning blur. There had to be *something* they could do!

Will!

Her brother's face popped into her mind as she emerged onto the bridge and saw her parents and Major West already there—but not Will. *He* hadn't been captured, she remembered now. Smith had brought Judy and their father and Major West back from the Vault—

—*but not Will!*

He was still out there somewhere!

And if anyone could figure out a way to kick Dr. Creepo Smith's mental butt, Penny thought, it was her little brother. He probably already had something worked out and was hacking into the ship's control systems or maybe the robot. He was just biding his time before launching his attack. Probably he'd send the robot in first. The robot was something Smith *couldn't* control, no matter how much of a brain boost he'd gotten from the Vault. Will would be sending some commands to the robot any minute now, as soon as—

"I see you are all determined to waste your valuable time attempting to change my mind," Smith said, looking casually around from the navigation console. "Very well, as long as you're all here, there is something I should show you. Perhaps it will inspire you to use your time more efficiently."

With the tap of a finger on a single control, Smith brought the viewscreens dimly to life. Penny squinted at the shadowy image but couldn't tell what she was seeing. The generally circular shape reminded her of the Vault and the surrounding park, but—

"You must excuse the lighting," Smith went on, "but only one of the world's moons is in the sky tonight. And of course there is no longer any artificial light being produced by the Vault. I imagine our computer can do some of its customary magic with the images, however, and make things clearer."

He nudged another control and the screen brightened, the contrast increasing a shade at a time until—

Maureen Robinson gasped.

"You recognize it, I see," Smith said softly.

And then Penny did too. It was the Vault—or what was left of it: a scorched pancake of whatever the material was, melted and resolidified like a lava flow. Here and there in the surrounding area were still-intact trees and benches and statues, but the Vault itself was—

"*Where is my son?*" Maureen Robinson asked through gritted teeth. "*If you've killed him—*"

"I'm truly sorry, dear lady," Smith said, "but it was his choice to enter the Vault—and to remain. I allowed Major West adequate time to retrieve him, but the boy's metallic guardian refused—"

"The bastard's right!" West broke in. "That pile of recycled junk refused to tell me which cubicle Will was in so I could get him out! It kept insisting Will wasn't in any danger!"

"But *you* did *that*!" Maureen glared at Smith as she waved a hand at the destruction on the screens.

"The boy had been in there for hours," Smith said, his voice placating. "He had experienced several weeks of subjective time, at the very least. I know how it works. So does your husband. In any event, I doubt very seriously that the child was still alive. Almost certainly he had at least been driven mad by then. By his own choice." He shrugged with a touch of regretfulness. "So you see, if he *was* still alive, I did the boy a favor."

His words were greeted with stunned silence. Penny felt sick, literally, as she wondered how she could ever have sided with Smith on *anything*! Or for any reason, even for the promise of an instant return to Earth! Her brother had been a pest as long as she could remember, but he'd been *her* pest! *Her* brother! Smith had no right—

The viewscreens flickered, drawing every eye back to them. Smith reached for the control panel, but instead of causing the image to restore and steady itself, he blanked all the screens except the relatively small ones above the navigation console.

"Time to finish your packing," he said softly.

"Then you really do plan to leave us here?" John Robinson asked, his voice flat and emotionless.

Smith nodded. "Anything else would be impractical."

"It was 'impractical' for *us* to let *you* live, after what you tried to do to us," John said.

An almost invisible smile played across Smith's shadowy face. "I wouldn't even think of disputing your state-ment, Professor. You are of course entirely correct."

"Then certainly—"

"The only certainty, Professor, is that I have absolutely no intention of repeating *your* mistakes. Surely you can comprehend the logic of my reasoning." Smith glanced at his watch. "You have forty-five minutes. I suggest you get cracking with your packing, so to speak, while I park the vehicle for your disembarking conve-nience."

Smith turned back to the navigation console, seem-ing to ignore everyone as he took the ship down. When West started moving toward Smith's back, however, the major's heart skipped a beat—literally—and he halted instantly.

Smith smiled quietly and completed the descent with a feather-light touchdown. Then, turning back to West and the Robinsons, he made a shooing gesture with his hands. "Forty-two minutes," he informed them, "and counting."

A grating sound from the vicinity of the airlock undid Smith's smile. A puzzled frown replaced it, and all eyes darted in that direction. Smith reached for the laser pistol that still lay on the console, but with his fingers just short of their goal, his entire body went numb and stiff.

He couldn't pick up the weapon, he realized, let alone aim and fire it. He doubted he could even stand. Or speak.

Then he and everyone else recognized the sound of the outer airlock door being opened.

But as they gazed in that direction, it was the elevator door, not the airlock door, that opened wide, allowing the robot to emerge and lumber across the bridge toward Smith, whose eyes widened in shock and surprise.

"I will take custody of that, Dr. Smith," the robot rumbled as it reached the navigation console. While Smith looked on helplessly, the robot grasped the laser pistol in its pincers. "We wouldn't want anyone to get hurt, Doctor, now would we?"

A moment later, Smith collapsed to the deck, unconscious. As he did, the exterior viewscreens flared into renewed life—and were filled not with the shadowy image of the melted-down Vault they had last seen, but with a well-lighted image of a virtually undamaged Vault. The only visible blemish was the hole the robot had burned in it a few hours earlier.

And even *it* looked as if it were in the process of healing.

While everyone was still blinking in puzzlement, the airlock's inner door swung ponderously open.

2 9

Will Robinson fought to keep from breaking into a huge grin as he stepped out of the airlock onto the bridge. Now that he'd pulled this off, there was no way they'd be able to avoid taking him seriously!

Absolutely no barfing way!

As if to prove his point, Penny broke into an ear-to-ear grin and dashed across the bridge toward him.

"*I knew it!*" she practically shrieked as she grabbed him off his feet in a wildly energetic, whirling hug. "I knew you and that robot had something up your sleeves all along!"

She set him down almost as quickly as she'd picked him up as Will gave her a mental nudge. Being appreciated by your goofy big sister was nice, but *she* wasn't the one that counted.

"What happened, son?" John Robinson asked. Everyone else, Will noticed with well-controlled glee, still seemed stunned by his sudden appearance. "We thought you were in the Vault, and then we saw Dr. Smith had destroyed it."

"You just *thought* you saw all that," Will said after a short but barely bearable pause.

"An illusion?" His father's eyes widened. "*Your* illusion? You can do that now? That easily?"

Will shrugged. "I can do it, but it's not all that easy."
Yet.

"But I had to let Smith *think* he'd zapped the Vault,"
the boy added with a shrug, "or he'd never have brought
the *Jupiter* back down here."

"What about the Rellkans?" West asked abruptly.
"The four that followed you into the Vault—*they* weren't
an illusion, and they were in pretty bad shape last I saw."

"They're okay," Will said impatiently. "Or they will
be in a few days. I got them to wake up, anyway, which is
the important part. They're with that bunch that tried to
ambush Smith and got put to sleep instead. I woke them
up too."

"Ambushed Dr. Smith?" John Robinson said, frowning. "What—"

"It's a long story, Dad. Just take my word that all the
Rellkans are okay. What we have to worry about now is
taking care of Smith. Before he wakes up."

"I can delay *that* happy event as long as you'd like,"
Judy said, "as soon as I get my medkit out here. Or Smith
into sickbay."

Don West grimaced. "If you want a solution to the
Smith problem—a *permanent* solution—I personally
vote for a plasma rifle."

"We've been over that territory before," John Robinson said stiffly. "I haven't changed my mind, even under
these circumstances."

"Besides," Will cut in, "there's no need for anything
like that now. Or to drug him, which we don't dare do
anyway. Drugs in his bloodstream might mess things up.

258

All we have to do is get him into the Vault before he wakes up and—"

"*Into the Vault?*" Penny looked as if she couldn't believe her ears. "Letting Smith in the Vault is what caused all the trouble in the first place!"

"What the Vault gives," the robot volunteered, "the Vault can take away. Praise be the Vault."

"That's not funny, Robot," Will snapped over his shoulder, then turned back to his father, ignoring Penny. "But he's right, Dad. There's a bunch of the cubicles that do just the opposite of the ones we were in. Put Smith in one of those and he'll be—deprogrammed, I guess you'd call it. Or retrained, maybe. But whatever you call it, he won't be able to poke around in people's heads anymore."

"And you know this how?" West broke in, eying Will suspiciously. "Come to think of it, how did you get out of the cubicle *you* were in if the robot didn't let you out? You're not saying that *Smith* let you out?"

"Of course not!" Will said, repressing an impulse to zap West, maybe make him stand on his head for a while. "The *Vault* let me out! That's what it does when someone completes a course. Or a first lesson, I don't know. Whatever it is, Smith *didn't* complete his, not even in two tries, so the Vault wasn't ready to let him go. Somebody on the outside had to open the door and drag him out before class was over." Will shrugged his narrow shoulders. "But I finished the course or the lesson or graduated or whatever, so it let me out. But it also told me a lot of stuff after the training part was over, while I was . . . recovering, I guess you'd say. And when it was sure I was okay, it opened the door and let me out. Maybe so I could keep Smith from wrecking the place."

"You think it knew—" John Robinson shook his head, like pushing a reset button. "You think the Vault was aware of Smith's plan, then?"

"*I* don't know. There *is* some kind of AI program that showed itself once I completed whatever it was I completed. Like I said, it told me a whole bunch of stuff. Or implanted it in my mind, I guess. All I'm sure of is, once I got outside, I remembered all this stuff that I sure didn't know when I went in."

Will glanced at Smith, still sprawled limply on the floor. "Look, we're wasting an awful lot of time here. We should be getting Smith plugged in there—before it's too late. I *think* I could handle him if he wakes up, but I'm not sure. This time I caught him off guard, with the illusions and everything else. He didn't know I was even alive, but if he wakes up now and starts fighting me—"

"You weren't in the Vault nearly as long as Smith," West persisted in a skeptical tone. "So how is it you completed the course and Smith didn't?"

"How should I know? Maybe I'm a fast learner. Maybe it's easier for kids to learn new things. Maybe old dogs have trouble with new tricks. Or maybe I just knew what it was trying to teach me, so I didn't have to be killed nearly as many times as Smith was before I found the right track."

"Smith knew what to expect too, the second time around," West pointed out.

Will shrugged, then suddenly grinned. "Maybe it's because this business of getting into people's heads is a lot like hacking into a computer. Only you don't have to mess around with a keyboard or a hacker's deck or anything like that. It's just your mind and the other guy's mind, and all you have to do is *think*. Now can we get going with Smith?"

Will was prepared to do a little impromptu hacking and nudging then and there if West kept resisting, but the pilot seemed to have run out of arguments, at least for the time being.

Five minutes later, with the robot carrying Smith effortlessly, Will led everyone to the center of the Vault, a meter-wide column surrounded by a circular area, more a doughnut than a hallway, just large enough for four cubicle doors and the radial corridor in its perimeter wall.

"These are the deprogrammers?" West asked suspiciously as Will herded them all, robot included, to stand near the column.

Will only grinned, and touched the column a meter above the featureless white floor. A moment later the central section of the floor, a geometrically perfect circle around the column, faded from white to gray and started to sink, like an elevator without walls. Only a mental nudge from Will kept West from clambering up and onto the surrounding floor as they began to sink. As a result, West spent most of the descent glaring at Will, who did his best not to grin too broadly as he explained that there were at least a dozen levels to the Vault, all looking pretty much the same.

Three identical floors down, their "elevator" stopped.

One of the four doors in the surrounding wall was open, waiting. Without hesitation, the robot carried Smith across the intervening two or three meters and gently set the doctor down inside the cubicle.

"Will!" John Robinson said sharply. "Are you absolutely positive that this won't increase his—"

Robinson frowned as the cubicle door closed itself.

"I'm positive, Dad," Will replied, still grinning.

By the time they were all back in the *Jupiter*, Major West was certain that Will had been poking around in his head at least twice, perhaps three times. At least that was how often his head had itched—inside. They weren't the same as Smith's blunt-force takeovers, and he might not even have noticed them, if he hadn't been on the lookout after the first one, on the descending elevator.

That first time, there had been no doubt in his mind. The moment the floor started to sink without warning, his battle-trained reflexes kicked in and he'd automatically moved toward safety, intending to haul as many of the others as possible with him. But his muscles froze before he could actually move and before his lips had even parted to shout a warning.

And that had been that. When they were down one floor and the opening to the main floor was unreachable, the itching had stopped and his muscles responded normally once again.

The other two possible times weren't tied to anything specific he'd tried to do. The only indication that anything had even happened was the tickle, as if Will was just checking in. The way a jailer checks the cell of a sleeping inmate every so often, West thought with a flare of irritation, just to be sure the inmate isn't up to something.

Or just to prove that the jailer can do whatever he damn well pleases, whenever he pleases.

On the *Jupiter*, everyone gathered on the bridge, where Judy could keep an eye on the Vault's power drain readouts. If they began to drop rapidly, it meant—according to Will—that the deprogramming was probably coming to an end and they should get back to the Vault to be on hand when Smith emerged.

Meanwhile, Will seemed delighted to hold court and tell everyone what he'd learned.

"For one thing," he said, "you know what the Vault used to be? It was the Rellkan version of a university."

"A war college, you mean?" West suggested.

Will shook his head. "A university. A computer-controlled, virtual reality university, the biggest one on the whole world. The entire city was sort of a campus."

West frowned. "You're saying the Rellkan method of teaching was to torture students until they accidentally got the right answers?"

Will laughed. "Of course not. That's just this one program. It's designed to force people into using whatever latent mental powers they have. But those powers are buried so deeply they had to do really drastic things to—to flush them out. All the regular courses, like science and history and stuff, were pretty much like regular classrooms, except every student had his own teacher.

Each cubicle was programmed for one particular student. And he could *live* the lessons. Not only that, the programs weren't just plain old programs, they were some sort of AI that really interacted with the students, way more advanced than the AI I've been trying to get to work in the robot. It really learned from the students, not just the other way around."

"All very interesting," West said, "from an academic point of view, but what I'd *really* like to know is, what the hell happened here two hundred years ago? Who were these Invaders that are supposed to have killed virtually everyone off? Did your chatty little instructor tell you any of that?"

"As a matter of fact, he did," Will said, and then, grinning even more broadly, looked around at the group, as if waiting for a cue.

"Well?" Penny snapped when her brother had held his silence for five or ten seconds that seemed like minutes. "Are you going to tell us? Or do we make guesses and you tell us if we're right?"

Will's grin faded, but only slightly, and he shrugged. "It's sort of complicated, at least what I've remembered so far. Or maybe it's just disorganized. As soon as I remember one thing, something else pops up, and it's hard to keep track of what goes where. It's sort of like getting a history book dumped on you a page at a time, without any page numbers."

"Just do the best you can, son," Maureen Robinson said, and John nodded.

Will pulled in a breath. "For one thing, Dad, you

were right about their superhypergate. It's a few steps up the ladder from yours. If you jump through theirs, no matter where you end up, you can find your way back. It's got some kind of hyperspace transponde system. You jump through the gate and you can end up anywhere, just like when the *Jupiter* jumps. Aiming it was one thing they hadn't figured out how to do yet. But the gate sends out a pulsed signal all through hyperspace every few minutes, so when a ship jumps back into hyperspace, it latches onto that signal and gets pulled back to the gate."

His father nodded. "That would take tremendous power," he agreed, "to virtually blanket hyperspace. It would be like . . . building a radar powerful enough to cover half the galaxy."

For a moment, with his father taking his words at face value rather than being skeptical or condescending, Will seemed to glow. "They built it three or four hundred years ago," the boy went on, "and they used it to jump all over the galaxy. Trouble was, they weren't ready for what they ran into."

"The Invaders?" West asked.

Will shook his head. "Not at first, anyway. For a long time it was just your run of the mill nasties, I guess. Nobody trusted anyone else, and they were all armed to the teeth and inventing new weapons all the time."

"Like Earth for the last few centuries," John said glumly.

"Something like that," Will agreed. "And the Rellkans couldn't cope. They didn't have wars—or hadn't for several centuries, anyway. And not all that much violence of any kind. But they had to be able to defend themselves."

"The Vault?" his father asked.

Will nodded. "Like I said, almost all their schools had been computer-controlled virtual reality for at least a century. And somewhere along the line, *someone* — or a whole lot of someones — figured out how to use it to train people in mind control."

West shook his head, frowning skeptically. "Are you sure about that, Will? If the Rellkans were so nonviolent, how'd they come up with a training program like that one? It sounds like *the* most violent thing I've ever heard of, killing people over and over, hundreds of times. What could have made them even *think* of such a thing?"

"How should *I* know?" Will asked, bristling. "It's not like I'm an expert on Rellkan history! As far as I can tell, all I got was a crash course of highlights. Besides, how else *could* it have happened?"

"Maybe they found it," Judy volunteered. "If they were jumping all over the galaxy through their super-hypergate, maybe they just stumbled across the technology somewhere." She shrugged. "Just like we stumbled across the Vault here."

"It's a possibility," Maureen Robinson agreed. But she went on, solemnly, "It's also entirely possible they *did* think of it themselves, especially if they already had some evidence of the existence of such powers. In some ways, it makes psychological sense. Nonviolent cultures often produce people who do violence to *themselves* when they come in conflict with warlike cultures. Just look at the

Buddhist monks last century who literally burned themselves alive to protest."

"You're right," John said, nodding thoughtfully. "It's entirely possible they had evidence of such powers, which probably manifested themselves in times of extreme stress. And since these virtual reality teaching machines existed everywhere, it's only logical that someone would try to design a program that would make these powers manifest themselves. And what better way than by inducing huge amounts of stress?"

Judy shrugged. "Maybe, but I still like the idea that they found the technology or the programs on one of their jumps. Remember, you said the bodies you inhabited during this training weren't anywhere near human. If the programs were designed to be used by humanoids like the Rellkans, why would they put you in totally alien bodies? Having the things that kill you be absolute horrors makes sense, but why your own bodies?"

"It doesn't *matter* who thought of it first," Will broke in irritably. "The Rellkans are the ones who started using it! They just wanted to be able to defend themselves without having to kill people right and left! All right?"

"Except," West said, "they obviously weren't very good at it. Otherwise they wouldn't have all been killed off by these mysterious Invaders." He frowned at Will. "Any ideas about *that*? Do you even have any idea who the Invaders *were*? Or *what* they were?"

Will returned the frown, which abruptly became a scowl, and suddenly West's brain began to itch and his heart began to pound.

3 0

His own heart pounding, Will jerked back from West's mind, wondering where the burst of stomach-wrenching anger had come from.

And wondering what would have happened if he hadn't stopped himself.

"Sorry," he mumbled, not meeting West's eyes, which now looked more annoyed than frightened.

"Just stay out of my head! Okay, kid?"

"Perhaps," Maureen Robinson interrupted, "we should continue this discussion later, after Will's had a chance to get some rest. Considering everything he's been through—"

"I'm okay, Mom," Will said, looking up sheepishly. "I don't know what happened, but I'll be more careful. Besides, I don't have any idea how long these memories are going to stick around. For all I know, they could disappear the first time I take a nap. They don't even *feel* like normal memories. More like something I dreamed."

"I agree with Will," John Robinson said. "The more knowledge we have, the better basis we have for determining our actions, so we shouldn't risk losing any. Go ahead, son. *Did* you pick up anything about the Invaders?"

Will felt another surge of sourceless anger and even a bit of fear twist at his stomach, but this time he was ready for it and kept his reactions under tight control.

"Not a lot," he admitted. "It's all kind of fuzzy. Or maybe it's that there's a whole bunch of different memories and they don't all agree. And I haven't had a chance to really *look* at them yet. I'm not even sure I can. Like I said, they almost feel like dreams."

"Just tell us as much about them as you can, fuzzy or not," his father said. "We'll sort them out together."

Will nodded, still keeping a tight rein on his reactions to the puzzling emotions. It was like trying to keep from automatically closing your eyes when someone tries to put eyedrops in. Or from screaming on a roller coaster. It can be done, but it's never easy. Sorting through and verbalizing his new, dreamlike memories wasn't much easier, but that too eventually proved possible, despite the way they seemed to move or change shape whenever he turned his mental back on them.

Whether the mind control training programs were found on another world or developed by the Rellkans themselves, the Rellkans used them extensively for at least a hundred years. What most amazed the others, particularly West, was that whoever got their hands on the programs first didn't simply keep the secret for themselves and quietly take control of the planet. For most humans, the temptation would've been too much to resist. Many would've simply wanted the power. Others would've wanted to "make things better," not necessarily for him or herself but for everyone. Earth might've been turned into a benevolent dictatorship or an oppressive, even Hitlerian dictatorship, but it almost certainly would have been turned into a dictatorship of one kind or another.

But that apparently wasn't the way the Rellkans operated. For starters, the very concept of a professional military was alien to the Rellkans, so virtually every one of them eventually took at least one lesson. They ended up with the ultimate version of a citizen army.

And it seemed to have worked. For decades would-be Invaders were turned back without even realizing they had *been* turned back.

Until two hundred years ago.

Then the Rellkans decided that no matter how successful they had been, having to deal with the endless stream of warlike and mistrustful worlds the hypergate gave them access to wasn't worth the stress and danger it entailed. So they would destroy the hypergate as soon as they could recall all of their own ships and give all non-Rellkans in their own system a chance to leave.

And they did just that, but not quite quickly enough.

Something came through the hypergate in the moments immediately before it was destroyed. It wasn't something their ancestors had encountered in their explorations, as some of the present-day Rellkans believed, something so terrible they destroyed the gate in an unsuccessful attempt to keep it out. It was something totally unexpected and apparently had nothing to do with the decision to destroy the gate.

That was where Will's memories became even more

dreamlike, and also extremely uncomfortable for him to explore. The sourceless mixture of fear and anger were almost unbearable every time he tried. The few simple facts he *was* able to dredge up didn't give them anything new, just confirmed what he and the others already assumed about what the surviving Rellkans had told them all: Whatever it was that came through the hypergate possessed an indeterminate number of Rellkans, and as a result, direct or indirect, all but a handful of Rellkans were slaughtered over the next decade.

The possession, of course, was simply mind control, probably the same kind the Rellkans themselves had been employing for centuries. But the Invaders apparently were better at it and virtually always won. Also, since Rellkan instruments did not register any ship or ships coming through the hypergate, there was widespread and fearful speculation that these beings—now known only as the Invaders—had been incorporeal. Either that or their physical bodies had remained at the other end of the hypergate link while only their minds made the actual trip.

As for motives, Will's newfound memories suggested that the Rellkans had not even made a wild guess. Will and the others were less restrained.

Judy, for instance, had a variation of a theory she'd already advanced. The Invaders might be the ones the training programs were originally stolen from—assuming the Rellkans had indeed stolen the programs rather than designed them themselves. That would account for the Invaders being better at mind control than the Johnny-come-lately Rellkans.

"I wouldn't be surprised," Judy said, "if the so-called Invaders simply came to reclaim their property. But they were trapped here when the Rellkans destroyed the gate."

"That would be enough to make anyone cranky," the robot, which Will had insisted be allowed to sit in on their discussions, remarked, "not to mention suspicious."

"Suspicious?" John looked directly at the robot for the first time since it had been looming over them all. "Suspicious of what?"

"Coincidence, of course, John Robinson. Coincidence is the hobgoblin of logical minds, one of which I happen to possess, artificial though it may be."

"Excuse me?" John eyed the robot skeptically.

"Of course," the robot said, "but for what?"

"I meant—what the devil are you talking about? What coincidence?"

"The coincidence of timing. Do you not find it remarkable that the Invaders arrived at virtually the same moment the gate was to be destroyed?"

John shrugged. "The present-day Rellkans think their ancestors knew the Invaders were coming but waited too long to shut the gate down. If they're right, there's no coincidence, just cause and effect. And bad luck."

"Or perhaps the Invaders destroyed the gate themselves," the robot suggested, "to keep the cavalry from arriving and saving the day."

"Cavalry?"

Will grinned. "He just means that if the gate had stayed open, maybe some white hats would've come through and zapped the Invaders. And rescued the Rell-kans. Of course that would mean the Rellkans were the bad guys."

"Precisely, kimosabe," the robot agreed. "However, which scenario is more likely to be correct? Which event was cause and which was effect? Logical minds want to know. Which came first, the invading chicken or the scrambled gate?"

"Don't push it, Robotman," Will said. "But he does have a point, Dad. Nothing I've been able to remember could prove it either way."

"What *I* want to know," Don West said, "is what happened to the Invaders, what*ever* they were? After they nearly wiped out everyone on the planet, what happened to them? Did they go away? Did they die out? Did they go into hibernation? What?"

Will shook his head. "No idea. The fact that they're not still here is enough for me."

"And who says they *aren't* still here?" Don asked, glancing around the group, his eyes settling on Judy. "I know you guys get a good laugh from some of my ideas, but if Will's right . . . He said these Invaders might be incorporeal, or maybe just minds projected through the hypergate. Are you telling me you can guarantee that nothing like that is still hanging around?"

"Of course not," Judy said uncomfortably. "But there's absolutely nothing 'incorporeal' about the Vault or anything in it. It's nothing more than computer-controlled virtual reality. Extremely advanced, obviously, and capable of mimicking human thought processes, even learning from people who enter the cubicles. But I hope you're not suggesting that these Invaders—or the minds of a bunch of two-hundred-year-old Rellkans, for that matter—are actually *living* in there?"

Don shrugged and turned to Will. "What about it? Do your new memories have any clues?"

Will shook his head, but even as he did, a doubt crept into his mind. Judy was obviously right about the Vault and everything in it being computer controlled. But once you got to *this* computer's level—head, shoulders, and kneecaps above the *Jupiter*'s computer and the robot's latest AI programs—you started wondering just what life had that the computer didn't.

Except that will-o'-the-wisp people called a "mind."

Several of which might have been floating around without bodies if the Rellkans were right and some sort of incorporeal beings—patterns of energy?—had come through the gate two hundred years ago.

Could something like that have taken up residence in the Vault's computer? Where did it say that a free-floating mind—if such a thing existed—had to take up residence in an organic brain rather than an electronic one? For that matter, considering the semiorganic nature of the cubicles themselves and most of the buildings on this world, who was to say the Vault's computer *wasn't* organic? In which case—

"Will?"

Snapping out of his reverie, Will saw Judy hovering over him, a concerned frown wrinkling her brow.

"You okay, Will?"

Swallowing uneasily, he shrugged. "I'm not sure," he said, addressing all of them. "I'm just starting to wonder if maybe something really *could* be living in the Vault. Maybe even what's left of the Invaders. Especially if Judy was right about them being the ones who designed the program—and coming here to take it back."

It would explain why something in his mind seemed to be doing everything it could to steer—scare?—him away from specific memories of the Invasion and the Invaders. Maybe it was trying to keep him from concluding that there might be some remnant of the Invaders still in the Vault.

And now in himself! Will thought with a shiver.

In any event, this "something" obviously had something to hide.

Something he was going to darn well uncover! Will abruptly decided.

By the time he finished explaining the mix of logic and hunches that had led him to his decision, his father was shaking his head. "I can't let you do it, Will. Even if you're right—*especially* if you're right—it's much too dangerous."

Will looked up with a startled scowl. "Dangerous how?"

"Really, son!" John Robinson sighed loudly, the condescension plain in his tone, at least to Will. "Are you forgetting what happened to those hundreds of millions of Rellkans two centuries ago?"

"But that's just it, Dad! We don't *know* what happened to them! That's what I want to find out!"

275

"But what if you're right? What if the Invaders really have survived in some form? What if, as you seem to be saying, they want to keep their existence a secret?"

"All the more reason to find out what's going on! Besides, I still don't see what's so dangerous. I mean, if they do exist and if they wanted to zap me, they would've done it already. When I was being killed right and left in the Vault, for instance. If they have any control at all over the machinery in there, all they had to do was freeze up the door to my cubicle or shut off whatever kind of life support it is that keeps you from being suffocated when that cyberglop comes out of the walls and wraps you up like a mummy. And anyway, now that I'm out here, what can they do?"

"Anything they feel like, perhaps, if they really *are* in your head. You just said you thought they were fighting you, trying to keep you from exploring certain memories."

"Come on, Dad! They didn't do anything to me while I was in there getting make-believe killed a few thousand times, so what're they going to do to me now that I'm not even hooked up to their machine anymore? Whatever it is, I can handle it. Okay?"

"I know you believe you can, son," John Robinson said, "and you may be right. But don't start thinking you're invulnerable. That's probably how the Rellkans felt two hundred years ago. Just consider that it was sheer luck you weren't killed a few hours ago, when Smith tried to laser the Vault. If it had taken just a few more minutes to finish your lesson, Smith would have—"

Will laughed. "I'd been out of there for hours, Dad!" he blurted. "I was never in any danger. And neither were any of you."

His father frowned with puzzlement. "But I assumed—"

"So when *did* you get out?" West broke in. He was frowning too, but was more annoyed than puzzled. "And what the hell were you doing all that time?"

"Yes, Will, what?" his mother asked, her tone deadly serious.

Will realized then that he'd put his foot in it. For a moment he wondered if he could take them all over and do something with their memories, but he quickly dismissed the idea. For one thing, he doubted he could manage it. He was still learning how things worked, and he'd had enough trouble creating a few illusions—when nobody knew he was even doing it. Now they all would know and would resist and—

And he'd be in even deeper than he already was. Maybe this mind control business wasn't all it was cracked up to be.

3 1

When he'd emerged from the Vault cubicle a few hours earlier, Will confessed with embarrassment, he'd been both surprised and relieved to find himself feeling almost normal. A little shaky, maybe, but nothing like Smith, who'd been practically comatose when he'd been dumped out the first time. Or even like his father, who'd only been in a cubicle for a couple of minutes.

For a second or two he'd wondered if something had gone wrong and the Vault hadn't worked on him, but then things began sorting themselves out in his head. He *had* been killed over and over, just as he'd been expecting and dreading. But the memory of it didn't bother him, at least not nearly as much as it should have. It was dull and distant, as if it had happened to someone else— or as if it had happened to him, but a lifetime ago, not just a few minutes ago.

There was a buffer zone of some kind, he'd realized, between the multiple deaths of his training and his release from the cubicle. It was as if he'd been sent to a recovery room after surgery instead of being booted directly out onto the street—the way Smith apparently had been. A recovery room where someone or some*thing* had filled that buffer zone with memories he couldn't quite get a grasp on, sort of like a doctor explaining all the technical aspects of the surgery he'd just undergone. And more.

Lots more.

The biggest surprise, however, came when he looked at his watch. Only an hour had passed. Later, he would figure it out, but right then he was confused. The robot, which he found still on sentry duty at the gradually healing hole in the Vault's outer wall, didn't have anything useful to contribute except to point to the four unconscious Rellkans stretched out on the ground.

That was when the first of the dreamlike memories surfaced. Or maybe "congealed" was a better word. Either way, he suddenly knew that these Rellkans, like their ancestors, weren't compatible with this particular aspect of the Vault. That was why their ancestors had survived: They had never gotten their lessons.

Will also knew that to save them he had to get inside their minds and drag them back from wherever they were trapped.

He also realized, with a shiver that went all the way through him like an icy mist, that he actually knew how to do it. After those thousands of virtual deaths had forced the basic mental powers out of hiding, he'd apparently been given memories of how to make use of them, a sort of in-your-head, available-when-you-need-it ops manual. And now, faced with the unconscious Rellkans, he knew how to help them.

When he'd done as much as he could for the four

Rellkans—it would take hours for them to return to normal—he had the robot pick him up and head for the *Jupiter*, full tilt. Halfway there, however, he ran into West and secretly dug out of West's mind what was going on back on the *Jupiter*.

"So that was *you* in my head out there, not Smith!" West interrupted angrily. "Why the hell didn't you just *ask* me what was going on? What's the idea of poking around in my brain?"

West shook his head when Will could only shrug and mumble sheepishly, "It seemed like a good idea at the time."

Which, Will realized with a sinking feeling, was really all he dared say about nearly everything he'd done in the last couple of hours: *It seemed like a good idea at the time*. Sending the robot back to the Vault with instructions to wait for West and then make West think that he was still in one of the cubicles. Going onto the *Jupiter* and instead of just zapping Smith and ending it right there, secretly messing with everyone's mind, even giving Smith a hint that enabled him to get the ship's navigation system working again so he could move it to the Vault.

And it *had* seemed like a good idea at the time. As long as he made absolutely sure he could zap Smith and put an end to things any time he wanted to, what was wrong with stringing things out a little? For one thing, it was just plain fun. And what was the harm in giving everyone a little extra scare before stepping in at the last minute like the cavalry and saving the day in a *really* dramatic way? After years of being the baby brother who always got the short end of the stick, who could blame him for wanting to fine-tune the rescue of his family and turn it into something they would never forget?

Something his *father* would never forget!

But now . . .

Instead of feeling like the big hero he'd been planning on, he felt smaller than he'd ever felt.

To Will's complete surprise, though, no one lectured him, not even the still-frowning Major West. But then, maybe they were afraid to, now that they knew what he was capable of.

And he *had* saved the day. There was no getting around that. He'd managed to escape from Smith and reach the Vault when no one else could, and he'd forced himself to go into a cubicle and let it kill him a few thousand times while it trained him.

And he'd taken care of Smith. Maybe he shouldn't have wasted time with what amounted to a practical joke to make himself look like an even bigger hero, but it hadn't been *that* bad. Kind of neat, really.

Besides, he thought, it had proven once and for all that he could take care of himself.

"Dad, about what we were talking about before— after all this stuff I did, you can't still think it's dangerous for me to keep trying to find out what happened to the Rellkans."

John Robinson shook his head sadly. "I'm afraid your . . . prank proved just how dangerous it really is, son."

"What!?" Will couldn't believe his ears. He'd

expected his father to be ticked off at what he'd done, but hadn't expected *this*. What he'd done might've been, well, immature, but it hadn't been dangerous. He'd been in control of the situation every second since he'd come out of the Vault. He'd been *in control* and had made sure that no one—absolutely no one, not even Smith—got hurt. Didn't that count for *something*?

"I'm sorry, Will, but what it proves to me is that you're even more prone than I thought to taking needless risks for nothing more than a whim. A practical joke."

"Your father's right, Will," Maureen Robinson said softly. "If you're correct about these so-called Invaders still being present in some form or other, who knows what dangers you could run into if you stir them up? Who knows what could go wrong? They killed nearly the entire population of this world."

"But Mom—"

"No argument," his father said sternly. "It's simply too dangerous. It's not as if we need to know precisely what happened to the Rellkans. It would be interesting, but interesting isn't worth that kind of risk."

"It's my risk, not yours!" Will flared, all his former contrition gone as he barely restrained the same angry impulse that had nearly laid West low a few minutes before. He forced himself to pull in a deep breath. "What *do* you want me to do, Dad?" he asked. "Just turn off my brain and not ask any more questions?"

John Robinson swallowed audibly. "Of course not," he said. "But before you delve into the Invaders' secrets, think about what the real purpose of these deprogramming cubicles might be. Haven't you wondered?"

Will blinked at the apparent change of subject. "Of course I've wondered! But I thought you just told me I wasn't *allowed* to wonder about stuff like that!"

"Suppose," his father went on, ignoring Will's sarcasm, "that the deprogramming wasn't so much to get rid of the powers the Rellkans had gained, but to get the Invaders out of their minds? In order to get rid of one, perhaps you have to get rid of both."

Will shrugged when his father fell into an expectant silence. "Possible, I suppose. So what?"

"So, you might want to be deprogrammed yourself, the same as Smith."

The words hit Will like a physical blow, his stomach feeling as if it had dropped into his feet.

So that was it!

They wanted him to go back to the way he'd been before! They were just *pretending* to believe his idea about the Invaders still being around. What they were *really* doing was trumping up an excuse to dump him into one of the deprogramming cubicles! Not that he could blame them for being worried. The low kid on the totem pole was suddenly on top, and they didn't like it one bit.

They were scared of him!

Will shook his head. "Thanks for the concern, Dad, but I can take care of myself—*now*. And there's no way you can make me give that up!"

His father swallowed nervously, and Will couldn't help but enjoy the feeling it gave him. All regret about his joke was gone, except that, even more than before, he wished he hadn't slipped up and told them about it.

"I'm sorry you feel that way, Will," his father began, but before he could say more, the boy turned and stalked off the bridge.

"Is it okay if I come in, little brother?" Penny's muffled voice came through the closed door of Will's cabin.

"Not if Dad sent you to talk me into going back to being your dorky little brother again."

"So when did you stop being dorky? Doesn't look to me like that brain boost of yours did you a whole lot of good, commonsense-wise."

"You know what I mean!"

"I guess. Now are you gonna let me in or not?"

A brief pause, and then: "Okay, come on in. If you trust me not to zap you or whatever."

The door opened slowly and Penny's face, big-eyed and framed in the usual untidy strands of jet-black hair, peeped in. "So what's your next plan?" she asked with a grin. "To shoot yourself in the *other* foot?"

"If all you're going to do is practice your putdowns on me—"

Penny gave a snort of laughter as she came in and closed the door behind her. "You're saying you *meant* to do that? To tell Dad and everyone about your dumb stunt? Come on, tell me what *really* happened to you in that cubicle. Sure, it gave you the power to zap people and all that, but it must've taken away a bunch of other stuff—like knowing when to keep your mouth shut."

This time he almost laughed, but he just shook his head. "You heard what happened," he said. "It just slipped out, okay?"

"And you couldn't just make us all forget what we heard? That's not part of your new weapons system?"

He shrugged. "Maybe I could. But it'd take a while, and I'd have to do each one of you separately, and then I'd have to make you all not notice the missing time. The only really easy stuff is knocking you out. And stopping your heart. That's a piece of cake. According to what I saw in Smith's head, anyway."

Penny grimaced. "I don't suppose there's any way you could turn just that part off?"

"Not that I know of. But I'll be careful. Don't worry."

"Easy for you to say. What if something just slips out and you accidentally wipe someone out?"

"It doesn't work that way."

"You're sure? Didn't you almost clobber Don? Anyway, what if there really *is* one of those Invader ghosts up there in that lost and found you call a brain?"

"There isn't. It's just memories. And even if there is, I'll keep it on a short leash. Now why are you here? Did you just come in to bug me?"

Penny shrugged and lowered her eyes for a second. "Actually, I was wondering if this supercharged brain of yours was going to be any help finding our way back home."

"What made you think of that?"

Another shrug, this one elaborately casual. "Well, you know what Smith was planning. Take a few chances and make a bunch of blind jumps instead of limping around in snail space and getting nowhere."

"Smith was planning a search like that? Or were you planning it for him?"

"A little bit of both, I guess. But you heard him before all this started. He wasn't all that worried about ending up in the middle of a star or whatever. So I figured—"

"You figured once he took over, he'd jump the *Jupiter* every chance he got and sooner or later we'd come out near a mall."

"Something like that. Well? What about it? Smith was right. We'll *never* get home if we stick to snail space. Even if we *knew* which way to go. We could be thousands of light-years from home."

Will shook his head. "Dad's the one who knows about hypergates, not me. He invented one, remember?"

"And he wants to stick to snail space! But you could change his mind. In a manner of speaking. You could have us jumping again by this time tomorrow."

"Sure. And when we pop out of hyperspace in the wrong place and get turned into a bunch of dissociated subatomic particles, we'll be really *moving*! In a million different directions all at once! That'll be fun!"

"You're a real chicken, little brother, you know that?"

"At least I'm a live chicken, and I intend to stay that way. Look, if you want to take your turn in the Vault and then change Dad's mind yourself, be my guest."

She blinked, as if the thought had never crossed her mind before. "How bad *is* it?"

"While it's going on? You heard Smith. Like you say, do the math."

She shuddered. "How did *you* get up the nerve to go in?"

"Actually, I didn't. I had to order the robot to force me in." He grinned. "You want me to order him to stuff *you* in?"

For a moment Penny looked as if she were considering it, but then she shook her head with another shudder and headed for the door, saying, "Maybe there *are* worse things in the universe than worlds without shopping malls."

3 2

For several seconds Will Robinson kept his eyes pressed tightly shut, hoping the noise would simply go away. But the sounds only grew louder, until he suddenly realized what they were: the hiss and crackle that could only come from the arcing energy halo that often sprang into spontaneous life around the robot's metal pincers. The realization drove all thought of sleep from his mind as he sat bolt upright in his bunk.

His eyes, almost painfully wide-open now, darted to the source of the sound—the door to his cabin. The door he had firmly sealed before finally finding a way, despite the uproar his world was in, to force himself to get some much-needed sleep.

A spot on the door was glowing. He could feel the heat on his face, and a moment later the glow became a widening hole, through which the robot's arcing pincers were visible.

"Robotman!" Will shouted, leaping from his bunk. "Whatever you're doing, *stop it*!"

"I'm sorry, kimosabe, but I can't do that." The robot's thundering voice almost drowned out the crackle of its pincers as it continued to enlarge the hole, just as it had earlier burned a hole in the outer wall of the Vault.

"Holy Takeover Scenario, Robotman!" Will shouted over the din, but that didn't work either. The robot didn't even respond, just continued pouring more energy at the molten hole in the door, enlarging it at an increasingly rapid pace.

Then, abruptly, it was lumbering through the opening. "We can do this the easy way or the hard way, kimosabe," it said, its now-quiescent pincers extended in the boy's direction. "It's up to you."

"Do *what* the easy way? What's going on, Robot? What do you want?"

The robot hesitated. "I'm not sure, strictly speaking, that I am capable of wanting anything, Will Robinson. What I have been instructed to do is to deliver you into a deprogramming module."

"*What?* Who—" He stopped, realizing who must have given the orders. "Dad? He ordered you to do this?"

"Affirmative, Kimosabe Will. Now are you coming or will I be required to transport you?"

"Knock off the kimosabe crud, you traitor!"

"I'm sorry if you find it offensive, sahib, but all terms of address are a result of programs you yourself designed and installed. As are my varying patterns of speech. I recall that you were quite proud of your ingenuity at the time. However, all that is irrelevant to our current situation. If you do not willingly accompany me to the Vault, I will have no choice but to drag your spindly little Robinson carcass over there. I will of course exercise the utmost care to avoid causing injury to the aforesaid

Robinson carcass in the process. I hope you understand. It is, ultimately, for your own good."

"Don't give me that!" Will snapped, backing away as far as he could in the small room. "Dad just doesn't trust me! Big surprise!"

"It's not that, son." His father, seemingly appearing out of nowhere, was standing in the corridor looking in through the cooling perimeter of the hole that had once been the door. "It's too dangerous to allow you to go on."

"But what about Smith? You can't dump me in there before Smith gets out of the Vault! What if he isn't completely deprogrammed? What if he's still dangerous when he comes out. You don't know—"

"The depraved Dr. Smith was released hours ago," the robot said. "His deprogramming was a spectacular success. He has become, metaphorically speaking, a pussycat."

As if to prove the point, Smith appeared in the corridor, peering over John Robinson's right shoulder, looking solicitous. "It's all for the best, child," he said in a saccharine voice that Will didn't believe for a second. "Surely you don't want to take a chance on resurrecting the Invaders."

"Don't be stupid, Smith!" Will snapped. "*If* they still exist, I can handle them! Besides, don't *you* want to know what really happened?"

Smith shrugged. "The knowledge would not effect me personally one way or the other. Therefore, it is of no importance."

"Dad! You can't—"

"Time's a'wastin', kimosabe," the robot said, its pincers darting out faster than Will had ever seen them move. Before he could even twitch, he was clutched rigidly to the robot's chest, just as he'd been when the robot saved him from capture by Smith.

"I'm sorry, Will," his father said, "but I have no choice. And it *is* for the best. Try to understand."

Wheeling about, the robot lurched through the opening into the corridor, past his father and Smith. It was only then that Will understood. Smith's deprogramming *hadn't* been successful! *He* was doing this! Smith was controlling John Robinson who was in turn controlling the robot.

Forcing himself to calm down and stop struggling with the robot, Will reached out to Smith's mind.

And found himself looking out through Smith's eyes at the robot's back as it lumbered along the corridor heading for the *Jupiter*'s airlock. But Smith's thoughts were as bland as his words had been. The deprogramming really *had* worked. Not only that, as the robot said, it had turned Smith into a pussycat.

It was as if Smith had been lobotomized, Will realized with a new chill. He'd lost not only the mental powers the Vault had tortured into him, he had also lost most of his personality.

And the same thing would happen to *him* if he couldn't stop the robot from dumping him into a deprogramming cubicle! Surely his father could *see* that!

Unless . . .

Abandoning Smith, Will sent his mind darting into

his father's. There was no resistance, but even as he started to search through the surface memories, he felt his father begin to speak.

"It won't work, son. I did what you did when you enabled the robot to rescue you from Dr. Smith. It will not respond to anyone, not even to me, until it has completed its task. Until you are safely in a deprogramming module."

"*Dad!*"

"It *is* for the best, son. The Invaders—"

An idea came to Will out of nowhere, and he abruptly withdrew from his father's mind. The robot was moving out through the airlock into a sunny Rellkan morning. The Vault entrance—now completely healed—was less than a hundred meters away, the restored door wide open.

"Robotman! Listen to me."

"Of course, kimosabe. I always listen, but if you're still—"

"You're not allowed to let a Robinson come to harm. Is that right?"

"Of course. But if you intend to argue that putting you in a deprogramming module will cause you harm, that hound won't hunt."

"Then I won't. But it *will* harm my father, who's also a Robinson."

The robot didn't hesitate. He was already entering the Vault and heading along the radial corridor toward the central elevator. "Why and how will your entry into a deprogramming module harm your father?"

"Because, Robotman, *I'll kill him*! I'll stop his heart. It'll be a piece of cake! And you can't stop me! Except by *not* putting me into a deprogramming module!"

"How sharper than a serpent's tooth—" the robot began, but Will cut him off.

"I *will* do it, Robotman!"

"He won't!" John Robinson called from somewhere behind them. "Pay no attention to him. Will wouldn't kill his own father."

Then they were at the same cubicle Smith had been placed in. It was already open, as it had been for Smith.

"I'm doing it now!" Will shouted. *"I'm stopping his heart! You'll be responsible for his death if you don't stop!"*

And as he spoke, Will reached out—

—and stopped John Robinson's heart.

"Look, Robot! Look!"

Suddenly, Will was struggling against the robot's unbreakable grip as he was forced into the cubicle. Just as he'd been forced into the training cubicle the first time, but that time the robot had been following his own command.

"Don't you see what you're doing, Robot?" Will shouted *"You're killing my father!"*

"No, Will Robinson," the robot thundered, its mechanical voice somehow infused with emotion. *"You* are killing your father. He was right. An Invader *did* survive within the Vault and now resides within you. It is controlling you, just as thousands of them once controlled the Rellkans, making them slaughter their loved ones. I have no choice but to carry out your father's wishes even though it means his death. It will prevent the even greater harm the Invader would cause to yet other Robinsons if it is not exorcised."

"*I can still save him!*" Will screamed, redoubling his struggles, thrashing violently in the robot's grip. "*Let me out and I can save him!*"

Suddenly, instead of holding him firmly within the cubicle until the door could be closed, the robot's pincers were gripping his shoulders, shaking his entire body like a rag doll.

And it began shouting at him—

—in Penny's voice!

In a split second, then, the cubicle and the robot vanished. Penny was leaning over him, strands of her jet-black hair flailing the air as she shook him like a madwoman, shouting in his face:

"*Wake up, Will! Smith killed Dad! You've got to do something!*"

3 3

Lurching upright on his bunk, Will felt the room spinning around him. Penny grabbed one arm and dragged him into the corridor before his head had cleared, screaming at him to hurry.

"What happened?" he managed to get out as he careened along after her, his shorter legs unable match his sister's galloping stride.

"He just *fell over*!" she gasped as she ran. "His heart stopped, just like when Smith did his stupid demonstration! Judy's doing her doctor thing, but she can't get his heart going! Smith must've gotten out of the Vault and zapped him, so I figured you're the only one who can unzap him!"

The realization of what had actually happened hit Will like a bolt of lightning: *It wasn't Smith! It was me!*

His heart was pounding more from guilt and fear than from exertion as he and Penny lurched into the sickbay. Their father was stretched out on the bed, a half-dozen wires pasted on him while Judy rhythmically hammered on his chest and Maureen leaned close and forced air into his lungs. Major West stood just behind Judy, ready to take over the chest compressions if she tired.

Despite their efforts and the wires, the monitors all showed flat-line.

"Do your thing, little brother," Penny said between gasping breaths. *"Please!"*

Will could feel the drumbeat of his own heart as he closed his eyes, fighting to calm himself and concentrate. Finally he was able to reach out mentally, much as he had earlier.

But this time he couldn't make contact. He could sense—"see"—the other minds—Judy's and his mother's hovering close together, Penny's and Major West's at a slight distance—but not his father's. His stomach seemed to sink to the floor.

He was too late.

His father was dead—beyond recall.

Unless . . .

Opening his eyes, Will darted forward to the head of the bed. With his hands, he gripped his father's head the way the hand in his mind had tried to reach out and grip his father's mind.

Finally, he felt it. It was so dim, so faded and exhausted, it was almost undetectable.

Forcing himself to be calm, Will backtracked through his memory to the moment when, in his nightmarish dream, he had stopped his father's heart—apparently both in the dream and in reality. He couldn't put into words what he'd done, but he didn't have to. He just had to do the reverse of what he'd done before.

Just as he'd done in the virtual reality nightmares of the Vault, again and again.

A moment later his father's heart lurched into sputtering life. A single beat thudded in his chest, and his lungs pulled in a single gasping breath. Another beat and then another, until finally it had a regular rhythm.

But the *mind*—

The mind was still faint and feeble, fading further every moment, slipping through Will's mental fingers like fog.

Will could feel his fingers stiffen as his palms pressed harder against his father's temples, as if to physically reach into his brain while his mind squeezed just as hard on the insubstantial fog that was his father's mind until—

Abruptly, without warning, the minds were one. A thousand memories swirled around him unseen as Will teetered on the edge of the same dark abyss into which his father had been about to descend. Without knowing how he was doing it, Will pulled backward with all his mental strength as the images darted and swirled around him like a maelstrom, and suddenly he was being pulled backward by some unseen force until—

He was looking out through his father's eyes, seeing his mother's face swim into view, hovering over him, Judy's worried face visible over her mother's shoulder. He could feel the pressure of two small hands on his temples.

His own hands.

He withdrew.

An instant later Will once again found himself in his own—and only his own—body, which half slumped to the floor as both his mental and physical grips on his father were released.

Catching himself, he managed to stay on his feet. "You can stop now," he said to Judy and his mother. "I got his heart going again. I think he's going to be okay."

A second later Penny was hugging him and lifting him off his feet, and this time Will didn't mentally nudge her back.

When she got around to setting him down, their father was blinking and sitting up as Judy pulled the monitor wires loose.

"What happened?" he asked, grimacing at the residual pain from Judy's long series of chest compressions.

"Smith!" Judy said. "He stopped your heart, just like he did in that demonstration of his, but this time he didn't start it back up again. Will saved you."

"Thank you, son." Will's eyes met his father's for a moment, then lowered as John Robinson turned back to the others.

John shrugged into the dark brown T-shirt Judy had removed to attach the monitor wires. Then they were all headed for the bridge to check the energy readouts on the Vault.

Will hung back, knowing that once they reached the bridge and saw from the energy readouts that Smith was still in the Vault, helpless, he was going to have to confess—again.

And this time he couldn't tell them that he'd been in control the whole time. This time it wasn't just a joke that hadn't harmed anyone. This time he'd lost control entirely and had very nearly killed his father.

No, he *had* killed his father!

It was only thanks to Penny's hunch and a lot of sheer luck that he'd been able to undo his own massive screw-up and bring his father back to life.

He hadn't meant to do it, but he *had* killed him.

He had accidentally killed his own father.

Except . . .

Then it got even worse. In the nightmare, *it had not been an accident*! He'd *meant* to do it!

Impossible! Even in a nightmare, he could *never* purposely kill his father!

Never!

It just didn't work that way!

Unless . . .

Unless the robot in the nightmare had been right!

Unless his father's fears about the survival of the Invaders had been justified.

Unless an Invader *had* survived in the Vault for two centuries and now lived somewhere deep inside his own mind!

The thought sent an icy chill coursing through Will, touching every part of his body, inside and out. But at the same moment, a wave of relief swept over him.

He hadn't killed his father!

The Invaders had!

He had saved his father! *From* the Invaders!

Picking up his pace, Will raced after the others. Entering the bridge, he saw Judy scanning the energy readouts. She looked both puzzled and relieved.

"The Vault's still at the same level it's been since we put Smith in there," she announced.

"So he's still in there," West said, "still having his mental fangs pulled."

"It looks that way." She turned from the console and started for the airlock. "But we better check his cubicle just to be sure."

"He's still in there," Will said, the words coming out with difficulty. "It wasn't Smith who stopped Dad's heart."

He stopped, the words freezing in his throat.

"So who was it, then?" Judy asked, frowning. "Smith's the only one with that kind of power. Except for you."

Will swallowed audibly, feeling as if he were about to jump off a cliff. "You were right, Dad, about the Invaders still being around. In the Vault. And in me now."

In fits and starts he told them about the nightmare and all the rest. Finally he stumbled to a halt and looked around. "So I guess I better go back in after all, and get my head cleaned out. Before that thing makes me do something I *can't* fix."

John Robinson nodded. "Good idea, son. As soon as Smith comes out and we're sure his powers are all gone. But until then, I think we should examine this a little more closely. For example, did you actually *feel* the Invader at any time?"

Will shook his head uncomfortably. "Not really. But what else—"

"And you say the robot in your dream actually *told* you about the Invader? In so many words?"

"Pretty much, yes." Will's growing uneasiness was the

same feeling he'd had when he'd been trying so hard to explore the recovery room memories. Until now he'd assumed it was some sort of protective action by the Invader, trying to keep its presence a secret by making him avoid certain parts of those memories. But now the Invader's existence was out in the open. "What are you getting at, Dad?"

"I'm not entirely sure, son, but when you were — bringing me back, I suppose — I got a glimpse of some of those memories you told us about, the ones you say the Vault must have implanted in your mind. . . ."

"And . . . ?" Will prompted when his father paused. He felt even more nervous now, and still didn't know why. He told himself it had to be coming from those implanted memories he hadn't been able to fathom, but which, during the brief joining of their minds, had been shared with his father, who apparently still had some form of access to them.

"And," John Robinson went on, slowly and deliberately, "I think I know who — and what — the Invaders were. And what they still are."

Impulsively, Will reached out with his mind and gripped his father's.

The Invaders! his thoughts screamed at him as he tried to pull back, to release his father's mind. His father had been right! Not only had they survived, but they were desperate to keep their very existence a secret! Desperate enough to kill him — *again!*

But they weren't quick enough. His father's thoughts flooded Will's mind, and suddenly *he* knew the truth as well.

In that instant, all the computer-enhanced self-deceptions that had permeated the implanted memories vanished.

And the Invaders stood revealed for what they were.

Or weren't.

It was of course pure coincidence, but only a few seconds later the readouts monitoring the Vault's power usage dropped precipitously. Apparently it was finally finished with Dr. Smith.

34

It was nearly midday when Kelwyn and Zolkaz warily approached the *Jupiter*, still resting where it had put down the night before, looming threateningly over the Vault. They'd almost refused to come when Major West sought them earlier that morning. After their own clumsy attempts to help the strangers in their conflict with Dr. Smith, in fact, they were on the verge of ordering an evacuation, sending all Watcher families back to their villages.

Despite some brief and confusing assurances by the young Robinson boy, they had no idea what had happened in the hours after they were rendered unconscious, presumably by Smith. For all they knew, Smith had been victorious, which wouldn't be all that surprising, since his only opposition was that same boy, a child little older than Zolkaz's own granddaughter.

Now, Zolkaz wondered if West's invitation was a trap of some kind, if he had simply been one of Smith's automatons, blindly carrying out his orders. Seeing that the entrance to the Vault had been completely healed did not reassure Zolkaz. It meant that whatever machinery existed within the Vault was still fully functional, and he could not be sure which of the strangers was now controlling—or was controlled by—that machinery.

Only when the boy and his father emerged from the huge ship did Zolkaz begin to believe that West's invitation to return to the Vault for an apology and for some possibly important news might be just that and nothing more.

Dr. Zachary Smith, by order and by preference, stayed on board the *Jupiter*, out of sight, watching the two Robinsons and the Rellkans on the viewscreens. He'd emerged from the Vault a few hours before, not an entirely changed man, but not quite the same man who had first entered the Vault either. He still bitterly resented the loss of his powers and held in contempt the rampant and counterproductive emotionalism of the Robinsons, but now he could at least vaguely comprehend its source. The time that his mind had spent occupying theirs and unwillingly sharing their thoughts and memories had apparently affected not only them but, unfortunately, him as well.

By his own interpretation, Smith was now cursed with the beginnings of empathy—a new and disturbing tendency to imagine how an action of his would appear to someone else. He even had a tendency to see his opponents as fellow human beings like himself, rather than the faceless and irritating obstacles to his own goals that logic showed them to be.

With a shudder, he remembered feeling a flash of relief upon realizing, the night before, that the infuriating Robinson child hadn't been killed in the illusory destruction of the Vault.

He would continue to fight such feelings, of course, but he very much feared he would never regain the pure, emotion-free state of complete sanity he'd previously taken for granted.

John and Will Robinson met the two Rellkans at the edge of the area Smith had scorched into a landing field the night before. Already the grass was regenerating, as was the partially melted walkway and a completely melted bench.

The first minutes saw the exchange of apologies: the Rellkans, for the very existence of something as potentially deadly as the Vault; John Robinson for most of Smith's actions and some of his own and Will's.

Then the Robinsons got to the news they were bringing, which filled both Will and his father, for different reasons, with misgivings.

"We thought it best," John Robinson began, "if we told only the two of you. Then, if you wish to share it with the others, that is entirely up to you."

"And why should we keep it to ourselves?" Kelwyn asked, though Zolkaz remained silent, his earlier uneasy expression returning.

"I'm not saying you should," John replied. "You know your people better than I. I'm only saying that I don't feel that I have the — the *right* to spread this information around indiscriminately."

"I must say, John Robinson," Kelwyn said with a faint

smile, "you make this news of yours sound most intriguing."

"That's not quite the word I'd use, but—" John broke off, resetting his thoughts with a shake of his head.

"Based on information Will was . . . given during his session in the Vault," he went on, "we have good reason to believe that the Invaders never actually existed."

"You mean they really were, as some believe, totally incorporeal?" Zolkaz asked.

"Not just incorporeal. Nonexistent."

Kelwyn looked puzzled and Zolkaz frowned. "If the Invaders didn't exist," he asked, "then who slaughtered hundreds of millions of our people two hundred years ago?"

John Robinson pulled in a breath. "*Apparently* they killed each other. As a result of—"

"Nonsense!" Zolkaz broke in angrily. "Other worlds have wars and pointless killing! *We* do not! That is why our ancestors finally chose to close the gate, to shut out such madness!"

"I'm sorry," John resumed, "but we also have reason to believe that the gate was not shut down by your ancestors. It was destroyed by someone from those other worlds. The memories—"

"*What* memories? How can you, who has never set foot on our planet until days ago, claim to *remember* what happened here centuries ago? Unless—" Zolkaz broke off, gasping. "Unless you and your kind *were* the Invaders! And now you have returned to complete our destruction!"

"No, it's nothing like that! Just give us a chance to explain, to make you understand."

"And what guarantee do I have that anything you say is the truth? That you are *not* the Invaders returned?"

John Robinson sighed. "None, I suppose. Except that if we *were* the Invaders returning to finish the slaughter of your people, we could have done that at any time." He gestured at the scorched ground under the *Jupiter*. "We could have searched out your villages and incinerated them all. Even *Smith* didn't try anything like that!"

"Then where do these memories you speak of come from? How can you remember things you could not possibly know?"

"The Vault. When my son—"

"The Vault? You have told us the Vault is a training device. A device that brings people's latent powers to the surface. What does that have to do with these things you say you remember?"

"When my son was in there, he received more than just the training that Smith received. He appears to have actually communicated directly with the Vault—the machine that operates the Vault."

"You're saying the Vault itself remembers these things?"

"In a manner of speaking, it *does* remember. It is, after all, a completely interactive device. The training it performs isn't rigid and inflexible, the same for everyone who enters. Think of it as a human—or Rellkan—teacher. It learns from each person it trains and then trains the next person just a little differently. But it's able to learn thousands of times as much as any individual. It can remember what's significant in the thoughts and lives of all of the millions who passed through it two hundred years ago. And now some of those memories, some of those attitudes and fears, have been picked up by my son. It could have been accidental on the part of the Vault, or maybe it was all part of the training. It might even be the result of a malfunction. All I know—all *we* know—is that it *did* happen, and my son now remembers at least a small part of what went on during the so-called Invasion. Or what the last few Rellkans who entered the Vault *believed* happened."

Zolkaz turned sternly to Will. "Is this true, child?"

The boy shrugged uneasily. "So far as I can tell, yes."

"And you—remember that the Invaders did not exist? You 'remember' that our people simply slaughtered each other?"

"Not exactly, but—" Will swallowed nervously, averting his eyes from the Rellkans, then pulling in his breath. "It happened to *me* too! I did the same thing your ancestors did. When you have that sort of power, it's just so *easy* to kill someone! You don't need a real *reason*. All it takes is a moment of anger." He shuddered, remembering. "Or a bad dream. That's how I killed my father. I—"

Zolkaz snorted loudly. "Now I know you are all mad or fools. Your father stands before me, alive and well!"

"Because he brought me back," John Robinson said. "My heart was stopped for several minutes, but once Will realized what he'd done, he was able to bring me back."

"*And I blamed the Invaders!*" Will burst out. "I knew

I couldn't have done anything that terrible myself, not even in a nightmare! So I decided the Invaders had somehow survived within the Vault, and one of them had gotten into my mind while I was in there. It was the Invader, not me, who'd killed Dad!"

"Which was pretty much what the Rellkans did two hundred years ago," John Robinson said. "Some Rellkan, somewhere, killed another using this newfound power. It's so easy to do, it amazes me that it took decades for it to happen. On Earth, if people found themselves with this kind of power, we'd be slaughtering each other by the thousands before the day was out. But you didn't, not for decades. And when it did start, the killers felt just the way Will did. They simply could not bring themselves to believe they had done something so terrible. So they—or their subconscious minds—came up with the idea of the Invaders, incorporeal creatures who came through the gate before it was destroyed and possessed people, driving them to kill other Rellkans. It was easy to believe, considering how many *real* Invaders you'd had over the decades since you'd built the gate, the greedy and warlike races that had come through and were driven back without even realizing what had happened to them. It was especially easy to believe since it apparently started almost immediately after the gate had been destroyed."

Zolkaz had seemed overwhelmed while John had talked, but now he shook his head in denial. "You said the gate was destroyed by others, not by Rellkans. Why? It doesn't make any sense!"

"I'm not sure," John Robinson admitted, "but then,

we're not absolutely sure about any of this. But I think what happened is that the Rellkans, once they found they were able to repel and manipulate the *real* invaders of your world, began sending—well, 'missionaries' is as good a word as any. They sent their most able Vault graduates out through the gate and tried to reform the home worlds of those who'd tried to take *your* world over.

"And someone out there must have found out what was happening. Or lots of someones. In any event, their only choice, as they would have seen it, was to destroy the gate in order to keep you from sending out even more of these missionaries."

John Robinson shrugged. "That's how I interpret it, anyway. And I'm certain it's how Earth would have reacted if its inhabitants had discovered that someone was getting inside their heads in an effort to reform them. We wouldn't have accepted forced reform in a million years. We would've figured out some way of getting rid of the reformer."

"I can show you," Will offered abruptly, nervously, "if you'll let me."

"By taking me over and getting into my mind?" Zolkaz shook his head sharply. "No, thank you!"

But Kelwyn was less rigid, more trusting.

Over Zolkaz's strident objections, she, in effect, invited Will into her mind. And Will did his best to share his newfound memories with her.

When he withdrew, she shuddered at the memories that were now hers as well.

But all she said was, "I sensed there was a way that

the Vault could be converted back to what it was before it became part of the Rellkan defense system. That it could once again be the university it once was. Is this true?"

"Maybe." Will looked up at his father. "But not until I get the same treatment Smith got."

"You're willing to give up the powers it gave you?"

Will nodded solemnly. He'd been thinking about since it became clear to him what had happened to the Rellkans. If *they* couldn't handle it, there was no way *he* could. He'd already demonstrated that. He'd killed his father *once*, and next time he might not be able to bring him back.

And he also knew that he could not keep his dreams—or his subconscious—under the kind of rigid control that would be required to keep it from happening again. To his father or his sister or especially Smith or someone like him.

The kind of power he possessed simply made it way too easy to kill people.

For that matter, he thought ruefully, it made virtually *everything* too easy. It would be like having a magic wand you could just wave to let you hack into any computer anywhere with no effort on your part. Where was the fun in that? It was the sort of thing Dr. Smith would enjoy.

Will shuddered at the thought of any similarity between himself and Dr. Smith. It was almost as scary as thinking about killing someone and not being able to save them.

No, he had no choice.

No choice at all, not if he wanted to be able to live with himself.

He *had* to give up the powers—all of them.

"I'm willing," he said, finally.

His father may have breathed a well-controlled sigh of relief, but then he smiled. "You may not have thought I noticed, Will, but I know you get upset now and then about being little and no one taking you seriously." He glanced at the Vault entrance. "You'll never have to worry about that again, son. What you're doing now makes you bigger than any of us will *ever* be."

Will swallowed away the lump that had suddenly formed in his throat, then turned and headed quickly for the Vault entrance, hoping he made it into the cubicle before he came to his senses.

EPILOGUE

"It's my way or the highway, Dad!"

With the lightest of mental nudges, Will sent his father walking obediently toward the *Jupiter*'s airlock.

Luckily, before his father could cycle the lock and step out into space, Will woke up. His whole body went limp with relief as he realized it was just another stupid dream.

At least it hadn't been quite as bad as the last one.

Or the one before that.

In another week or two, maybe they'd be gone altogether. Maybe he could finally quit torturing himself after each one, wondering if way down deep he wasn't like Smith after all, just wanting his powers back so he could boss everyone around.

Not that he couldn't use just a *little* of the power. No matter what his father and the rest of them had all told him when he was trudging back into the Vault to be deprogrammed, things had drifted back to normal pretty quickly. His father soon started brushing off most of his suggestions, just the way he always had: "I know you're very bright, Will, but you simply don't have the experience needed to properly evaluate this sort of thing."

Whatever the specific "this sort of thing" happened to be.

And Penny— Well, Penny was just being Penny. She probably didn't mean—

Suddenly, all thoughts of his dream problems vanished as he heard the whine of the hyperdrive generators beginning to build up a head of steam.

An instant later he felt the whole ship shudder as the hyperdrive segments extruded and locked into place with a series of metallic thuds.

What now? he wondered, his heart pounding as he leaped from his bunk and raced into the corridor, almost colliding with the robot. He tingled all over as if he could actually feel the buildup of the hyperdrive force field.

The last thing he heard before he and the entire ship were once again thrust into the limbo of hyperspace was the robot's enthusiastic but totally unhelpful greeting: *"Geronimo, Will Robinson!"*